SOME REVIEWS OF GARRY KILWORTH'S BOOKS

His characters are strong and the sense of place he creates is immediate. (*Sunday Times* on *In Solitary*)

The Songbirds Of Pain is excellently crafted. Kilworth is a master of his trade. (*Punch Magazine*)

Atmospherically overcharged like an impending thunderstorm. (*The Guardian* on *Witchwater Country*)

A convincing display of fine talent. (*The Times* on *A Theatre Of Timesmiths*)

A masterpiece of balanced and enigmatic storytelling…Kilworth has mastered the form.
(*Times Literary Supplement* on *In The Country Of Tattooed Men*)

An absolute delight, based on the myths and legends of the Polynesian peoples. (Mark Morris on *The Roof Of Voyaging*)

A subtle, poetic novel about the power of place – in this case the South Arabian Deserts – and the lure of myth. It haunted me long after it ended. (*City Limits Magazine* on *Spiral Winds*)

The Iron Wire

A novel of the Adelaide
to Darwin telegraph line, 1871

GARRY KILWORTH

infinity plus

Copyright © 2014 Garry Kilworth

Cover design © Keith Brooke

All rights reserved.

Published by infinity plus

www.infinityplus.co.uk

Follow @ipebooks on Twitter

No portion of this book may be reproduced by any means, mechanical, electronic, or otherwise, without first obtaining the permission of the copyright holder.

The moral right of Garry Kilworth to be identified as the author of this work has been asserted by him in accordance with the Copyright, Designs and Patents Act of 1988.

ISBN-13: 978-1500779429
ISBN-10: 1500779423

This novel is for the Australian author John Brosnan (1947-2005) a great writer and a good friend, whose ashes I returned to his homeland in 2006, scattering them in a Victorian vineyard.

Also for my fellow telegraphists
(the Blood-and-Custard Boys)
who served with me in the RAF
from the mid 1950s through
several decades.

Acknowledgements

Enormous thanks to Bill Glover, whose extensive knowledge of the Adelaide-Darwin Overland Telegraph Line was generously imparted during the writing of this novel and who read the draft. Bill's name was passed to me by Bill Burns, whose name was passed to me by someone whose name has sadly gone from my mind. Thanks to those people too, as well as John and Elaine Edwards who took two strangers into their Darwin home for several weeks and treated them like family. Finally, thanks to Carolyn and Peter Worth, who drove me all round the Top End in an RV while I gathered local colour and gave me a plane flight over that area of the Northern Territory for my 70th birthday present. Adelaide, I had already visited you in 2006 and found you delightful.

BY THE SAME AUTHOR

Novels
Witchwater Country
Spiral Winds
Standing on Shamsan

Science Fiction Novels
In Solitary
The Night of Kadar
Split Second
Gemini God
Theatre of Timesmiths
Cloudrock
Abandonati

Fantasy Novels
Hunter's Moon
Midnight's Sun
Frost Dancers
House of Tribes
Roof of Voyaging
The Princely Flower
Land of Mists
Highlander (novelisation of film script)
A Midsummer's Nightmare
Shadow-Hawk

Young Adults' Books
The Wizard of Woodworld
The Voyage of the Vigilance
The Rain Ghost
The Third Dragon
The Drowners
Billy Pink's Private Detective Agency

The Phantom Piper
The Electric Kid
The Brontë Girls
Cybercats
The Raiders
The Gargoyle
Welkin Weasels Book 1 – Thunder Oak
Welkin Weasels Book 2 – Castle Storm
Welkin Weasels Book 3 – Windjammer Run
Welkin Weasels Book 4 – Gaslight Geezers
Welkin Weasels Book 5 – Vampire Voles
Welkin Weasels Book 6 – Heastward Ho!
Drummer Boy
Hey, New Kid!
Heavenly Hosts v Hell United
The Lantern Fox
Soldier's Son
Monster School
Nightdancer
Faerieland Book 1 – Spiggot's Quest
Faerieland Book 2 – Mallmoc's Castle
Faerieland Book 3 – Boggart and Fen
The Silver Claw
Attica
Jigsaw
Hundred-Towered City

Horror Novels
The Street
Angel
Archangel

Short Story Collections
The Songbirds of Pain
In the Hollow of the Deep-sea Wave
In the Country of Tattooed Men
Hogfoot-right and Bird-hands

Moby Jack and Other Tall Tales
Tales from the Fragrant Harbour
Dark Hills, Hollow Clocks
The Fabulous Beast

Fantasy Novels as Kim Hunter
The Red Pavilions Book 1 – Knight's Dawn
The Red Pavilions Book 2 – Wizard's Funeral
The Red Pavilions Book 3 – Scabbard's Song

Historical Fantasy Novels as Richard Argent
Winter's Knight

Historical Sagas as FK Salwood
The Oystercatcher's Cry
The Saffron Fields
The Ragged School

Historical War Novels
Jack Crossman series
The Devil's Own
Valley of Death
Soldiers in the Mist
The Winter Soldiers
Attack on the Redan
Brothers of the Blade
Rogue Officer
Kiwi Wars

Ensign Early series
Scarlet Sash
Dragoons

Memoirs as Garry Douglas Kilworth
On my way to Samarkand: memoirs of a travelling writer

AUTHOR'S NOTE

At the age of fifteen years I was taught to send and receive Morse code at around 25 to 30 words per minute, a skill which I still retain at seventy though possibly at lower speeds. It is, in this technological age, an art that is completely redundant. There are more blacksmiths shoeing horses than telegraphists sending dots and dashes. Yet there was a time when communication by Morse key was at the cutting edge of technology. A time when a good telegraph operator was highly regarded and lauded as a man of science. The early 1870s was such a time, when the overland telegraph was constructed from Adelaide in South Australia to Port Darwin in the Northern Territory, a distance of over 2,000 miles of barely explored wilderness.

Only one man, John McDouall Stuart, had crossed the red heart of the continent before those construction crews set out to perform the fantastic feat that would take them well over two years to complete. They had to find trees for poles – 36,000 of them – to carry the wire, water to survive the harsh, arid outback and they would come into contact with a stone age people some of whom had never seen a white face before these strangely clad men tramped across their hunting grounds leaving a high-strung length of wire behind them to sing in the outback winds.

I believe that what made this enterprise unique was the fact that these 'explorers' were not actually explorers, but ordinary working men. Labourers who forged a path through a hostile landscape seen by only one pair of European eyes prior to theirs, building a communication link that would immediately connect Adelaide with two far, distant cities, London and New York.

Cities that could only physically be reached by a long and dangerous sea voyage of up to four months. With the overland telegraph line and subsea cables there was almost instant communication and it was as if the vastness of the globe had been tamed and brought to heel.

This book is a work that was created gradually over several long visits to the amazing, sweeping, mystical land that is Australia and includes one motorcycle ride of 4,000 kilometres through the Queensland outback. It is an historical novel: that is to say a warp of fiction woven into the weave of history. Once this has been done it is of course quite difficult for any reader to separate truth from untruth, even though named real people interact with creatures of my imagination and events that actually took place mesh with inventions that have only taken formation in my head. I extend my apologies to any descendants of the pioneers whose ancestors speak words I have put their mouths for the purpose of my story and whose characters have been reshaped by my pen. I have tried to imagine the trials they went through, the problems they had to solve, and to have them react accordingly. In fact, these are not those actual men, even though they bear the same names and share the same tremendous spirit of wild enterprise and high adventure.

On a more personal note, this novel has been a very special journey for me since it draws on a number of situations I have had to accommodate in my own life. At aged thirteen a friend and I became separated from a scout group and we were lost without water for almost two days in a desert region in what is now South Yemen. My experience in the wilderness at a young age has heavily influenced any plots involving wandering characters trying to find their way out of lonely wastelands.

When I grew to adulthood I found myself working closely as a member of a small group of men, often in isolated and sometimes bleak circumstances. As an RAF airman telegraphist, not yet in my twenties, I spent a year on a small remote coral island in the centre of the Indian Ocean. The way many men handled what they regarded as boredom and deprivation was to slip into a state of apathy and indifference. However, fortunately for me one close friend shared my views and saw the romance and delight in a unique experience. The subsea life was superb and I had the opportunity to read every book in our well-stocked island library.

Later still I had the responsibility for leading a group of servicemen, the nature of whose work caused us to travel clandestinely to remote, hostile areas of the Middle East. The humour, escapades and scenarios were sometimes extreme but have provided fodder for my writing ever since. I have also lived in and had a love affair with the Far East and Australia where I spent time with my daughter. The biggest attraction was always making an expedition into the outback – it felt like the widest most isolated open space on the planet. The sky, the horizon, unexpected trees, animals, outcrops of rock, Aborigines, all had impact.

My fascination with telegraphy continues to this day, despite progress to satellite communications and computers. I feel it is one of Man's greatest achievements. Global communications are now essential to our sense of well-being and security. The concern I experienced when I unexpectedly lost contact for several weeks, with my wife who was working in a remote area of India, was profound.

I worked for seventeen years within the RAF and eight years facilitating communications with Cable and Wireless Ltd. I hope when you read this book you will share the wonder of the very beginnings of global communication.

Garry Kilworth, 2014

THE ROUTE OF THE OVERLAND TELEGRAPH

This is an account of my part in the remarkable construction of the Adelaide to Port Darwin overland telegraph line. The tale was for a long while simply a savage beast in my chest which has now managed to claw its way out and onto these pages. I have no faith in the idea that anyone will read them.

Alexander McKenzie (Telegrapher)

Garry Kilworth

ONE

There was a warning shout from one of the Afghan cameleers. Someone was out there in the darkened wilderness. I'd heard the sounds too: a loud rattle of stones accompanied by a long, low moan. The faces of the work crew turned in the direction of the noises. Fear surged through me, as the thought of a native attack pierced my head. Then a strange mixture of both shock and relief swept through the camp as a minute later a lone white man staggered into the firelight. Tall and lean, his thick beard red with bull dust, we saw him blink rapidly in the flickering glow thrown over the scene by the fire and lamps.

'Help me,' he croaked, and reached out a hand.

For a few moments the whole crew simply sat as if stunned. To a man they stared at him while he swayed back and forth. I was close enough to see his bloodshot eyes, which contained a dazed and bewildered look. Then he began to fall forwards and would have crashed to the ground if Mr Roberts, the sub-overseer, had not swiftly sprung up and gathered the collapsing body in his arms.

As dawn broke the crews went out to look for suitable trees to cut for the poles and then to dig holes to put them in. Everyone in the camp had a regular job to do, except me, the telegraph operator, the line not yet being completed. I was given the task of ministering to the man, who was clearly exhausted, wasted, and near to death. Had he not found us when he did, he would have been gone within hours. I saw to his immediate needs, the most urgent of which was to get some water into him. Not too much in the beginning, but enough to revive him. I soaked a rag for him to suck on, rather than trying to pour water down his throat. By midday he was able to open his eyes and attend to my questions.

'What's your name, shipmate?' I asked him.

He came up from a lying position onto his elbows and stared into my face with a belligerent look in his eyes.

'Why d'you call me that? I'm no sailor.'

I shrugged. 'Force of a habit from the voyage. I'm not long off the boat from England.' I knew men dropped half of that word when greeting each other in Australia. 'All right, what do I call you?'

He looked up at the canvas ceiling. We were in one of the company tents and though the air was stifling inside, it was better than being out under a blazing sun.

'Where am I?'

'This is Section E of the overland telegraph project.'

A misty light came into his eyes and he coughed and lay back again, still staring up at the top of a tent pole.

'Ah, yes. O'course.'

He seemed satisfied with that, but I was still curious.

'You still haven't told me your name.'

'Not that it's any of your business.'

I felt a flash of anger go through me.

'This is my bloody camp you've wandered into and that makes it my business. Don't bother to feel grateful that I've just saved your life for you.'

He grunted out a half-laugh. 'I won't. Your camp, eh? You the big man?'

I felt my face redden with embarrassment. 'I'm not the overseer. I'm the telegraph operator.'

He nodded. 'I could tell you weren't a worker by your soft skin, when you was swabbing my face.'

'And I could tell you were an idiot by the way you went and lost yourself in a wilderness where water's scarce.'

A ripple went through his frame.

'By God, I'll...' In his rage he tried to struggle to his feet and I knew he wanted to attack me. The spittle sprayed from his mouth as the effort overtook him and he fell back again, his eyes still blazing.

'Take it easy,' I said, more quietly now, knowing that men with heatstroke often died after one or two days, even though they seem to have recovered. 'You're not out of the woods yet.'

'I know that,' he gasped. 'This is my country. I've lived in the outback most of my life. I don't need no soft-bellied English telegraph operator to tell me things I already know. Fuck you.'

'Fuck you, too. Now, take some more water...'

A short time later Mr Roberts came to the tent and asked how the invalid was doing. I told him he was coming on fairly well. Then the sub-overseer knelt by the man and asked him his name. To my astonishment the answer came immediately and without any resentment in the tone.

'Walker,' came the reply. 'Sholto Walker.'

There it was! Meek as you like. A different man lying there than the one who had spoken to me just a few moments earlier. He even looked different. Gone was the arrogance and hostility from his prostrate posture. In its stead there was a mildness that attracted pity from the observer. I was astonished at the change. Here was an actor who could have played Shakespeare's Hamlet with ease.

I looked at Mr Roberts. Somehow it seemed to me that *Sholto Walker* was not the man's real name. Perhaps the *Sholto*, which had come out of his mouth smoothly and easily. But not the *Walker*. It was too obvious. The fellow had *walked* into our camp. But this deceit must have passed over Roberts who evinced no evidence of scepticism. He simply nodded, gravely, and continued with his questions.

'How did you get here, Walker? Are you from another crew?'

'Yeah. Section D.'

'What's the name of your overseer?' I asked, quickly.

Sholto Walker suddenly screwed up his eyes and cried out, 'Christ my head hurts like hell. Feels as if it's goin' to explode.'

Roberts nodded and patted Walker's shoulder, sympathetically. 'You take it easy.'

Outside the tent, Mr Roberts said to me, 'He might make it, you never know. He seems a decent sort. There's no sense in sending him back to D. We can use him here, if we can get him back on his feet. Woods's loss is our gain, I say.'

'You don't think there's something strange here, sir?'

A shorter man than me, Roberts looked up and straight into my eyes.

'Why is that? Why would think that?'

'I don't know, I've just got this feeling.'

The sub-overseer sighed. 'Oh, feelings – well, I can't see what he would have to gain, riding off into the wilds. That's tantamount to committing suicide.'

I knew that Mr Roberts, and Mr William Harvey the chief overseer, were both under a great deal of pressure. The work was behind time and all their effort and concentration needed to be on the job. They would have no time for idle reflection, no time for fancies and suppositions.

I was going to say something further, when I suddenly remembered the company tent was just a few feet away. Mr Harvey would be in there, with his maps and instruments. That's the funny thing about people and tents. Because tents serve the same purpose as houses, which have thick walls of wood or stone, people must think they have the same properties of dulling sound. They'll talk loudly within a tent, without realising they can be as plainly heard outside as if they too were in the open air. Every word Roberts and I had exchanged must have been heard by Mr Harvey and of course the man who called himself Sholto Walker.

A final resigned wave of the hand and the sub-overseer scuttled away to take care of more urgent and important tasks.

Sholto Walker, a decent sort? How would Roberts know that from a few moments' acquaintance? Indeed, he could not.

However, I was prepared to be charitable. Walker might very well have been as good a man as any other, for all I knew. Perhaps my poor bedside manner had annoyed him? A man in pain is often bitter with people around him, even with those who are trying to help him. Time would, as always, reveal more, given that Walker lived. We had already lost a man through sunstroke and heatstroke. The body is forgiving of most abuses, but won't last long without liquid. You can starve it for a long period without harm, pickle it with alcohol, shatter its bones, even puncture its organs to a degree, but deny it fluid and it will perish.

That evening the men returned to the camp after a day's poling. They were dirty, dishevelled and heavily bearded. Their clothes were torn and filthy, and not a few of them looked worn and ill. We had already trekked for more than a thousand miles from Port Augusta over rough, inhospitable country, trudging over ironstone hills and across gum-tree plains with our bullock carts, horse wagons and saddle horses. Friendships had been forged, but also hostilities had flared. The manual workers were beat and yet the main job had only just begun. Controlling the emotional politics that flowed like lava through a group of men glued to each other over a period of eight months, ordinary men suffering all the privations and hardships of an alien, unfriendly wilderness, was probably the most difficult part of the overseers' duties. Harvey and Roberts, both surveyors by profession, with Forster their cadet, were used to handling men, but in conditions less aggravating.

The Afghan camel drivers seemed to fare better, but they were contained men and if they had their woes they kept them private. At least, they didn't share them with us. We had undergone hardships that would have threatened the sanity of the toughest of men. The route across central Australia through which only one small party led by a man named John Stuart had forged a path just over ten years previously, was being poled from end to end for the Overland Telegraph Line. When it was finished, a single line of galvanised wire would stretch from Adelaide to Port Darwin, a distance of nearly 2,000 miles, held in the air by over 36,000 poles. The thought of those figures made my head spin and I wondered if we were just foolish children setting out on an impossible enterprise.

'Come and eat, Alex. I've got yours here.'

I had been hailed by young Tam, seventeen years of age, originally from Ayrshire. Thomas saw me as a fellow Scot, my surname being McKenzie. However, I was born in Suffolk, England, and had no connections with Scotland, and in any case now saw myself as an Australian. I was happy to put the old country behind me and forge my career in this exciting new land which had so much to offer.

'What's for supper?' I asked, sitting down beside him. 'Don't tell me — red blanket and beans?'

His boyish grin went almost from ear to ear.

'You've got it. Booyoolee beef and beans. Everything begins with b tonight.'

'And most nights.'

Tam pointed at the tents with his spoon.

'How's the invalid?'

'Still breathing,' I replied, swallowing the mush in my mouth. 'I'll tell you one thing, Tam. That gaunt bloke that wandered in here last night certainly doesn't seem grateful for being saved.'

'Och, he's probably off his head at the minute,' said Tam. 'I wouldna want to be lost in this wilderness alone. I'd turn gie mad inside a few days.'

'How was the poling today?' I asked, changing the subject. 'You get much done?'

Tam shrugged. 'The ground's like brick and there's a lot of mulga about which is nay gude for the poles.' His face suddenly became drawn and pale. 'Aye,' he added in a distant tone, 'and there was a man out there. A dead black. Just lyin' stretched out on the red rock, his feet and hands gone. You couldna see his face at first, for the flies, but when Johnson brushed 'em off we noticed the birds had eaten his lips and eyes.' Tam's chest heaved once, before he added, 'Who would do a thing like that, cut a man's hands and feet away from his body?'

'We're strangers in a strange land,' I answered. 'There's a great deal we don't understand – and maybe never will.'

TWO

Looking down at this destitute man who called himself Sholto Walker, made me appreciate how fortunate I was in life. I was certainly lucky to have been given an education at a Board School, giving me the tools I needed to escape a life of farm labouring. Apart from this, I was not born into a family with wealth or prospects: my father at the time of my birth was a horseman on a Suffolk farm. My mother had inherited a sizeable plum-tree orchard from one of her uncles, but that was the extent of the family's assets. When my parents both died of the typhus within two weeks of each other, I sold the orchard and used the money first to purchase my training as a telegrapher, then my passage to South Australia. In Adelaide I met with a cousin who had emigrated before me and he put me in the way of obtaining work for the South Australian government on a project managed by a Mr Todd, also an immigrant.

How exceptional I feel being a man of science! Me, a farm worker's son given the privilege to be part of this astonishing and mysterious world of electricity. One of a band of elite, special beings with magic in our fingertips. Wild lightning, that used only to crackle across and crease the sky with its savageness, has now been tamed and forced to flow in wires. The sparkling freshness of it fills me with almost uncontainable excitement. Why even that strange new word 'science' is unknown to the ears of those country folk I knew in my childhood. I think my grandfather still calls it 'philosophy'. Yet here I am, a student of the code first devised by the American, Mr Samuel Morse, privy to a secret language known to only a very few on this earth, part of a fantastic enterprise to allow men to speak to each other though they be separated by thousands of miles, nay, half a the distance around the globe.

No wonder I feel special and honoured. I'm one of a new breed of men: an electric communicator. I lift the alphabet from paper and it surges through my blood to my hand and down the wire to another like me. Soon there will be no more wars, for a maharajah in India is now able to speak instantly with the Prime Minister in London and their differences can immediately and amicably be sorted out with little fuss or misunderstanding. The telegraph operators of this world are the future ambassadors of peace. And more, for trade will increase and explode across the whole surface of the planet. Even now there are ships driven by steam engines, powerful steel machines that travel on rails, factories and farms with mechanical devices that improve our existence and make this world a marvellous place on which to spend our lives.

Looking up at the vast canopy of stars, I wondered if they talked to each other with their spikes of light. Who knows what's out and up there, in that blackness decorated with glittering pebbles? If we can leap mountains and seas with our inventions. If we can penetrate every nook and cranny, every crack and canyon in the earth with our voices. If we can whisper across Asia and over Europe and be heard by our fellow men in the Isles of Britain, then impossibilities become probabilities and nothing is beyond the scope and vision of men. I cannot adequately express the emotion I feel that wells up inside me when I think of our profession. Surely we are the new wizards, working magic with flexible electric wands and cryptic keys? I have become a magus overnight.

'If you're expectin' me to die, you've got a long wait.'

Walker's eyes were on my face, red-veined, glaring.

'Damn, you're awake,' I said with a groan. 'I did think of cracking your skull with a rock, before you woke up.'

Walker sat up, fully now for the first time, and stared around him at the darkness. I wondered what had disturbed his sleep. Several of the men were filling the night with loud snoring. The livestock was restless too and there was snuffling and shuffling coming from the makeshift pens. Or had he indeed felt my gaze on his grizzled features?

'What am I doin' out here?'

'Mr Harvey, the overseer, thought you'd be better in the open air for a while, since the air in the tent's thick and stale. It's cool out here. Mr Harvey thought it would do you good.'

'Mr Harvey, Mr Harvey,' he said in a falsetto tone. Then in a normal voice, 'By God, you're an arse-kisser.'

'And you're your own man?'

'Yes, by God I am.'

'Got you a long way in life, hasn't it?'

There was no answer to this. He simply lay back down and stared up at the night sky, before saying, 'Your Mr Harvey knows what he's talkin' about. This is better. Look at those stars swimmin' around up there, like fish in a black bowl. Millions of 'em. Millions and millions. And so far away. Takes away the breath of a free man. Makes him feel as if he's got plenty of space to move around in.'

'You something of a poet, Mr Walker?' I asked, surprised by the depth of feeling in his tone.

I could see his features in the light from the embers of the dying fire. They were full of scorn.

'Poet? That *would* get me a long way in life.'

A thorny devil came out of the rocks and made its jerky way towards the fire. Then it veered off, its course directly towards us. Its strange faltering walk made it look as if its legs were rusted at the joints. Every so often it stopped and its head went from side to side, checking I supposed for danger. I had never seen one at night before and the firelight picked out its mottled red, brown and yellow markings making it appear quite a beautiful creature in its way. The rose-thorn spines covering its body would put off any predator who thought about swallowing it whole. However, there were creatures around who weren't interested in eating it, just killing it for what it was.

'Put the rock down,' I said to Walker, who was just about to crush the lizard. 'Leave it be.'

'Don't fuckin' tell me what to do.'

'I will while I'm carrying the pistol,' I told him. 'You'd better start getting some manners around me, mister. I don't give a damn who or what you were before you stumbled over us, this is a telegraph camp and I'm an important man around here. Maybe I might persuade Mr Harvey and Mr Roberts to investigate how you've finished up on our laps.'

I could tell by the look on his face that this had gone home. He took one last glance at the thorny devil, which had changed course again, now heading back for the pile of stones out of which it had emerged, then threw the rock away. It landed on a soft patch of sand with a thud. Walker then lay back down and closed his eyes.

Within a few minutes Sholto Walker was breathing heavily in a deep sleep and I was feeling I was a little nearer to understanding this belligerent man. Clearly he had a secret which he did not want discovered. I doubt very much whether the overseer or his deputy would actually be interested in anything I said about him, but he did not know that. He was not a man with any great knowledge of engineering projects. My superiors were concerned only with getting the job done within the time stipulated. They would not expend valuable energy on investigating the history of a single man who had caused no trouble, simply on the whim of one of their telegraph operators.

I took out my pocket watch. It was one o'clock and the camp was mostly asleep. There were two guards on duty, north and south. To the east was a steep, high escarpment and any native attack from that direction would need good climbers with alpine equipment, the latter which the Aborigines were unlikely to possess. The west was covered by the Afghans, who were light sleepers.

One of the Afghan camel drivers, Farzin, died of natural causes two days go and he was buried near a dry creek which we named after him. We left his burial to his fellow drivers. They washed the corpse in water and then wrapped it in white cloth. They placed him in his grave on his right side with his face to the North-west. Then the drivers did something that horrified me. They slit the throat of Farzin's favourite camel. It crashed to the ground and bled to death, snorting and moaning. The camel was then buried alongside its dead driver. The overseer was angry and went to the Afghans and a long discussion took place, the content of which was not passed on to the rest of us. We did learn that this was some kind of ritual which could not be avoided.

In the glowing embers of the fire I made a jug of coffee, then poured it into three tin mugs. It was hot and I had to wear poler's gloves to carry the mugs to the guards. I sat with one of the guards, a man named Wilson, while we drank our coffees. Wilson was Australian born but his father was an ex-convict originally from a village called Stogumber in Somerset, England. He told me his father was a lamb-stealer and had got away with his nefarious trade for a long time before he got careless and was caught. He would wait for the lambing time then, on a dark night, take one of the newly-born. The farmers often lost one or two of their lambs to foxes and wild dogs, and so did not investigate too thoroughly. Wilson's dad would keep the lamb alive, feeding it with bottled milk, until he was ready to slaughter it.

'He came on too bold,' he said, sipping the coffee. 'Started sellin' the meat stead of keepin' her just for the family. Travelling magistrate called him "a greedy, unprincipled criminal" and then he heard the magistrate went straight to the inn and ordered seven jumbuck chops with his spuds and greens. Said all that talk had got his taste juices flowin'. Somethin' a bit - what's the word – disrespectful there, eh?'

'Contemptuous?'

'Yes, that's more like it. Fat bastard went around the West Country, chuckin' men in jail, hanging em, sending 'em to the colonies and getting paid handsomely for it, and my dad was s'posed to be the greedy one. Anyhow,' he continued philosophically, 'We're better off out here. Got a good job and the country's wide open, ain't it? Anythin' could happen. I've heard that men got rich overnight at Poverty Point. Could happen to anybody if he's a lucky enough bugger.'

Poverty Point was at Ballarat in Victoria, where gold was found twenty years ago. Men had flocked to the area and some, a few, had made themselves rich. Jim Gwilliams, the Irishman down on the C Section crew, had become one of the wealthiest men in Australia at the age of fifteen years. He had still been in his school clothes when he uncovered a nugget the size of a tea cup. Naturally he had a wonderful time for about five years, but by the time he was twenty it had all gone. Some had been swindled from him, he lost a vast amount at the card tables, a goodly sum was spent on unnecessary and fleeting luxuries, and after he learned to drink, a vast amount went on filling other bellies with whisky, because most men, the Irish especially, do not like to drink alone.

I finished my coffee and bid Wilson a good night. I then went to the tent which I shared with seven other men. The air was rank under the canvas, but then none of us smelled of lavender. We seldom had the luxury of a good wash and we wore the same filthy clothes day-in, day-out. There were mouths with bad teeth in that tent and men who broke wind with a natural and unbridled ease. One of the older polers had a urinary problem and smelled constantly of dried piss. Those who did not snore breathed heavily and John Scully's throat was never empty of phlegm which relentlessly babbled and bubbled away in his gullet. It was not a place I enjoyed spending time in and always made myself tired enough to fall onto my blankets and thus to sleep. I would willingly have slept outside, under the stars, if it were not for my fear of snakes.

The one blessing was also a curse. Alcohol was banned in all the sections working on the overland telegraph by order of the Superintendent of Telegraphs, Charles Todd, the man responsible for the success of this enterprise. Any bottles of liquor found at the beginning of the construction had been smashed by the overseers. I missed my beer and sometimes I dreamed of that first jug of ale that would slip down my throat after it was all over, but I saw the reasoning behind the prohibition. Many of the men working on the line were habitual drinkers and there is nothing like alcohol for raising blood temperatures and causing trouble. I could see the craving in the eyes of a good number of the men when they smoked their pipes, for men do like a relaxing drink to accompany their smoking. I felt it myself, badly sometimes. But in my more sensible moments I was glad there were no drunks to roar and cause havoc once the day's work was done.

I woke the next morning to the reincarnation of a camp. There were the sounds of men talking, kicking at objects in their way, yelling at each other, and – loudest of all – noisily clearing their throats and noses. (With no women around to disapprove of ungentlemanly habits, men tend to throw their manners and niceties to the wind.) Domestic animals too, were defecating, urinating, moaning and groaning. The clatter of tools and cooking pots added to the cacophony. I was the last one out of my blankets and emerged from the tent still wearing the dirty clothes I had slept in. Directly opposite me, on a gentle slope, stood a big red kangaroo, watching the scene of the camp coming alive with an expression of mild interest. The wonder was that no one had yet shot him. He bounded off after another minute, as if that very thought had been transmitted to him by an invisible telegraph wire.

'Beautiful, eh?'

I turned to look at the speaker, a man who could have doubled for King Charles the First, with his long curly black locks and thick black beard that was growing every more fuzzy and wild by the day. It was Tim Felix, probably the most intelligent man in the camp, the overseers included. He was of medium height and build, and not particularly adept with a spade, but everyone marvelled at the size of his brain. Not that one needed to be a professor to rise above the intellects in Section E, but I would guess that even in academic society Tim Felix would have been regarded as a little more than above the ordinary. Tim had obviously been studying the same animal from a few feet away from me.

'Yes – but good to eat, too.'

'Ah, the age-old contradiction.'

I went to the water point and took a long draught, then stared around me at the landscape. There were sand hills humping the topography like whales' backs emerging from a red sea. Kangaroo grass decorated the base of these massive lumps, along with mulga scrub and spinifex. As always, the feeling of infinite space filled me with awe and worry. The sense that the landscape went out on all sides and had no visible end was disquieting. At times like these I was aware of the presence of my soul, which anywhere else would be a stranger to me. There was a bird soaring above the terrain, stirring a sky full of white cloud-puffs, too high to tell what type, though it looked to me like a kite. It was a clear, sparkling morning around fifty Fahrenheit which would grow to over seventy-five on reaching noon.

'You can assist the wire-fitters today,' said Roberts, as he passed me by. 'Walker's able to look after himself now.'

I spun on my heels.

'You're not leaving him alone in the camp.'

Roberts stopped in his tracks. 'He won't be alone. Cookie's here.'

'Yes, but he'll be too busy to keep an eye on Walker.'

Robert's fists went onto his hips, his arms perfect triangles.

'What is it with you, McKenzie?'

'I don't trust the man. We don't know anything about him. He comes wandering into our camp in the middle of the night, straight out of wilderness a thousand miles square? There's got to be more to it than that. If he was from D Section, then why doesn't he know the name of the overseer? Or his deputy? There's something not right about this. I think we should find out more about him before giving him the freedom to walk about the camp, looking into anything he pleases.'

Roberts looked exasperated. 'I haven't got time for all this. We're trying to cross a continent with a wire here. The Queensland Government is screaming for attention, saying they want the telegraph to go from Normanton and down across their state and I'm supposed to shilly-shally around with a poler? Do what you're told, McKenzie, and stop fretting me with all this unwarranted suspicion.

'Yes, sir,' I replied.

He turned back towards his destination and stumped off, still grumbling to one of his men walking with him. There were nineteen workmen, in all. Twenty, if you counted Sholto Walker. Others came and went to and from the depot located at Alice Well, down past D Section. Then there was me, and the two overseers. I was there to do line checks occasionally, ensuring that what the crew had erected actually worked. Our stretch from Barrow Creek to Tennant Creek was only around 150 miles. The whole line would eventually cross 2,000 miles, so ours was a relatively small part of the whole. Yet, you try to tell men who have been planted dead in the middle of desert country at the beginning of winter that they have an easy job and there's no need for concern. Harvey and Roberts were as anxious as men waiting for their wives to give birth to their first child. They both had permanent furrows on their foreheads that a ploughman would be proud of on his field.

From what I understood, the most difficult section would be from Palmerston down to Tennant Creek, the Northern Section, over 630 miles of the hardest country imaginable. There were rivers to cross, wetlands to negotiate, wild open country to tame. So far as we knew they had not yet planted a single pole. If they did not get going soon the wet season would be on them and they would bog down for sure. Rain came down like a biblical flood in the north and deep, sucking mud made any progress across the landscape an impossible venture. I was glad to be in the red heart of the continent, despite all its contrary moods.

We started work immediately after breakfast. A third of the men were sent out to find suitable trees and cut poles. The rest, except for the cadet Forster and me, went to dig holes and erect those poles that were ready-shaved to go into the ground. A few days previously Afghans and their camels had brought up more galvanised wire and insulators. We had already poled five miles. I had to get up to the top of the poles that were already embedded and pin up the wire and the insulators. It was awkward rather than backbreaking work. It was when I was up the second pole of the morning that I saw them in the far distance.

'Aborigines!'

Forster had obviously been dreaming and had drifted away to somewhere else.

'What?' he said, lifting his head to look up at me. 'What did you say?'

'There are blacks out there.'

I stared into the haze. It was only around 70 Fahrenheit, but snakes of heat rippled upwards from half-buried rocks distorting my long view. I could see several men, or possibly women, just standing on the desert staring in our direction. Dark, naked shapes, some with sticks or spears in their hands, others unarmed. How aptly they fitted into the landscape, as if they were part of the yellow-and-red ochre plain. Part of the bush and scrubland with its occasional creek running like a deep, jagged scar between two lines of dwarf trees. There must have been a dozen of them. At first there was no movement among them, which gave their appearance an eerie aspect. Then one of them gestured towards me with his arm. They must have been able to see me quite plainly, perched near the top of my pole, my dark, wide-brimmed hat on my head, my gingery beard gleaming like old bronze in the sunlight.

Still there was no forward, or backward, movement. They continued to stand and stare. Surely we must have been the first white men that these people had seen? Stuart, and more recently Ross and others had been through before us, but there was no reason to suppose the Aborigines in this region had crossed paths with them. How did they see us? As pale copies of real human beings? Ghosts perhaps, or something else unnatural and not of their world? I had no knowledge of their beliefs and had no way of guessing how we would be perceived. I knew that in other parts of Australia there had been battles and men had died on both sides. Were there lines of communication between the native tribes? Perhaps they had heard about us, giving rise to hostility from them?

'What are they doing, Alex?'

Forster brought me back from my musings.

'Nothing.'

'They must be doing something?'

'Just standing there, looking at me.'

'Shall I run and tell Mr Harvey?'

His face had an eager look and I knew he was thinking that as a messenger carrying exciting news such an action would raise his profile amongst the men. They would be pleased to grab a rest in the middle of the morning, while the surveyors pondered on whether to do anything about this new situation.

'No, they're way up ahead. Go and fetch me a rifle from the camp.'

Forster's face lost its colour. 'Christ, you're not going to shoot them?'

'Of course I'm not, you idiot. It's just a safety measure.'

Forster took to his heels, his feet drumming on the hard earth.

Once he had gone, I suddenly felt vulnerable. If I stayed up the pole I could keep the Aborigines in sight. But if they decided to attack I would have to get to the ground first before I could run. I had seen Aborigines use their boomerangs with great accuracy and effect from a fair distance and if they got a little closer to me I was a perfect target on top of this pole. I was undecided whether to go down or stay where I was. Then it occurred to me that a friendly gesture might help to keep the situation calm. The natives did not yet appear aggressive.

I smiled and waved. 'Hello there! G'day!'

The words sounded ludicrous the moment I used them.

Several of the group took some steps back. One of them, a youngster I think, even ran away a few paces. Finally, after staring for a few more minutes, the group turned and began walking slowly away in the direction they had come. They were too far off for me to hear if they were talking. Then Forster was back with a rifle and a pistol.

'Shall I throw one up to you?' he asked, excitedly. Clearly his first misgivings about shooting natives had changed to expectancy.

I shook my head. 'They've gone.'

He looked disappointed.

Later that day I visited Mr Harvey and Mr Roberts at their tent. They had a makeshift table on which they had spread a map. Mr Roberts had a prismatic compass in his hand along with a pair of dividers. They looked up at me as I ducked under the canvas entrance.

'Yes, McKenzie,' said Roberts in an unfriendly tone. 'It's not about the man Walker, is it?'

'No, sir, it's not.' I informed him of what I had seen that morning, being careful to mention that there was no sign of hostility from the Aborigines.'

Harvey said, 'Blacks? Why didn't you come to me straight away?'

'I saw no need to interrupt the work, sir. As I've told you, they weren't aggressive. If they had shown any desire to attack I would've sent Forster running for you.'

'In future I would prefer to know immediately.'

I nodded. 'I'm sorry.'

He shook his head. 'No, no, there's no set down procedure for this kind of thing, but we need one now. They might have returned in greater numbers. You did what you thought right, but hear me, in the future I would want to know straight away.

Roberts,' he said to the sub-overseer, 'will you see that the rest of the crew are aware?'

'I will indeed.' Mr Roberts gave me a steely stare. 'Is there anything else, McKenzie?'

'No, that's it.'

As I left, I turned round and said with a smile, 'If that's the first time they've seen a white man, it must have given them a very strange idea of us.'

Harvey asked, 'What d'you mean?'

'Well,' I said, chuckling, 'they must be asking themselves if all white men sit on the top of poles and wave their arms about.'

'You waved your arms about?' said Roberts, frowning. 'What did you do that for?'

I was tempted to reply, 'Semaphore', but I could see neither man was prepared to be in the least amused.

'Oh, just a friendly gesture.'

Roberts raised his eyebrows, but Mr Harvey had already dismissed me from his mind and was back to studying the map.

I left these serious and worried men to their cartography and walked back to the camp fire, the smell of mutton stew in my nostrils. A drover had arrived in the afternoon with a small herd of goats. A welcome sight and a change from gamey meat.

That evening revealed one of those spectacular sunsets that take away man's breath with its awesome beauty. A fiery sky that eventually turned to rust before the shades of night swept across the hills and plains. The mysterious landscape of the Australian wilderness had added its own elemental rufus hues to enhance the scene I felt privileged to be witnessing. A wonder of the natural world that a man in London or Dublin could never imagine, nor even find in his dreams. Were I an old man, my time come, I would have happily died under that amazing sky.

THREE

The next morning, on my way to my daily ablutions, I almost trod on a spiny creature.

'Bloody hell, hedgehog,' I muttered. 'What're you doing, wandering around here?'

'Echidna,' said a sharp voice, from behind me.

I turned to find Walker there, now on his feet, standing much taller than me. His narrow features were framed by a dark beard streaked with white. Two large ears stuck out through his long, lank hair on either side of his head. But it was his eyes which grasped my attention, drilling into my own with an intensity that caused a chill to run through me.

'What?' I asked, failing to understand. 'You said something.'

'I said that fellah there is an echidna, not a hedgehog. What the hell's a hedgehog, anyway. Some kind of a pig that sleeps in a hedge?'

'In a ditch, under a hedge. Echidna. Right.'

'Watch!'

Walker nudged the animal with his toe and it immediately began to burrow into the sand. Within a minute or two it had completely buried itself. I turned my attention back to the man in front of me.

'So, you're back on your feet.'

'Looks like it, don't it?'

'Are you staying? I mean, to work.'

'Why not? Mr Harvey seems to think it's a good idea. It don't matter to me whether I work for him, or for Mr Woods.'

I nodded. 'I see you've finally found out the name of Section D's surveyor.'

He leered. 'Not found out, McKenzie. I worked for him, remember?'

'So you say.'

His face clouded. I was continually amazed how quickly this Sholto Walker could alter his expression. Those terrible eyes narrowed dangerously.

'Are you callin' me a liar, McKenzie? No man calls me a liar and walks away with the word still in his mouth.'

'Prove it,' I said. 'Prove to me now you worked for Woods.'

'How?'

'The name of the sub-overseer?' I asked, quickly. 'And his cadet?'

He stared at me and after a few seconds the savage expression vanished into nowhere.

'Even if I am lying,' he said, grinning with long teeth, 'no one will take any account of your ramblings. You're not liked a lot, Mr Telegraph Operator. Not by most of the blokes round here, or Roberts, either. He thinks you're a bloody nuisance, most of the time, and I'm one to agree. You're a fucking mosquito, McKenzie.'

I flushed. It was partly true. I was not a favourite of Mr Roberts. To the rest of the men I was part of the management and therefore on the outside.

'So, you were lying. You never worked for Woods.'

'I'm sayin' *if* I'm not telling the truth, which I maintain I am, and I'll punch the lights out of any man who says different.'

I stared at him, wondering if I could take him in a fight. Although I was now a professional telegrapher, I had been raised on a farm, doing heavy labour. I was smaller but stockier than the lean, whipcord-muscled man before me. There was no certain outcome either way. It was not something I wanted to test, but if it came to it then there was no foregone conclusion that he would walk away the winner.

He said with a sneer, 'You'll never make an Australian, McKenzie.'

'And why's that?'

He gave me a lopsided smirk. 'Your eyelashes are too long, sweetheart.'

'That observation says more about you than it does about me, Walker.'

By this time the echidna had re-emerged and was quietly waddling away up a slope. Walker suddenly turned and kicked the animal like a football, sending it flying through the air. It struck a rockface and fell broken and bloody to the ground where it lay unmoving. I gaped. When he had first put his boot to the creature, to make it bury itself, the toe had been gentle against its rump. This attack was vicious and savage, totally unnecessary. Walker then turned back towards me and stared into my eyes with hooded lids and a twist to the corner of his mouth. I knew then that his unprovoked assault on the creature had nothing to do with the animal itself. Walker was giving me a message as to the nature of his character and indeed I was stunned and chilled by the callousness of the act.

I turned and walked away. It would do me no good to brawl with this belligerent newcomer. There were fist fights in the camp occasionally and once, even a spade fight between a couple of diggers whose tempers had finally blown like overheated boilers. You couldn't get two dozen tough labouring men living cheek-by-jowl in the outback without that happening every so often. However, those clashes were between the polers, axemen and wirers. I was supposed to be a responsible member of the staff. And I wasn't unique. I could be replaced if I caused enough trouble to concern my bosses. I desperately wanted to be one of the first operators on this historic line that crossed from the bottom to the top of my chosen country. There was no way I wanted to risk being sent back to Adelaide. I think Walker had worked all this out and knew he need not fear my suspicions. I had to learn to keep my mouth shut and leave him to his lies.

After breakfast, the gangs were just getting ready to go out to work on the line. Suddenly there was a shout of alarm and a group of about half-a-dozen men scattered. I soon realised what had caused the panic. On the ground near where they had been standing was a four-foot long snake coiled amongst the stones.

'That's a bloody taipan,' cried one of the men. 'One nip from that bastard and your wife'll be wearing black, Joe.'

Bates, who had a long-barrelled rifle slung over his shoulder, unslung it and said, 'I'll soon sort the bugger out.'

Without asking whether it was a good idea he took careful aim and fired at the creature. Immediately afterwards there was confusion as Bill Turmaine fell to floor with a high-pitched scream. The snake disappeared into a crack in the ground, clearly unhurt, while Bill was rolling in the dust holding his foot. When we clustered round him, I saw that there was a huge hole in his boot and blood was seeping through it.

Mr Roberts came running up.

'Who fired that gun?'

Bates said, 'Me, sir. There was a snake…'

'Jesus and Mary,' muttered Roberts, bending to look at Bill Turmaine's foot. 'You've shot one of your mates.'

I realised then that it must have been a ricochet. Bill was still yelling blue murder and there were tears streaming down the big man's cheeks. No one seemed to be doing anything to help him. Roberts seemed more interested in chastising Bates for causing the accident, telling him he was an idiot of the first water.

'Hadn't we better get Turmaine into a tent and have a look at his wound?' I said. Then without waiting for an answer I bent down and tried to lift the injured man. He was heavy, so someone else took the other side of him and we managed to heave him up and carry him to the nearest tent. Turmaine was simply weeping now and hammering his own thigh with his fist. The man who had assisted me now spoke to Bill in a harsh tone. 'Shut up, you Mary – what are you, a girl or a man?'

I saw then that my helper was Sholto Walker, who continued to berate our patient after we had laid him down on a blanket.

'Stop whining, for Christ's sake. It don't hurt that much.'

Turmaine was furious. 'How the hell would you know?' he shouted through his tears. 'I'm the poor bastard who's shot.'

'I been shot once or twice, worse than that little scratch. I know what it feels like and I didn't scream like a mummy's boy. Let's have a look at it.' He bent down and unlaced Turmaine's boot, then eased it off his foot, not without a renewed bout of yells and tears.

'Jesus, what a baby,' Walker snorted. 'I've seen braver two-year-olds.'

Once the boot and the sock were off, we inspected the wound together. The bullet had smashed a pit in Turmaine's ankle that made my stomach churn. The rock which had caused the ricochet had of course mashed the bullet into a distorted shape. The hole was huge and torn at the edges. Bits of shattered white bone were visible within the wound, which continued to dribble blood onto the blanket. However, that was not the extent of his injury. There was a second, larger hole down by his heel, which Walker inspected quite roughly, causing Turmaine to hit him on the shoulder with a clenched fist.

To my surprise, Walker took no notice of the blow and simply stuck an exploratory forefinger into the first hole, twisting it about for a while, then into the second hole, doing much the same. Turmaine struggled violently under this invasion of his raw wounds, whimpering and snarling by turns, trying to get a purchase on Walker's throat.

'Hold 'im down by the shoulders,' Walker ordered me.

'What?'

He shouted now. 'Do as you're bloody-well told.'

I knelt and forced Turmaine's upper body down, gripping his wrists and pinning his arms to the ground.

Finally Walker made pincers of his forefinger and thumb and dug deep inside the first hole again, coming out with some bits of woollen sock soaked in blood in his nails. He continued with this exercise entering the ugly wound several times, while Turmaine lay back in a sweaty half-faint, until Walker finally desisted. The smell of stale perspiration and urine filled the air in the tent and I wanted to gag. I stared at Turmaine's loins and saw a wet stain spreading over his crotch. I held my breath, forcing back any impulse to retch, knowing it would be made a great deal of by this stranger in our camp.

'What was all that about?' I asked him.

Walker shrugged. 'Well, he may still have to have that foot off, but I think I've got all the sock material out of the wound. It's that, if anything, that'll cause gangrene to set in. There's no lead in there, lucky for him. It came out of that hole under his heel. Better clean it up now and hope for the best.'

I said, 'How do you know all this – about cloth in the wound?'

'Oh my God,' he cried, in a tone of mock tragedy, 'I've given myself away.' His face twisted into a sneer.

Mr Roberts entered the tent at that moment, followed by Mr Harvey, which prevented any retort from me.

'How is he?' asked Roberts.

'Smashed ankle, sir,' said Walker in that ingratiating tone he used when talking with the overseers. 'Pretty bad, poor bloke.

I've done what I can to clean out the wound and cleared it of any foreign matter, but he's pretty crook. He needs to see a doc soon.'

'Well done, Walker,' replied Mr Harvey.

Both men stood over the supine body of Bill Turmaine, who had now given way to unconsciousness.

'Might I ask what kind of rifle was used?' said Walker.

Roberts replied, 'Oh, that? I think it was an old muzzle loader – a Minié I've been told by Bates. He brought it with him. Why?'

'Wondered about the calibre, sir. A Minié, you say? That's a point 702 calibre.' Walker held up his own calloused right thumb. 'About that size. It would rip into a man somethin' cruel, a bullet that size. No wonder the holes are so big.'

Harvey said, 'Holes?'

'Two,' answered Walker. 'One in, one out. There's no lead in his foot, as I told the telegraph operator here.'

I could not help myself. 'How is it that you know so much about wounds caused by firearms, Walker? And you seem to know a lot about weapons too. I've never heard of a Minié rifle.'

Sholto Walker looked suitably taken aback, which I knew was an act, before he replied, 'Not *all* weapons, McKenzie, just those used by the British army. I fought in the Crimean war, alongside one or two other Australians, doin' my bit for the mother country against the Russians.' He turned to face Harvey and Roberts. 'We had Miniés at first, but later they armed us with Enfields.' He turned back to me. 'I'm not surprised you haven't heard of them, McKenzie, if you haven't served.' He then picked up Bill Turmaine's boot, felt inside, and came out with a lump of metal. 'There it is,' he cried, holding it up for inspection, pleased with himself. 'Came out of his heel, but didn't have the force to go through the sole of his boot. Anyway, having seen such injuries before, Mr Harvey sir, I would recommend you get him to a surgeon quick. You don't want a man in camp with gangrene. One of us will have to saw his foot off and we ain't really set up for that, are we? No doctor here I suppose?'

Harvey shook his head, still staring down at the wounded man.

'The expedition's physician, Dr Renner's supposed to be somewhere down along the line, but we haven't seen him up here yet. No one else that I know of – not even a horse doctor. D Section has a man who used to be a hospital orderly in the army so's I understand. We could send him down there.'

'I agree,' added Roberts.

I could see how the overseers would not want a man with a smashed leg to remain in camp. Someone would have to nurse Turmaine, change his bandages, and indeed do something about removing his leg if the man contracted gangrene. Turmaine was a big responsibility now and Harvey and Roberts would want to pass that on to someone else. If we sent him to D Section they could hardly send him back again. They might pass him down the line to C or B or even A, but there would be no point in him being returned to the northern-most section in operation. I read in their eyes that they wanted to be rid of him as soon as possible.

Harvey said, 'He's still bleeding. That blanket is soaked. Dress his wound, McKenzie. Put a good firm bandage on it before he wakes up again and starts that yelling. Get one of the drivers to take the express wagon down to D Section. You go with him…'

'Me?' I interrupted. 'Why me?'

'Why not you?'

Roberts was nodding as if this was a good decision on the part of the senior surveyor.

'No reason,' I said, shrugging, 'but surely the driver doesn't need me to go with him?'

'No one likes to travel this country alone. You go with them, then report back to me, once he's in safe hands.'

FOUR

It was 6 June 1871. We were working northwards towards Port Darwin. Sections A,B,C and D had been in operation long since, also working northwards from their various starting points between Adelaide and what is known as the Red Centre of Australia. It was our job to reach a place called Tennant Creek. John Ross, the leader of the exploratory expedition, had preceded us along the route mapped by John McDouall Stuart ten years before, in order to make sure the landscape was suitable for poling. Ross, an experienced bushman, had reached the Roper River close to 370 or so miles south of Port Darwin by 19 May. All the sections were now working hard to complete the line by the coming New Year. A, B, C and D to the south of us and the Northern Section, coming down from Port Darwin.

We were the very centre of it all. I was at the centre of both a great enterprise and a great continent. How golden this seemed to me. How fortune had smiled on me to allow me to be part of this unique and glorious endeavour to cross a wilderness that had not yet even been conquered, only yet traversed by less than a handful of visionary pioneers. We were the conquerors, our shabby gang of ordinary men: wiremen, axemen, diggers, saddlers, blacksmiths, wheelwrights, coopers, cooks, drovers, drivers of horses, bullocks and camels, Morse operators and surveyors. We were slicing through new frontiers, building a wire road which whistled in the wind. Along that wire messages would travel using a strange invisible force called electricity.

And here am I, at the very crossroads, where the equator of our continent crosses a longitudinal length of galvanised wire.

At the same time as we were constructing the overland telegraph, a subsea cable was being laid from Java to Port Darwin, the harbour of the top end town of Palmerston, which would connect us halfway across the world to Britain. My mind whirled with the magnificence of this scientific venture. Soon I would be able to send a message to my beloved Sally, to be received in the heart of London.

I had gone to London from a village close to the Orwell River, to learn the science of the electric telegraph and to train to become what I am today, an operator of Mr Morse's code of dots and dashes, which is just like our ordinary alphabet and number system except in a different form. You can learn in a few days, perhaps a few hours, the corresponding sounds for each letter or number – dot-dash being A, dash-dot-dot-dot B, dot-dash-dot-dash-dot C, and so on, right through the alphabet and on into numbers. It's simply a memory game and not difficult at all.

However, when it's necessary to use it to send and receive a message, with a Morse key, you must have those codes locked in the intellect ready to be released without pause for thought. If you're to receive Morse code at thirty words a minute, that's a constant flow letters or figures, each of which has to be recognised and written down in less than half-a-second. There's no time for memory recall, only for intuitive recognition of a set of sounds. I have found it best to think of other things while sending or receiving Morse, such as what I'm to have for supper or possible names for my future children. If I even pause to think, 'Oh, that is dash-dot-dash-dash, the letter Y,' then a whole torrent of other letters has swept by without notice and are lost. It is my belief that Morse bypasses the mind and flows through the bloodstream from the ear to the hand without even bothering to employ the brain.

Sally, ah, Sally, she puts electricity in my blood.

We met while walking by the Thames. Sally's parasol blew away in the high wind and I chased it down, trapping it under Regent Bridge with an expert foot. She blushed when I presented her with the runaway and said she was very grateful to the 'kind sir' who had returned her property and would have walked away without further discourse had I not taken her gently by the arm and enquired where I might find a coffeehouse, being a complete stranger to the big city.

'Why sir,' she replied, while nervously spinning her parasol, 'there is one not very far from here, called Button's coffeehouse.'

'May I be so bold as to ask you to accompany me to this establishment?'

She blinked, furiously. 'No sir, you may not. I do not know you and I am not the kind of woman...'

'Please, please,' I said. 'I have no intention of being rude and can see you are a lady of fine manners. I would not upset you for the world, but,' I waved my hands in the air, 'how is a young man to get to know someone like you, if he knows no one in London at all? I am here to learn Morse...have you heard of the Morse code?'

'No, but that doesn't make me stupid.'

'Of course it doesn't, it's a very new thing, to do with electric current. I am able to send messages in the form of telegrams over an electrically charged wire. But that's by the by, what I mean to say is, I'm new in town and very lonely for just company, nothing untoward you understand, just to talk with another human being.'

She half-smiled at this and said, 'Well, I am certainly a human being.'

I laughed. 'That's the spirit. We are both human beings, who must communicate with one another.'

All the while we had been talking we had indeed also been walking, despite my companion's original refusal to accompany me. We now found ourselves outside a coffeehouse. The street was busy with passersby and traffic. Several times in my eagerness to be attentive to her words I had almost trodden in one of the piles of horse dung that littered the roads we had crossed. She herself had had to navigate carefully, since she wore a pretty cobalt-blue dress with a high lace collar and many flounces, the hem of which trailed along the ground around her feet. I was most admiring of her hat which perched high on her head, the gauze veil lifting in the breeze. She stood a head lower than me and this diaphanous item flicked back and forth under my nose.

I turned to my new friend and said, 'Would you join me in a coffee, please?'

Her look darkened. 'I can't go in there. You forget, sir, I am a woman.'

I was struck at how annoyed she seemed by my stupidity. Or perhaps it was because of the stupidity of male society, who would of course have created a fuss at a lady entering a gentlemen's sacred realm. One or the other, or both. Her frown was like a dark rain cloud having swept over what was previously a sunny sky. I noticed how clear and cream-like was her complexion, set alight by two beautiful eyes that were alternately hard as sapphires or as soft as the blue feathers on a jay's wing. How could I let her go now? I could not. I attempted to put things right. I did not want her to simply march away in a temper.

'Of course not, forgive me. I wasn't thinking. I told you, I am new to the city. There are no coffeehouses where I come from. Could we walk then? And perhaps find a park bench on which to sit and talk? I assure you I have no ulterior motives or awful intentions. I'm just excited with my new profession and want to share that excitement with someone. I have no one whom I can transmit it to here in London.

'Transmit? That's a funny word.'

'Ah,' I replied, 'a telegraph operator's word.'

'Well,' she said, clearly coming to a decision, 'we have not been formally introduced and my mother would have a fit if she knew I was being accosted by a strange man, but you have a nice face – yes, you have – a very nice face, and you seem to be sincere. There are the Riverside Gardens down by the water. It is quite open to view from the pavement above, so we shall not be secreting ourselves away.'

'Secreting? That's a funny word.'

She giggled. 'It's a lady librarian's word.'

'My goodness,' I said, 'you're a librarian? Why that's a modern profession too. You see we have a great deal in common...'

Ten minutes later we were seated in the gardens and I said to her, 'My name is Alexander – Alexander McKenzie.'

'A Scottish name. You don't sound Scotch, Mr McKenzie.'

'No, no, my grandfather came down to England in his youth and we are all virtually English now. I still have relatives north of the border and I still love to go to the country of my ancestors. It's very beautiful up there, especially in the Highlands. There are golden eagles and mountains covered in heather. Beautiful. But a man must make his way in these modern times. Things are changing Miss...'

'Whiting.'

'...Miss Whiting. We must seize our opportunities. One sentence has changed the world. *What hath God wrought.*'

'Indeed, you are a religious man, Mr McKenzie?'

I laughed. 'No, not as such. Oh, I'm as God-fearing as the next man – or woman – but that's not why I used those words.

That sentence was the first ever message transmitted in Railroad Morse by its inventor, Mr Samuel Morse. Railroad Morse is used in America but in Europe we now use the International Morse Code, which will of course change the whole nature of our society. We are hurtling into a future, Miss Whiting, where there will be no more idiotic wars because all misunderstandings will be immediately rectified by the use of telegraphy.'

'*What hath God wrought. Behold, the people shall rise up as a great lion and lift up himself as a great lion.* Numbers, Chapter 23 verses 23 and 24.'

'Miss Whiting?' I said, turning to her in amazement. 'It seems you *are* a very religious person.'

She smiled, wryly. 'Not especially, Mr McKenzie, but as the telegraph is your *forté*, so mine is books. The Bible, you will recollect, is a book, Mr McKenzie.'

'A rather large book. Do you know every chapter and verse?'

She laughed. 'Certainly not. But I am familiar with a great deal of it, since I was made to read the Bible every day as a child.'

'Well, you still astound me. I am all admiration.'

'Indeed, it seems I am here on the banks of Father Thames for a didactic discourse from an Anglo-Scot, Mr McKenzie.' But she said it with a twinkle in her eye. 'You forget I am a mere woman, with no pretensions to understand the male world of engineering and machinery. I prefer books. Books are what will save mankind from destroying itself, not machinery. Indeed, I was reading in the *Times* newspaper the other day that in the war in America they are using a machine called a Gatling gun, which fires one bullet after another in rapid succession, allowing the soldier operating the weapon to cut down humans in the manner of mowing corn stalks. I'm afraid I do not see machines as progress, Mr McKenzie, at least not progress that will enlighten mankind and allow nations to be at peace with one another without reserve.'

'Perhaps there are some machines which are for good and some which are best not invented?'

We talked for a long while, animatedly, sometimes hotly disputing one another's arguments. I had never met a woman like her. She was intensely pretty, but also very intelligent and knowledgable about many things. I am not one of those men who find intellect in a woman threatening. In fact I think it is necessary to a lasting relationship. Why would a man want to spend much of his time with someone who had little understanding of the world and its wonders?

I learned her Christian name was Sally. Sally Whiting, the librarian. We made a pact to meet again very shortly, though I agreed with her that we should find someone to introduce us formally, so that she could in good faith go to her parents and tell them that she had met someone through such-and-such a cousin who seemed a 'nice man'. It was important to her that she be open with her parents. She assured me that such a cousin would not be difficult to find, since she had 'dozens of them' living in places like Shepherds Bush and Catford, 'not to mention places south of the river, such as Greenwich'.

FIVE

'What hath God wrought.' I said aloud.

The driver of the horse-drawn express wagon, a more comfortable ride for our patient than a dray or a bullock wagon, glanced sideways at me before he spat tobacco juice over his right shoulder.

'Sorry,' I said. 'Thinking out loud.'

'Strange thoughts,' muttered the driver, flicking the reins.

'Sshrange thoughts,' echoed our passenger, who had been made dead drunk for the journey so far. Alcohol was forbidden the workers, but it seemed the overseers had access to 'certain medical supplies'. 'Sshrange fuckiin' thoughts. Go way, fuckin' flies. Fuckin' ants. Fuckin' sky…'

There was no road south of course. No road anywhere out here in the outback. Visible tracks, where we and others had brought up our wagons and other transport, but these were marked in the dust and travelled over rocky ground, through creeks, along animal trails, over passes between mountains. The wagon jolted and banged on the uneven ground, throwing Bill Turmaine back and forth. Occasionally he yelled as the pain penetrated the alcohol barrier, but for the most part he was out of it. I had instructions to give him more of the transparent liquid when he started to look like he was sobering up, which would not be for some hours. Naturally the driver and I had tested the 'medicine' and found it satisfactory and had then tested it some more. Now there was a danger that it would run out before we got Bill to a doctor.

We bounced and lumbered through that twilight world of the outback which seems empty of all but mystical scenery, seeing the occasional wild creature but no human being. Broken white trees like ghosts on the landscape. Red rockhangs and sandhills forming an ocean of frozen waves and swells.

I was forever trying to improve my acquaintance with the natural world, but lacked a tutor to whom I could direct my many questions. Most of the workmen on the construction party were no more knowledgeable than I was and often had nicknames for wildlife and plants, such as 'gum tree' for the eucalyptus, or 'boomer' for a big kangaroo. I heard talk about a creature they call a 'bunyip' which still remains a mystery to me. However even Tim Felix had grown weary of my inquisitive nature and I had ceased asking.

Equally I've little patience for the Latin labels that natural philosophers put on nature's wildlife and plants: they're of little use to common men like me. Latin seems designed to keep a wall between ordinary people and the subject. It's the language the clergy once used to maintain their exclusivity. While in a port on the way to Australia I asked a passenger the name of a crab-like sea creature I did not recognise and the gentleman told me, 'It is the *Palinurus vulgaris*, sir. Common in these waters.' Later, I asked a member of the crew, a birth-right Australian, the same question and he told me it was a *yabby*.

Finally, I found out the common name for this crustacean is a *crayfish*. I always seem to find myself in the middle of two layers of society, belonging to neither, despised by both. Here on the line the management do not see me as one of them and the labourers don't admit me to their circle either. So here I am, at the moment alone in the middle, squashed between two powerful forces: unyielding authoritarian granite on the top, thick dense puddingstone at the bottom.

My ignorance still needs enlightening. The echidna, which I thought was a hedgehog, is a good example. I suppose I should have thanked Walker for giving me the common name for that animal.

On the third day out Joe was in the process of complaining to me about two drivers of bullock wagons, who were women. He did not think his sort of job was a suitable one for members of the opposite sex.

'Not that they look like women,' he said, snorting. 'They're oversize girls with arms on them as big as a boomer's thighs. That Silvie Jones f'rinstance. Big girl. But ugly. Ugly as a frogmouth.'

'I heard she was a beauty,' I said, 'though I haven't had the pleasure.'

'Beauty? You can stare at that sea cow's mug of hers for hours and beauty you will not find, mate. Beauty? You must have been talking to one of them stockmen or drovers – blokes on outback farms who never see a human female from one year to the next. O' course they'll find beauty in women like Silvie, since she reminds 'em vaguely of somethin' they've been wantin' to encounter for the last twenty years. A creature they've almost forgotten existed in the world, leaving 'em wonderin' if this thing called a woman is somethin' their imagination dreamed up.'

'You think that's true?'

'A starvin' man will see a feast in a lump of stale bread. That don't make it a feast though. It's still a chunk of crust, ain't it?'

'Stop the wagon!' I said, abruptly.

Joe did as he was asked, instinctively I believe, but he subsequently showed his annoyance at being told what to do by swearing a couple of times into my face. Bill, in the back of the wagon, his medicine alcohol having been depleted, let out a bellow of pain.

'Sorry Joe, but I've seen something...'

I jumped down from the wagon and made my way through some spinifex. As I neared the place where I had seen a glint of metal, about a hundred yards from the wagon, the awful smell of putrid flesh attacked my nostrils. The corpse was rank, fouling the atmosphere with its fetid gases. My stomach churned and heaved. I kept going though and came upon a carcass half-hidden by the spinifex. It was a dead horse. The glint had been from the bridle bit which lay near the creature's mouth.

Covering my nose and mouth with my kerchief, coughing a little, I began to inspect the carcass. Studying the remains it seemed to me this had been a prime mount, a beautiful black Australian stock horse. The hide and the bones remained and quite a bit of the flesh had not been eaten by carrion. I was no farmer or breeder, any more than I was a naturalist, but I had seen mounts like this one in Adelaide market and I knew what I was looking at. This was no wagon-puller. This was a horse built for speed and endurance, not for dragging goods.

The saddle was still there, loosely hanging bearing down on the spine of the skeleton. It was a good one. Good leather, polished with use. The rest of the tack was there too. I took out my clasp knife, opened it, and cut away a unique-looking, elaborate stirrup, decorated with centripetal designs and flourishes. This I slipped into my trouser pocket. Then I walked away from the spot, eager to escape the stink and the flies, the maggots, and all the other members of the lower order of beings which were feeding gloriously on this bounty which had fallen from the sky. As I walked away a wedge-tailed eagle came down to investigate the cadaver, rooting around with its talons and beak. It was a marvellous bird, the king of the skies, the thunderbolt of Tennyson's poem, though I doubt the poet had ever seen an Australian wedgie.

'You finished?' asked Joe, irritably, as I climbed back into the wagon.

'Sorry, Joe. It was important.'

'So's gettin' this moanin' bastard in the back down to Section D. Giddup!'

That evening there was a light fall of rain, somewhat late for the season. When I rolled out of my swag in the morning the whole world was verdant with delicate green plants. Gentle, rolling waves of greenery as far as I could see. I breathed deeply, as if to inhale the beauty of this scene down into my lungs, to refresh my spirit and body. Dry, grit-like seeds, lying dormant for months, had sprung into life as if by magic. God's magic, I suppose many would say. It appeared to me that mustard and cress covered the landscape with a natural cloak. By noon it would be gone, crisp and dry, awaiting the next rainfall.

When we arrived at D Section, the domain of Mr Woods, he was none too pleased to have been handed an invalid. I had guessed as much. Now he was saddled with an invalid, which would just give him one more problem on top of those he already had.

'What the hell am I supposed to do with him?' he cried.

'Mr Harvey said you had a surgeon or someone like that,' I replied. 'He'll probably need that foot off. It's beginning to stink already.'

'We don't have a bloody surgeon. He knows we don't have a bloody surgeon. Is the wound going black?'

'Yes.'

'Bloody hell.' He beat his thigh with his broad brimmed hat, causing a cloud of dust to fly off his riding breeches. 'I've a good mind to send him back to Harvey, with a letter of No Thanks.'

'Turmaine will die before then. He's already raving.'

Woods snorted. '*He's* raving? I'm bloody raving. All right, McKenzie, not your fault. Who in God's name shot the poor bugger in the first place? Was it a fight or an accident?'

I told him the story of the shooting and Mr Woods's eyes rolled in his head as he contemplated the vagaries of Man. I liked Woods. He treated me with the sort of respect a telegrapher should be accorded. Not at all in the contemptuous way that Roberts did. I have no idea why Roberts disliked me so much – Mr Harvey was indifferent rather than hostile – but certainly it was refreshing to be spoken to as a skilled operator who was an important member of the team. There was no sneering dismissal of my views from Mr Woods as he listened attentively to what I had to say.

'By the way,' I asked, after passing on all the news of our problems and progress at E Section, 'did you have a man called Walker on your crew? Someone, who went missing? We had a Sholto Walker stagger into our camp and he claimed to have got lost. He said he had worked with D Section, though he didn't know the names of either of his overseers – your and Mr Jarvis's names. Said he got parted from the crew while out looking for timber, then found he was lost, though I don't know why any lost soul should head north in this country. Only a fool would not be able to see the position of the sun in the sky and work out a rough compass from that, and whatever else Walker is, he doesn't appear to be a fool.'

A frown appeared on the forehead of the chief surveyor before he finally said, 'I don't recall anyone of that name and we certainly haven't lost anyone. One or two accidents and illnesses, naturally, and men have been sent back down the line, but Walker? No. No Walker, not to my knowledge. You might have a word with Steve Jarvis. He might have some idea of a man up from the depot perhaps. Sounds a rum business to me and you sound suspicious of the man's story.'

'It just doesn't add up, Mr Woods, and I like my sums to end up with the correct answer.'

'Quite right, man. Quite right. See Steve Jarvis. Now, while you're here, could you test our line for us, back for about twenty miles? Young Bagot's got the equipment you need. Morse key, battery, relay, sounder and some other device. My operator has had to go back down the line to assist C Section, so I would appreciate your help.'

'I'll need a receiver. I don't need the sounder, but I do need a receiver, unless there's someone else here who can read Morse?'

'Not to my knowledge.'

I had a good meal, courtesy of D's cook, which was welcome after several days of biscuits and tea. There was some good, fresh lamb to be had, since some stockmen were passing through on their way north. A pair of brothers and their drovers were driving several thousand sheep, goats and horses all the way up to Palmerston. They had had to work their way up the continent from waterhole to waterhole, stopping at the construction sites on the way. That was something to admire, the initiative and courage of these two brothers, John and Ralph Milner. Having heard of the overland telegraph enterprise, they had decided to take advantage of the pioneering venture and set out on one of their own, crossing the mountain ranges and deserts with their stock.

Apart from filling my stomach I also grabbed some tobacco for my pipe, after running out on the way down. As I was walking through the camp I was approached by a shortish, wide-shouldered man in a bright red shirt. He was carrying a box and black folded board. A smile seemed deeply etched into his features as if the lines and creases of his face were set to a humorous disposition. It made me wonder if, underneath that expression, the man himself might sometimes be melancholy and yet be without the power to reveal it to others. The hair on his head was jet black and slicked down with grease which emanated a flowery-sweet smell even from twenty yards away. However, he looked a kiln-hardened man, well-muscled and tough, whose appearance and demeanour would make anyone think twice about calling him a fancy name.

'G'day mate,' he said, cheerfully. 'Want a game of chess?'

The offer made me blink in astonishment.

'No, why would I?'

'Just asking. You look an intelligent sort of bloke. I can't seem to find anyone up here who knows how to play.'

I shrugged. 'I know the moves, of the pieces, but you need more than that to play chess properly. I've learned that much. Anyway, I'm very busy. I've got work to do.'

'Hey, look – you the telegraph operator?'

I nodded.

'Well, when you go back – you come from up in E Section, right? Well, when you go back, take me with you, eh? I've got all I need from this crew. I'm a reporter, for the *South Australian Journal*. They sent me up here to get the stories from you blokes. So, when you're ready to ride up to your own camp, I'll come along, if that's all right with you.'

He said it as if even if it wasn't 'all right' with me, he was determined to come along anyway.

'Yeah, I'll give you the nod.'

'Thanks mate.' He grinned and reached forward to grip my hand far harder than necessary and shake it with his own, the skin of which was as calloused as the shell of a wild tortoise. ''Preciate it.'

He walked away and I continued my search for the local cadet, thinking that Harvey and Roberts would not thank me at all for bringing along a bloody news reporter to disrupt their workings. In which case I had no intention of taking him with me when I left. He would have to find some other idiot to lead him up there. All he had to do was follow the wire in any case, so he actually didn't need a guide. My feeling was that the wilderness scared him and he needed company. I was not a man who liked the responsibility of protecting others. I could look after myself, but I didn't want the job of acting nurse maid.

With the cadet Bagot's help I connected a battery and a Siemens telegraph receiver to the line in the camp. The receiver was almost ten years old, but it was still in very good condition. The battery's cells had recently had their copper sulphate solutions replenished so they were fully charged and ready for use. This is the magic of electricity. You take an empty canister, fill it with an ordinary fluid and hey presto you've got electricity. Mr Woods was a good overseer. He would have checked the cells himself and had the solution changed if the charge was low.

Inside a portable shack I stared at the main battery with a sense of wonder in my heart. Slivers of sunbeams streamed through cracks in the wall and brought the Meidinger cells to a sparkling array of light. There were eighty jars, and jars within those jars, packed with copper sulphate crystals, forming a block of vivid, sparkling blue colour five feet by four feet and standing ten inches high. Also within the glass jars were zinc cylindrical electrodes and lead plates. Here was the true reward of the alchemist: not base metal turned to gold, but to electricity. Those old would-be wizards seeking wealth through chemistry had been chasing the wrong grail. Gold had been the dream of men pursuing fame and fortune, but electricity was real, dependable money. This bank of 80 cells, easily produced, would give me 120 volts of pure, crackling energy to send down my line. Contained in these simple jars was a magical power that would carry messages across a wide wilderness. It would bring together men who were physically thousands of miles apart. They could 'talk' as if they were in the same room with each other.

Before leaving camp I completed the main single-wire circuit by earthing it, but I also had to set up a small local circuit for the Siemens telegraph receiver, which could not be connected to the main circuit. For the battery to this circuit I used a set of Leclanche cells contained in a porous pot. The circuit, being very small, had little resistance and therefore produced the high current needed for the receiver. A relay device helped to boost the power from the line.

Now I had to ride down the line and use my Morse key to test its effectiveness. If it was good, my message would be on the paper tape of the receiver when I returned in the form of dots and dashes. Finally, Bagot found me a good stock horse to ride down the line. This was my real work and I loved it. Not digging holes, not pinning wire, not escorting invalids, but sending and receiving Morse code.

'By the way,' I said to Bagot before I left, 'you're a local boy, eh? You know South Australia?'

'Some of it,' replied the youth. 'Not around here, though.' He stared out at the wilderness around him as if he were personally aggrieved by its presence.

'No, I mean down at the coast, around the Murray – out on the Yellabina and maybe the Nullarbor?'

'Yeah, a bit.'

'What do you know of any bushrangers around the area?'

At the mention of Australia's highwaymen, Bagot's eyes lit up. He was a typical youth. The idea of bad men vicariously holding up stages and robbing banks obviously appealed to his imagination. Gun battles, fleeing the law on a fast faithful horse, hiding up in the barn of an older friend with a beautiful daughter, this was the romantic stuff of a life of excitement and drama. I imagined these visions racing through the brain behind his eyes as he contemplated the subject. He was not yet quite old enough to appreciate the fact that actually pioneering a vast wilderness was a great adventure. He probably missed dances and parties with girls of his own age, and had had quite enough of bull dust in his porridge.

'Captain Midnight,' he said, emphatically.

I blinked. 'Captain Midnight? Is that a name from a romantic novel?'

'No, no, that's his name. Well, his *real* name is Tom Smith, but that's what they call him in the newspapers. Captain Midnight. He was in the Parramatta gaol, 'til he escaped. Now he's out there somewhere, robbing and killing. I heard he killed a constable in Melbourne, then rode this way. A sergeant, he shot. Bullet straight through the heart. They called on him to surrender in the Queen's name, but he fought his way out of the trap they'd laid for him at the Wonbobbie Inn.'

The youth's eyes were alight with passion, as he recounted the tale he had read in a newspaper, probably brought up on one of the supply wagons.

'And he rode this way, towards the Northern Territory?'

Jarvis screwed his face up. 'Naw – into South Australia. Who'd want to come up here?'

'I suppose not. When was this, by the way?'

'When?' he scratched his head. ''Bout a year ago, I think.'

'A *year* ago?'

'Yep, 'bout that.'

I rode out, along the line, southwards for twenty miles. It took me several hours as I had to walk the horse over rough ground and around huge clumps of spinifex. Finally I reached the point where I'd last checked the line, only to find a pole that had obviously been struck by lightning. The insulator was shattered and the wire dangled. Poles were normally buried four-feet deep, but this one had been dislodged from its base and leaned over precariously. It seemed that the wire-fitters had not been out this way in the last few days.

I righted the pole using the horse to pull it vertical, then I piled rocks at the base. Someone would have to come out later and do a more thorough and permanent job. I also managed to repair the break in the wire with a spare insulator from a pile that had been left hidden. According to a notice pinned to one of the poles, they were secreted under a saltbush. I found them easily. It was safe enough to leave such a sign, since it was certain the locals could not read English. The company's men didn't trust the Aborigines to leave the insulators where they were: the blacks might just take them home out of curiosity.

Mr Woods never called the Aborigines thieves. The natives, he said, 'took' things, but they did not 'steal' them. Woods had told me he believed the blacks had no concept of personal ownership. All things belonged to all men. I found that hard to understand, but I respected Woods and therefore I tried to respect his principles – though if an Aborigine had crept into my tent and had stolen my brass Morse key, I would have found it extremely difficult to treat the act philosophically. So far I had had no dealings with the local people, but I guessed that would not last out in the wilderness, which was more theirs than mine, even though they might deny ownership of it.

I connected my Morse key to the line. When I used it the action sent 120 volt electrical pulses along the galvanised iron wire. It felt good to have a key in my hand once again and to be using my skill. I was reminded every time I used a Morse key, that although Samuel Morse invented the original code, it was his friend, Alfred Vail who was probably responsible for the electromagnetic alphabet. Poor old Alfred was not much mentioned by Mr Morse, once the latter became famous.

It appears to me that great men are often jealous of sharing their fame once they have it. Look at the argument that raged between those two eminent explorers of the African Nile, John Speke and Richard Burton, both of whom did their part in their expedition, yet on returning each tried to claim all the glory. If two men who have shared tremendous adversity together and probably saved each other's lives, cannot share the consequent fame between them, then there is little hope for inventors who hardly ever leave their home shores.

Once I'd sent my test message – *What hath Man wrought* – I rode back a short way, but knew I couldn't get right back to camp before dark. I had no swag with me, so I had to sleep on the bare earth. I had water though and the horse wasn't fidgety. I shared my biscuits out between myself and the mare, though I doubt she appreciated my even-handedness and would have eaten the lot if she could've got hold of them. We humans often endow our animals with our own feelings and slip into the belief that they know when we are being magnanimous or unjust. They don't, of course. There may be a bond there, but it is devoid of emotion, I'm sure of that. I thought to myself, 'If I had a pet hound it would eat me if it was in danger of starving to death.' Then I had a second thought, which was that of course I would eat the hound if the circumstances were reversed – so that was no guide to love.

The stars came out in their silver clusters. I was no astronomer or navigator, but loved them simply for their beauty rather than their formations. Of course, I knew the Southern Cross, just as back in England I could have pointed out the Plough. The Cross is more important to me now than the Plough. According to authority I am still an Englishman but my heart is in this new land. I do not want to go back to that island some still call 'Home'. Queen Victoria remains my monarch and the British Government has rulership over me, even out here in the middle of the wilderness, thousands of miles from London's Houses of Parliament, but one day I'm sure Australia will throw off the leash and become a country in its own right. Perhaps even several countries, the Australian states being as large as several other nation states. Why, I'm told the British Isles would fit inside Australia thirty times and still there would be spare land around its edges.

These thoughts whirled in my head, as I tried to fall asleep on a soft patch of sand. In truth I was worried that a snake would curl up with me, seeking the warmth of my body. The temperature dropped at night down below 50 degrees Fahrenheit, which isn't chilly, but it's said that reptiles are cold blooded creatures and don't produce heat from within. They need some external agent like the sun or possibly a human being to warm them up and give them energy. I held the firm belief that snakes are far from grateful creatures and even though a man may assist them by sharing his body heat with them, those fortunate serpents would not feel obliged to desist from biting their benefactors.

Before I fell asleep I heard a deep, hollow, throaty, wailing sound coming out of the surrounding hills. What was out there in the wilderness that would make such a haunting noise? It was as if the wind had suddenly taken to temple chanting in a rhythmic moaning way.

On standing up I noticed there were fires on the hillsides surrounding my campsite. People. It was people who were producing those odd laments enhanced by an underlying, deep, thrumming sound. Then, after a while, a giant began using a hollow hill as an ocarina, playing a strange tune that floated on the back of the night air. I had heard these sounds before, when visiting an Aboriginal village. Music. Black people's music. They blew into the ends of long wooden pipes and what came out was not what we would call a melody as such, but naturally they seemed to enjoy the rhythm and tone of the notes.

So, the hills were alive only with people and not themselves animated or inhabited by horrifying, preternatural beasts. I was relieved and breathed deeply, smelling the night odours of the arid landscape, drawing comfort from the dry, piquant scents of crisp plants and dust. I was glad not to be in the midst of a mystical happening, but then reminded myself that I was not exactly safe from harm. Those people up in the hills might be hostile tribes bent on destroying the pale creatures who were erecting a strange high fence across the country.

I lay down to rest again with my cocked and loaded revolver close to my right hand, despite the fact that I might shoot myself in the foot by accident. And though the sounds in the hills had initially woken me up, they seemed now to have the power to lull me to sleep with their gentle cadence. Those deep notes were like holes in the night, into which my spirit could lightly fall and be soothed. My dreams concerned the beat of the heart of the earth, the globe being a live, good-natured being.

However, despite my feeling of complacency on falling asleep I woke yet again in the middle of the night with a rapidly thumping heart. Had I heard a loose rattling amongst the rocks? It could have been caused by many things: the wind, an animal, my horse, even a live man. But now I was gripped by night fears and sat up quickly, staring. I was surrounded by white figures, tall and wide, spreading their arms into the night, It was a few fast heartbeats before I realised they were stark, leafless trees. Probably gums. Even when I had worked out what they were, I remained in a state of terror. They were not dead men risen, but I was still scared.

Looking out into that starlit world of hollow shadows and mysterious gnarly rockshapes the height of humans I remained overcome with an intense fear of the unnatural, a sickening sense of horror clogging my windpipe. Despite the fact that I had travelled a thousand miles in the same wilderness, this was actually the first time I had spent a night completely alone. The music in the hills had fallen silent and I stared around aware that there was no company out there, only a malevolent darkness that might contain the ghosts or deathforms of creatures from the world beyond that to which I was now clinging with fingers like talons.

This was not my land. This was an ancient wilderness which seemed far older than the one in which I had been born. They may have been made at the same time, but the gruesome monsters of the spirit world had been subdued and subjugated by civilisation in my birthplace. Here they were still roaming the wastelands, strange unformed creatures whose only reason for being was to find unprotected men like me in order to rip the souls from their bodies so that they spent the rest of their lives in vacant despondency. Even in Suffolk I had, as a boy and youth, spent nights petrified by stories of dead men who sat and discussed their woes in dreary churchyards, and tales of ghosts who visited the living to obtain revenge for past offences. Out here, a plumbob in the centre of nowhere, my fears of the supernatural were manifold.

I stayed half-sitting for a long time, shaking in my blanket, too frightened to get up and investigate, too frightened to lie back down and go to sleep. It must have been close to dawn because before very long a grey light began to creep up over the horizon. I then managed to lie back and stare upwards at the fading stars instead of at the frozen figures of the monsters that surrounded my camp.

So, the night had been long, but no slithering beasts had come to share my patch of sand, nor unspeakable horrors to share my blanket. My handgun had not been fired accidentally: I still had all my toes. With my bleary gaze fixed on the distant horizon I watched the sun weld the earth to the sky. Soon afterwards I arose and holstered my pistol, then drank a good pint of water, making sure my mount had her share too. The weird throbbing music of the tribes in the hills didn't start up again and I could no longer see the smoke from their fires.

Perhaps they were all exhausted with dancing and eating and whatever else they did while listening to their musicians playing their strange ethereal instruments.

I started back towards D camp, arriving there around noon, going straight to the temporary shack to check the receiver. Indeed, my message paraphrasing the Bible was there and I was reminded of Sally and her 'great lion' quote that followed from my telling her of the first telegraph transmission. The dots and dashes on the receiver's paper tape were very faint, almost invisible, due to the fact that the ink from the inking wheel had almost dried up. Still, a trained eye such as mine could make out the marks and I reported to Mr Woods that the line was good.

'However,' I told him, 'there was a shattered insulator, which I repaired, but also a pole almost down. I righted the pole as best as I could, but you may want to send a gang down there to do a proper job. And I couldn't do a complete Britannia joint with the broken wire. It's overlapped and bound with thin wire, but not soldered yet.'

Once I had satisfied Woods, I snatched a breakfast of johnnie cakes and coffee, then went and found the youngster Bagot again. I discovered him with the farrier, helping to shoe horses. He seemed to be amazed by the portable forge which the blacksmith had brought with him on a wagon and didn't enjoy being dragged away from the white-hot heart of this small, grounded sun.

'Listen,' I said to him, 'you seem to know all about this Captain Midnight, the bushranger. What sort of horse does he ride?'

The youth's eyes widened. 'Horse? You mean does he ride a gelding or a mare?'

'Or even a stallion,' I added, with some asperity. 'No, I want the breed, or rather the colour.'

'Oh, they say he rides a bay.' He screwed up his face for a moment, then added, 'Or is it a chestnut? Brown, anyways.'

'Not black? Why would a man who calls himself "Midnight" ride anything but a black horse?'

'Ah, you mean midnight being black, as in dark?'

'Yes.'

'Well, I can't say for certain, but I think I read it's a bay or a chestnut. It would be fast, though, wouldn't it? A man running from the constables would need a fast horse, eh?'

So, I was no nearer to solving the puzzle that was haunting me. I let him go again and he returned joyfully to the intense heat of the forge where the farrier was shaping a shoe on his anvil, his hammer strokes sending red and yellow sparks showering onto the red and yellow landscape.

After making sure I stayed clear of the red-shirted newspaper reporter, I rode back to E Section alone, still not knowing whether Bill Turmaine was going to keep his foot or lose it to a saw. I don't think I really wanted to know the grisly details. I'm not a squeamish man, you can't be when you're on an enterprise of this sort. Accidents happen all the time and men sometimes even die. But I was not going to hang around D camp just to find out whether Bill was going under the butcher's knife. I knew the two surveyors would ask me when I returned, whether Turmaine's foot had been amputated, as would the other men on the crew, but they could get the news from someone else. I had better things to do than carry messages from an invalid's sick bed.

On the way back I went by way of Central Mount Stuart, delighting in the colours one could see in the mountain ranges from that grand plateau: hues of blue, deep purple and maroon. They looked like phantoms of themselves from a distance. It was the Australian autumn and as I passed over the plateau, some night-rain water was trickling through a gorge of naked rock. Down on the plains it was dry of course, with white-trunked gum trees standing like signposts pointing their bone-like fingers, sending travellers in every direction. Red loam covered the flat areas and red sandstone rock, and sandhills, humped the surface. Here was a land that equalled the sky for depth and distance, and made a man feel small but not insignificant, since he could trek from one end of it to the other and say he had conquered its vast emptiness.

SIX

At the time I was riding back to E camp, those south of our position were in full swing, poling and wiring. Preparing the poles was not just a matter of chopping down a tree, cutting off the branches and sticking it in the ground. Each pole had to be approximately twenty-three feet long, ten inches diameter at the base and six inches at the top. Once the branches and bark had been stripped from the pole, the bottom six feet had to be charred in a fire before being buried. This took time and energy and the work crews laboured under a hot sun, in difficult conditions, while being bothered by all those aspects that worry a man when he's away from home: is his wife still faithful? do his children miss him? is his brother-in-law cheating him out of his savings? has his best friend stolen his fiancée? is that rash around his groin just prickly heat or something more sinister? will he kill that annoying bastard who sleeps next to him or will he indeed be killed by someone he has angered? will the dog he left behind still be alive when he goes home?

These, and a thousand other similar concerns, swam through the heads of men every day, as they swam through mine.

A, B, C and D Sections were progressing well. On occasion there was a shortage of trees for the poles, and not every stretch of the way was blessed with water, but for the most part the sections were advancing, each towards the next one north of themselves.

The Northern Section, coming down from Port Darwin was another matter. They had started poling back in September 1870 and were now stuck having been bogged down by the wet season of short but tremendously-intense monsoon rains. The rainforest, with its hot humid air, steams over the summer months of December to March, and leaves working men limp and exhausted, hanging like boiled damp rags on their spades. Tempers are short and furious, like the intermittent deluges of water from the sky. There are mutinies and desertions that weaken morale and the heart of the project begins to rot.

The leaders of that crew had been removed and a new supervisor, a man called Patterson, was on his way by ship to Port Darwin to try to revitalise the work. The crew in the north was split into two sections, A and B. Party B was building the line between Port Darwin and Tumbling Waters, a distance of around forty-five miles. Party A from there to the Adelaide River, which was around forty miles. The teams had erected poles for 225 miles and wired 156 miles when the Government Overseer decided to cancel the Northern Section contract on the 3 May, 1871 and appoint a new man to take charge of the northern end of the project.

B party had originally progressed, but not without backbreaking work. They had to hack their way through heavy rainforest. They were troubled by winged assailants, the worst of which were the flies and mosquitoes. Those in the north are more vicious and cruel than those in the south. Diggers, axemen, wire-fitters – the whole crew – found themselves attacked by insects that bit or stung them savagely, investing their clothes with gifts of eggs and larvae, thank you very much. If the conditions were not enough to soak men's souls with despondency, there were not enough wagons and cattle to haul the goods, sometimes across a wetlands landscape in which bullocks sank to their thighs.

Men went short of food, short of sleep, short of patience.

Notwithstanding the privations and difficulties of the route, by December 1870 they had crossed the Adelaide River. That was when the rain came to wash the dirt from their faces, soak their clothes and fill their boots. So fierce were the downpours that men's hat brims were forced down to cover their ears and faces, plastered as it were, to their heads. They became, over the wet days, wrinkled pale creatures, almost drowning where they stood. Bread melted in their hands and other food was rendered inedible.

Relief supplies were sent up the Roper River by boat. On the way a tragedy occurred. An unwary member of the crew, lazing in the bows of the craft, was suddenly snatched and dragged overboard by a saltwater crocodile. The last his friends saw of him was his head and shoulders, his face screwed in pain and terror as he was pulled under by a pair of massive jaws. When a saltie gets you in its maw you are done for. These reptiles with their prehistoric greed and tenacity, will never let you go. They grow to an average length of seventeen feet. They have thick yellow teeth each the size of a man's fist, a massive muscled torso with a stone-hard hide, a lashing tail and a dragon's claws, and finally, the compassion of an avalanche. They take you down to the murky depths, tuck you under a submerged tree root. There they leave you to rot. When your flesh begins fall away from your bones, the killer returns to a succulent meal of decomposed human meat.

Yet, despite all the setbacks, by Christmas somehow the line had reached Pine Creek, over halfway to Katherine. On the way old imprints of wagon tracks were found where no wagons were supposed to have gone before, the Overland Telegraph Company's wagons being the first to traverse that region. Stories sprang up around these ghost tracks, to explain their presence. My favourite is that of a wagon train coming out of Queensland which never reached the only destination for hundreds of miles: Palmerston. What happened to the people is probably less interesting than what happened to the wagons. Humans and livestock would have been prey to wild creatures, but predators do not eat wagons. Did they sink in the mire during the wet? Were they broken up and used for firewood by the Aborigines, the ironwork going to make knives and spearheads? Perhaps one day, someone will discover them hidden under a rock pile or swallowed by vines and creepers and waxy-leafed plants?

When the construction crews did finally reach Katherine, the wet had truly set in and floodwaters halted their progress. By March the men had had enough and voted to strike. This they did on and off, for a while, until finally the two leaders were dismissed by the chief overseer and eventually Mr Patterson was sent to sort out the mess. I didn't envy him. The Northern Section would prove monstrously difficult to conquer and time was against the new leader of that enterprise.

SEVEN

Mr Roberts was surprisingly affable, almost friendly, when I reported back to him. When I explained that I had to check the line for Mr Woods and that was the reason for my tardiness, he shrugged and told me it was not important. He asked me about Bill Turmaine and I told him nothing had been decided before I left D camp.

'Ah, poor man,' said Roberts, tapping his thigh with a measuring stick, 'I doubt he'll keep that foot.'

'What about Bates?' I asked, asking after the man who'd fired the rifle, 'is there going to be an enquiry of any sort?'

Roberts pursed his lips. 'Oh, it was an accident, wasn't it? The snake was dangerous, after all. Just an unfortunate incident. You can't try a man for something like that. Yes, he was foolish and perhaps negligence comes into it somewhere, but I don't think Mr Harvey will take it any further. And of course, we have the new man, Walker, to replace Turmaine. He's a good worker, the new man. You did well to keep him alive, McKenzie. Strong man. Determined. We could use a few more like him.' He sighed, before adding, 'But we won't get 'em, not way up here. Those sections south of us will filter out the best of them, before they ever reach us, should we need more workers. By the way, you need to check the fresh section of the line. Do that, will you?'

'Yes Mr Roberts, I'll do it this morning.'

E camp had moved geographically while I had been away. Several more miles had been poled in my absence and the tents had been struck, carried northward by camels, then erected again in a new area of sandhills and scrub. I think both surveyors were feeling good about the project. The men too greeted me as if I had been missed. Tam was especially happy to see me, but that didn't surprise me, for he's an affectionate young man and enjoys social contact. A wide smile stretched his already broad Celtic face. He pumped my hand, vigorously, then struck me on the shoulder with a calloused palm.

'Hey, Alex? How's things?'

The gangs of men were just gathering their tools, ready to go out and work at their various tasks on the line. I could see Walker bending to pick up an axe. Others were calling to me, asking me about Bill Turmaine, but I shook my head and told them I knew nothing more than the fact that he had been delivered safe and sound at D Section. So far as I knew, I said, there was no doctor there, but I was sure one would be found sooner or later.

At this remark Walker whirled and faced me.

'Where, under a bush?'

Someone started laughing, but then cut short the sound.

'There's Dr Renner, somewhere down the line,' I replied, 'and to my understanding he doesn't hide under bushes.'

'But then your understandin' is a bit limited, eh? Otherwise, you'd know exactly where this Renner is, wouldn't you, mate?'

Tam frowned, looking first at me, then at Walker, finally he chimed in with, 'Och, no one knows where the doctor might be at any one time, Sholto. He's away an' up and down the line and can't be in the right spot at any one time.'

Walker nodded briskly. 'You're right, Tam. Sorry if I sounded a bit sharp there, McKenzie. Wasn't thinkin' too well. Are you coming then, Tam? You and me are a team today again, eh?

We're the best axemen they've got in this part of the country, bar none.'

Tam smiled at the bloody bloke, who seemed to be able to twist every other man round his finger except me.

Tam grinned at him in obvious pleasure. 'I'll be with you in a wee while, Sholto. I just want a word with my friend Alex here.'

Walker replied earnestly, 'I won't start without you, Tam. I like my best man by me when the work needs to be done.'

I could see how this kind of flattering talk could seduce a youngster like Tam and I realised what Walker was doing. Sholto Walker had taken a real dislike to me and even though it would be in his interest to befriend me the way he had others in the camp, he could not help succumbing to the enmity he felt towards humanity. It was a draught of succour to him, trapped as he was in our company. He had to have at least *one* outlet for the hate and bitterness he felt towards authority and I had been chosen as this vent. I was the fringe man, in the camp, belonging neither to the management, nor to the workers. I was on the edge, outside any closed circles, and therefore an easy target. Had I been a poler, the other polers would have come to my defence. Had I been an axeman, or a wire-fitter, they would have closed ranks against him. Even the cook was untouchable, being a good one and the provider of food, and therefore held in some affection by the rest of the men.

There was also the fact that I was suspicious of him and he probably guessed I was intent on investigating his recent history. So he made sure he was a 'great bloke' to the other men and, because Tam was my closest friend in the camp, had decided to wean the youth away from me. He wouldn't do this with outright lies, but I'm sure was hoping to rely on my attitude towards him to 'prove' to Tam that I was an unreasonable person. By showing hostility to Walker I would be risking Tam thinking that I was unjust and irrational. A cold feeling went through me as I realised what was happening.

'Tam,' I said, ignoring all the warnings that I'd just given myself, 'be careful of that man – he's not what he seems.'

The youth raised his eyebrows. 'Sholto? Och, he's a gude man, Alex. You should see him use the axe. He's aye strong.'

How does that translate into character, I asked myself, but wisely did not press my case with the Scot.

'I'm sure you're right. Take no heed of me, Tam. I'm somewhat weary after my long ride and my thinking's fuzzy at the moment. I don't suppose you could help me check the line this morning?'

Tam's face fell. I knew he enjoyed assisting me with the connections and batteries. He was a quick learner too and liked it when I praised him for it. However, there was no getting him away from Walker this morning.

'Ah, sorry, Alex. I've made my promise to Sholto.'

'So you have. So you have. I forgot. Well, you'd better keep that promise, eh? I'll see you at supper and tell you all about my ride down to D. You would have enjoyed it, Tam. The landscape, when you're alone, is majestic. The colours…'

'Aye, aye, but I must rush. See you later, Alex.'

He strode off with the axe, this broad shouldered youth, eager to employ himself at the art and science of felling timber.

My only other real friend in the camp was an Afghan cameleer. I'm not sure how many Afghans there were, up and down the line, but two of them were regarded as the main men. My friend was not one of these two. He was called Afeeza Kabir and he came from a country called Balochistan, a place I had never heard of until I met Afeeza. I still have no idea where it is on a map and keep promising myself that I will increase my knowledge of geography. One day I'll study a globe and see where the big camelman was born and raised. I know one thing, though he said it is near Afghanistan, it is not part of that country. We called all the camel drivers 'Ghans' but they came from many different countries: India, Egypt, Persia and Turkey being four of those nations.

This effusive man had brought some of my Morse equipment up the line on one of his camels and he had taken to me instantly. I have found that friendships formed between two men of different cultures are often more tolerant of idiosyncrasies than those made within a culture. My eccentricities – my obsession with electric communications and my love of long words – did not bother an Afghan camel driver so much as it might a poler or surveyor from my own nation. The latter might regard me with suspicion, thinking I was trying to impress. Afeeza, however, also talked big, praising himself for his own skills, which may have caused many of his own kind to screw up their faces in contempt.

The two of us then were brothers under the skin and therefore hit it off perfectly. So well, that the next time I saw him he had a wonderful gift for me, which he called an 'astrolabe'. This astonishing instrument consisted of a set of flat brass concentric circles that fitted perfectly into one another, forcing me to admire not only the art but the engineering of the piece. The surfaces of the discs were etched with an astronomical map of the night sky and there were two pointers attached to curved brass arms that swept over the whole discus. Afeeza told me the device was used as a compass in his own land and could show a lost man the way. I was amazed at the attractiveness of the astrolabe, not caring what its purpose was, but simply admiring it for its aesthetic value, for its intrinsic beauty. It was a jewel of the Orient that I had been given, shrouded in mystery and mysticism. I felt like I was carrying a key to another world in my pocket, which would one day open the doors of the East and reveal to me Alibaba's cave of Levantine treasures.

THE IRON WIRE

Afeeza was a big, barrel-chested man with a great black doormat of a beard which reached his waist and spread on either side of his ribcage. Like the other cameleers he wore a turban, but not one of those you see on the heads of maharajas or Sikhs. Afeeza called his headgear a *lungee*. There was nothing grand about it at all. It was much like a piece of torn cloth wrapped around and over itself. His long coat he called a *kurta* and there were other names for the rest of his clothing which have since slipped from my memory. His face, that part not covered by facial hair, was like tanned leather, out of which shone the brightest pair of blue eyes I have ever seen, even on the Scandinavian sailors I've met. Where he got them is a mystery to him and his family, since he told me his father has deep brown eyes and his mother the same.

'My older brother said I was sired by a pie-dog, but that was because he was jealous of my strength,' Afeeza once told me. 'My brother was too stupid to see an insult to our mother in this remark and I beat him until he knew that what he had said was a terrible offence.'

That day, after I had finished checking the latest addition to the wire, I went to the part of the camp where the Afghans had their tents. Somewhere up and down the line there were a hundred or so camels. In our camp at that time there were about thirty of the beasts and a five cameleers, one of them a boy of twelve. Two of them had arrived the day before, one of them being Afeeza. I found him at prayer, which for some reason embarrassed me and I had started to walk away when he rose from a kneeling position and called me back.

'Sikandar, my friend,' he called softly, while still moving the beads on his prayer string, 'wait for me. I am almost finished.'

Afeeza always used the Indian version of my name, Sikandar Jah, given to Alexander-the-Great when he conquered the Indus.

I stayed, sitting down with the other Afghans where they squatted on the ground. I felt awkward and probably showed it in my demeanour. Three men with swarthy faces stared at me, then nodded briefly. I nodded back. Two of them were chewing *qāt* in the way that we chewed tobacco. Afeeza had told me that *qāt* was a grass which grew in a country called Al-Yemen. It was supposed to help the person who was chewing the grass and swallowing the juice to think more clearly. However, looking at these two men, their eyes slightly glazed and their faces dull, I wondered if that were indeed the case.

I turned my attention to the young boy, who gaped with an open mouth at first, then grinned when I made a face at him. There were gaps in his teeth which made his expression comical and made me smile. None of the four spoke to me. It was not that they were unfriendly. They simply had nothing to say to a telegraph operator. Those who spoke some English would talk with the polers and axemen, whose work they understood, but I was a magician who toyed with lightning, an occupations they failed to comprehend.

The fact that I didn't really understand electricity either, and to my knowledge nor did most ordinary men, did not help the situation. They had seen my fingers playing with fire from the sky. That was magic. I'm not sure they were aware of the invisible flow of electricity along the wire, but often when I was making connections with the battery, or on the line, blue and white sparks would suddenly crackle and flash, making me yell occasionally, and that was enough evidence for them to come to the decision that I was a sorcerer making spells.

So we sat there in silence, away from the noises of the camp, but within the sound of the wind singing in the telegraph wire.

Fortunately Afeeza joined me quite quickly.

'Don't the others pray?' I asked, as he sat down.

'Of course, but I am always late. It is a source of grief to my mother. "You will be late for your own death," she tells me often. "I hope so," I answer her, "and perhaps he will get tired of waiting for me and go home."' Afeeza laughed, loudly, causing his comrades to stare at him in disapproval. 'But,' he slapped me on the back with a heavy hand knocking all the breath out of my lungs, 'here you are, my friend. You come to greet Afeeza. I am come up the line with much wire on my camels. Number eight gauge galvanised wire, coming from thousands of miles over the seas from England by ship and next by Afeeza's camels.' He puffed his chest with pride at being the holder of this knowledge. 'Now, we will drink tea together and talk about life.'

He said something in his harsh tongue to the boy, who jumped up and immediately went away, returning a little later with tea for everyone in the circle, pouring it carefully from a battered kettle into tin cups.

'When are you going to get a beard like Afeeza?' I asked the boy as he poured my tea. 'Will you grow one as large?'

'Bigger!' he said. 'Much, much bigger,' and giggled as he danced out of the way of Afeeza's swatting hand.

'So, you have come from the depot at Alice Well?' I said to Afeeza.

'Yes – and you have come from down there too, I hear.'

'A man was shot, accidentally.'

'So I hear. Foolish. But where you get men, you get guns, and where you get guns, you get accidents.'

Afeeza owned a beautiful Arab desert rifle, one of those long weapons with a short curvaceous stock. It was inlaid with mother-of-pearl and had silver mountings. Like most of the other Afghans, he was a crackshot. One of his team, a cousin of his, was cross-eyed and did not carry a gun of any kind, so I guessed this man was not up to the mark of the other cameleers. Even the boy had an old battered musket from some forgotten war. The Afghans also carried curved, wide-bladed daggers in their waistbands. These they called their *khanjars*. The sheaths were elaborately decorated with silver rings, coins and plate and had horn handles with solid silver bosses. I coveted one of those daggers and hoped one day to persuade one of the cameleers to sell me his *khanjar*, albeit it was probably a vain hope, for they loved their deadly possessions, keeping them in perfect condition.

'So,' I said to Afeeza, nodding in the direction from which he had joined the group, 'you pray every evening?'

'Five times in every day. How many do you?'

I thought about this. 'Once a week, on Sundays.'

'Ah, your God is very patient.'

'I'm not very religious, Afeeza.'

He shrugged and wafted a fly away from his nose.

'The shooting,' he said. 'What else has happened?'

I brought him up to date will all the news of the camp, telling him we were doing well with our poling and wiring.

'And when it is finished, you will talk with your countrymen in England?'

'Not *talk* exactly, but we will be able to send a message very quickly. The government in England will be brought as close to Australia as you are to me. They like to know what is going on right at this minute, so that they can make instant decisions on events in Australia.'

'So, your God is very patient, but your government is not.'

'As always, Afeeza, you are very astute.' I said.

He asked, 'What is that? Astute?'

'Clever. You have an answer for everything.'

This compliment pleased him a great deal and I was invited to eat with the Afghans that evening.

'Ramadan is now. I have not eaten all day, so forgive me Sikandar if I eat like a starved donkey.'

'Ramadan?'

'Religious. We must not eat between sunrise and sunset for one whole month. Now is Ramadan in the year 1288 in the Hijri.'

'1288? You have a different year to us?' I was at first surprised, then realised not without a minor shock that of course, different cultures probably had totally different calendars to us. No doubt the Aborigines were living in a completely different year to the 1871, in which white men lived.

'Oh, then you must be very hungry,' I said, lamely.

Since they had no cutlery, I was careful to copy them and use only my right hand. Afeeza had told me the left hand was used for dirty tasks and though I was tempted to tell them I washed *both* my hands I knew it would offend them greatly if I didn't follow their example. During the meal they chattered in a language I did not understand, which though as I said they came from different regions, they seemed to hold in common. When the meal was over I thanked them for their hospitality and went back to my tent, still feeling the effects of my ride back from the south.

'Sleep well, my friend,' called Afeeza as I walked away, 'but remember, Night is the brother of Death.'

What? What did that mean? Was Afeeza just quoting a Balochistan saying or was he warning me of something specific? My head was buzzing through lack of sleep. I was too exhausted to think too deeply about such things and needed rest before such mental trials.

When I entered the tent one of the men, a thick-headed sheep-shearer named Trout, was writing a letter under lamplight in a laborious fashion. He looked up and said, 'You wasn't at the supper.'

'No. I ate with the 'Ghans.'

'I dunno what you see in them bloody nigger boys. They talk a lot of gobbledygook and pick their noses.'

'So do most of our bunch pick their noses.'

'Yeah, but they are our bunch,' he replied, emphatically, 'not a load of lascars. That's the trouble with you, McKenzie. You don't like your own kind.'

'If they're anything like you, you sheep-shagging bastard, I bloody never will.'

He put down the letter and made as if to stand up.

'I've a mind to kick your guts in.'

My heart was racing and my brain was telling me I was being stupid, forcing a fight with an idiot like Trout.

'I'm standing here,' I said.

In the end, he didn't get up, but snarled, 'Yeah, well Walker will fix you before the work's done and I'll be there to watch and cheer. He's promised to knock the bellows out of you, mate, so I wouldn't sleep too easy of nights if I was you.'

I was both shocked and alarmed at this news.

'He has, has he?'

Trout stared at my face, which had probably gone a little pale, and a sneer registered in his expression.

'Ha, that's put the fear of Christ up you, ain't it?'

My heart was pounding again, but I replied, 'I'll fight Walker any time he likes.'

With that I turned and left the tent, to get some night air into my lungs.

EIGHT

When I rose the next morning and left the tent, there was a long roll of cloud crossing the sky. It looked like a comber of surf on a sea strand and seemed to go for a hundred miles in either direction. I was still staring at this awesome phenomenon when Mr Roberts approached me and looked up in the same direction.

'What's up there?' he asked.

'I'm looking at that cloud,' I told him. 'Have you seen anything like it before?'

His eyes took on a weary look. 'Many times. Now, McKenzie, have you got the results of yesterday's line checks?'

'Yes sir.' I gave them to him. 'Oh, and we need some copper sulphate crystals. The charge in the battery is getting low.'

'There's some on the way, I hope, by the next wagon. Also a batch of ironbark insulator pins from the Sarnia timber yard – at least, I'm praying there is, or I'll lose my hair…'

I began to see how difficult and stressful Roberts's job was. Of course, the ultimate responsibility for E Section lay with Mr Harvey, but Roberts's future career depended upon the success he made of his job under Mr Harvey and a good report was probably essential. If he, Roberts, had been given the task of ensuring wire and insulator pins – and indeed copper sulphate crystals – were readily available in the camp, then he would be reproved if there was a problem with supply, even if it was the timber yard's or the haulier's fault and not his.

'They must be sick of making insulators at Sarnia's yard,' I muttered, thinking about the wood turners who had had to make several thousand insulator pins.

'They're earning good money for it,' growled Mr Roberts, though not with any malice. 'More, I expect, than the four shillings and sixpence a day earned by our men. Wood turners! I expect you think you're too good for that kind of work, McKenzie, but someone has to do it.'

I took no offence at this remark. I did think I was too good for that kind of work.

After Mr Roberts had left me, Tam came over to speak. He had his axe in his hand and I knew by the way he was shuffling his feet that he expected me to disapprove of whatever it was he had to tell me.

'Wish me luck, Alex,' he said.

I raised my eyes to heaven. 'Not again?'

He looked hurt. 'Sholto says I can do it this time.'

I was going to say 'What the hell does Sholto Walker know about anything?' but I desisted.

'How much did you bet, Tam?'

He looked chagrined. 'Half a month's pay.'

'Well, that's not too bad. At least you'll keep the other half.'

'I might win,' he said, frowning at me. 'Have you thought of that, Alex? I might win against one of them at least.'

'One of them?' It was worse than I thought.

'Well, I'm taking on both brothers, y'ken Alex, and I think I've got a gude chance this time, as Frank has a bad chest.'

'And Freddy?'

'He's no got a bad chest.'

Frank and Freddy Clancy were two Australian-born axemen and anyone will tell you that axemen fathered and bred on this continent are without exception swifter and surer than any other axemen in the world, Canadian lumberjacks included. Even if the Canadians *were* better, it wouldn't help Tam, he being born and bred in Scotland. Tam was a big lad, with a big heart and as strong as any ploughboy coming from a Highland Perthshire farm, but he was no match for the Clancy brothers. They had taken more of Tam's wages than I had sent to Sally for her passage to the Antipodes, and they looked like taking a several more shillings from his meagre purse.

'Walker put you up to this?'

'Och, I had a dram with him last night and it just came up in conversation – it's no his fault, Alex. Look man, I've improved since the last time. I'm certain sure I can take one of them. Will ye no cheer me on, Alex. Will ye no support your Perthshire pal Thomas Donald?'

The word 'dram' was a falsity, since Charles Todd, the Superintendent of Telegraphs – the big boss and overlord of the whole enterprise – had stipulated there was to be no liquor of any kind in the camps of the Overland Telegraph Company's work gangs. What we had was coffee and tea, and the occasional bitter lime juice. When we had the latter there was an unspoken pretence that it contained alcohol. Thus men 'drank' together, as men need to do when they are discussing the world and its problems and putting the errors of the authorities to rights.

I reached up and swatted his tousled fair hair, standing on end, stiff with sweat and dirt. He was as eager as twelve-year-old boy.

'Of course I'll support you, you big dope.'

It just grieved me to see him taken in. However, I knew he had been working hard to improve his speed at felling black box on the way up through South Australia. Maybe he was ready to take on the brothers? I had no doubt Walker was set to receive some of the money that the Clancys expected to win and it would do my heart good to see him thwarted in that endeavour. Then a further thought occurred to me.

'Tam, did you promise any of your winnings to Walker?'

'Aye, I did that – he was the one who set it all up, see, so I felt obliged, Alex.'

'You didn't *need* anyone to set it up, Tam. All you had to do was challenge the Clancys. What did you need Walker for?'

Tam looked shame-faced at this and I knew I wasn't going to get an answer from him. So, Walker was set to get money either way, whoever won the contest. That was very clever.

My young Scot told me that the competition was to be early the next morning, before work started for the day.

'Six o'clock sharp,' he told me.

'Like an early morning duel,' I said. 'Axes for two, coffee for one. Or in this case, axes for three and coffee for two.'

'Whut?'

'Never mind, Tam.'

When the time arrived, it was indeed much like a duel was going to take place. Tam was stripped down to his shirt and the two Clancy boys naked to the waist, all three limbering up on the red earth. They each had their axes. I went to the Clancys and chatted with them before the chips started flying. I liked the brothers. Young men, they were always cheerful and full of zest and life, like many of those born on this vast untamed continent. Possibly the sunshine did it for them. Grey skies, dismal rain, long nights in the old country produced thinkers, inventors, men of learning, but when you have nothing to do but sit indoors by a fire then you have very little else with which to while away the time.

Not that those with an Australian birthright are not clever people, but they don't spend the majority of their days staring into the flames of a fire and wondering about the origins of Man. At this point in time this land needs men and women who will go out and do things – forge railways and telegraph lines, pioneer paths over unexplored landscapes, build towns in remote places – not scholars who sit without necessity and ponder on the size of the moon or the distances between the stars.

The Clancy boys came from a farm in Victoria, north of Melbourne. Although they weren't twins, they were never seen one without the other. They ended each other's sentences when they spoke and they were of course fiercely loyal. That's not to say they didn't argue with each other. They actually scrapped a great deal, sometimes the fights being quite vicious affairs that had to be stopped before one or the other got seriously hurt. But within an hour they were talking to each other again and it was as if no great battle had been fought.

'Go easy on my friend,' I said to them. 'You've taken a great deal of his pay already.'

'He challenged *us*,' said Felix.

'Not the other way around,' added Frank.

I nodded. 'I know, I know, but he was put up to it.'

'By Walker,' Frank remarked.

Felix added, 'But he's better than he was…'

'…and might beat us.' finished Frank.

'Not a chance,' I said, 'and you know it.'

They both grinned, their confidence full and complete, shining like the sun from their eyes and expressions.

It did not bode well for my broad shouldered and willing Scottish competitor that hardly anyone was taking bets. Normally men working on the line, or indeed working anywhere in Australia, are fanatical gamblers, especially on two-up, where three coins are tossed and bets are taken on the result. Today I noticed hardly any money exchanging hands. That meant the forecast was bad for Tam. No one wanted to venture a wager on him. I attempted to put some money on the Clancys, to try to recover what Tam would lose, but I could find no takers. The odd tuppence was laid down on my lad, in the very remote possibility that a Clancy might accidentally chop off his own foot during the contest, but apart from these small exchanges, the betting was non-existent.

Three ghost gums had been found, with trunks more or less of the same sized girths. A lone butcherbird was sitting in the branches of one of them and seemed determined to remain there. There is nothing quite as beautiful as the song of the butcherbird, but this morning everyone was irritated by the sound. We wanted to hear the thud of steel cutting into bark, the swish of the axe, the grunts of furious energy.

Sholto Walker had taken it on himself to start the contest by striking a metal pan with a spoon. This he did once the three axemen were ready, their bodies already gleaming with sweat, their arms like coiled springs. I could feel the excitement mounting in the morning air. My own breast was full of it and I could see the Afghans on the far side, awaiting the start of the match with just as much interest as any of us. Days on the line were for the most part simply hard physical work followed by unsatisfactory sleep. Men need entertainment and though we had campfire songs on some evenings, this kind of distraction from the daily grind was far preferable. Even the surveyors were there, standing apart from the men, but with a good view of the proceedings.

Clang!

Three axes dug their blades into the bark almost simultaneously. If anything, Tam's strike was a fraction of second ahead of his two rivals. Soon the wood chips fountained, raining down on the nearest spectators, all of whom were yelling like crazy. It was an amazing sight to see these three gods of the axe, racing each other to fell their individual ghost gum. The butcherbird had flown out in a panic on the first strike and was now a dot above the distant hillsides. One of the camels rose fairly gracefully from his genuflections and bolted. The young Afghan boy was sent after the runaway, cursing the beast and screaming his reluctance to leave the scene of the battle. Still the chips sprayed the scene until a sharp cracking sound was heard over the general din. It all went completely silent amongst the crowd for a few seconds as Frank's tree crashed to the ground, then started up again, only to stop once more as Felix's gum followed that of his brother's, and finally, just seconds later, the target of Tam's ferocious onslaught hit the ochre earth with a thud.

A huge cheer rent the air, causing a rodent of some kind to finally leave his lair in the rocks and go zigzagging across the dust looking for an escape from this bedlam of noise. Was this not supposed to be the gentle quietude of the wilderness? Where had these insane two-legged animals come from with their monstrous mouths?

Tam naturally looked despondent. I went over to him and gave him a wink. 'You did well, mate,' I said. 'Bloody well. Only a fraction behind the Clancys. I'm proud of you.'

'But I lost,' he said, mournfully.

He leaned on his axe handle, his head hanging low, the sweat dripping down and staining the earth. His long lank blond hair was covered in bits of bark and wood, some of it sticking to his face and bare arms. Many of the fragments were stuck to his shoulders. He looked as if he had been in a storm of splinters.

Walker came ambling over, his tall lean frame full of arrogance.

'Not up to the mark, eh?' he said, punching Tam on the arm. 'Next time though, mate.'

'Sorry, Sholto. Ah couldna get a head o' steam.'

Walker said, 'You went flat out, mate – they were just too good for you. But we'll get you there. They ain't invincible.'

'Make much money?' I asked him.

He gave me a menacing stare. 'What's it to you?' he said. 'You're always stickin' your beak in, McKenzie.'

Tam's head came up. 'Hey, Sholto, Alex is a friend of mine.'

'Well he should mind his own bloody business. I've got nothin' against telegraphers or whatever he calls himself, but they should keep their noses out. Fact is, Tam, I put a big bet on you, but I ain't complainin' about the loss, am I?'

'Och,' said Tam, looking even more upset, 'I'll make it up to you, Sholto – next pay day.'

'Don't worry about it, mate. As beaky here suggested, I did demand some money from the Clancys, for setting up the contest. A sort of management fee, if you like, but that's neither here nor there. Any man would expect the same. It was a fair and level match and I honestly thought you stood a good chance of winning. You didn't, but that's no fault of mine, nor yours. You did your best. I don't expect a fee from you, by the way, as you're in my stable. Mates don't take fees from mates, do they, eh? Now, you'd better go an' shake the hands of your opponents...'

'Right,' cried Tam, suddenly aware that he might be committing a grave breach of expected etiquette. 'I'll do that, straight.'

He marched off to the Clancys, who were cock-a-hoop with their win and wore grins wide enough to split their faces.

'So,' said Walker, glaring down at me, 'still fucking with me, eh McKenzie?'

In my trouser pocket I had the magnificently decorated stirrup I had cut from the tack of the dead black horse on the way to camp D. I'd been waiting for an opportunity to confront Walker with it. I pulled it out now and thrust it in front of his face.

'Seen this before?'

Instantly I knew by his expression that he recognised the item.

He took a few moments to gather himself, then sneered.

'That? Yeah, I've seen it before. Comes from a horse a bushranger rides. You haven't captured Captain Midnight, have you? Well, let me be the first to congratulate you, McKenzie. Big money on that man's head. Big reward there. What did you do, find him asleep and helpless?'

This speech took all the wind out of my sails, but I rallied quickly.

'And how would you know it belonged to Captain Midnight?'

He seemed amused. ''Cause I was one of the constables chasin' the bastard?'

I was taken aback by this clever reply. Somehow Walker always managed to get me on the back foot.

'You? You were a constable? I'm supposed to believe that?'

'Personally I couldn't give a monkey's arse what you believe. But you go ahead. Go and show it to Roberts or Harvey and tell them you think I'm the notorious Tom Smith. I'm sure *they'll* believe you, seein' as how you've got all this proof. I'll just stand here waitin' to be arrested.'

I suddenly realised how ludicrous my position was and realised that Walker remained untouchable. Indeed, I could have shown the stirrup to my bosses, but what would that prove? Nothing. There was no way to check whether Walker had been a constable or not. Not until the line was up and working all the way back to Adelaide.

'You gave up working as a constable?'

He nodded. 'Too dangerous, with bushrangers like Captain Midnight in the outback. Might get shot.'

There was nothing more to say. I walked away, feeling his eyes on my back, reminding myself that this man had sworn to the others that he was going to 'settle my hash' before the project was over. It might all have been hot air, but then if I was right about him being a bushranger, it might be serious. There was nothing to worry about for the time being, but when the project neared its end I would have to be vigilant.

NINE

Over the next few days and weeks, the poling and wiring continued. There were hitches of course, but in the main we progressed well. I checked the line every so often and sometimes we had to go back and repair the iron wire, or a pole or insulator. One night there was a magnificent sizzling storm – God showing me what *his* electricity could do, even without wires – which brought down several poles and smashed a good many insulators. At one point during the onslaught the whole camp stood outside and simply watched in awe as the blackness was lit up with a hundred lightning strikes at any one moment. Camels danced in fright. Horses and bullocks cried out, and kicked and shied in their makeshift corrals. Certainly I had never witnessed such ferocious storms as these back in Britain, but also the Australians among us were equally enthralled and overawed. This wilderness thunder came from a place more savage than ours. This lightning, these bolts of electrical fire, came from a deeper and fiercer sky than the one I was born under.

Then the rain came down as if a cataract had suddenly appeared above our heads and we all ran for the cover of the tents.

The period of rain was extremely brief. The earth flowered once again, then died, returning to bare dust and stone in a short time. Poling continued the next day. One man shot a rock wallaby, which provided a few steaks of a different nature to mutton. We had a Sunday evening of entertainment when men stepped up and revealed hidden talents. There were whistlers, harmonica players, singers, spoon-clappers, poets, actors and several others. One man recited the whole of Alfred Lord Tennyson's *Ulysses* which ends with lines that any worker on a venture such as ours would appreciate, '...*strong in will, to strive, to seek, to find and not to yield*'. To my surprise Walker sang a convict's song which I had never heard before, but which I have since heard many times. It was called 'Moreton Bay' and the words are these:

> 'I've been a prisoner at Port Macquarie
> At Norfolk Island and Emu Plains
> At Castle Hill and at cursed Toongabbie
> At all these settlements I've been in chains
> But of all the places of condemnation
> And penal stations in New South Wales
> To Moreton Bay I have found no equal
> Excessive tyranny each day prevails.'

This rendition was greeted with hoarse cheers and a stamping of feet. I've found that in Australia, men from the colonies here are more ready to side with the criminals than with the police. I suppose it might seem unsurprising since this land is a place to which such people were shipped to serve their jail time, yet many of those who were sentenced to servitude in the penal colonies were not real criminals. They might have committed transgressions according to the law of the land at the time, which have since become quite minor offences. Setting fire to a haystack. Shooting a hare on private land. Stealing a pie from a butcher's stall. All reprehensible acts, but none of them too dreadful. So the perpetrators of these crimes, you would expect to be, underneath it all, decent citizens on a normal day. And the colony of South Australia boasted that only free men settled there. It was not a penal colony in any sense.

Yet the police and judiciary on this great island are despised, while murderers and killers are seen as misunderstood folk who are entitled to carry out heinous acts of revenge on society because of the grievous sins committed against them by governments and authorities. They become folk heroes and legendary champions, but I would guess only to those who know them by hearsay, not to those who are done to.

Walker sang the song well, his voice deep and gritty. I cheered along with all the others once he had finished. His eyes were sparkling as he stood and received the applause. I believe he was thoroughly enjoying his moment on the stage and was relishing being the centre of attention. He reluctantly relinquished the spotlight for the next performer, a big-bellied bloke who presented us with imitations of, first a bullfrog, then a booming bittern and finally a musk-ox giving birth. These were all deep, throaty interpretations and since no one present among the audience even knew what a musk-ox was, let alone what it sounded like giving birth, we were hardly good judges of his talent. However, this deficiency on our part was no bar to imagination and we could well conjure a musk-ox in our minds and envisage what it would sound like when calving.

The evening was a great success and even the usually staid Mr Roberts performed, presenting his workmen with a comic story about a man who was dangling his foot over a canoe going down the Roper River, known to be swarming with saltwater crocodiles. After a while the fool says to his friend, 'Hey, Joe, a croc's just bitten my foot off.' His shocked fellow canoeist turns to him and asks, 'Good God, which one?' The reply comes, 'I don't know, all crocodiles look alike to me.' We all laughed at this story, but injury and death was ever present on such ventures as ours and there was a faint sense of apprehension in the air as we applauded this cautionary tale from one of our bosses.

Two days after the outback theatre a pack of dingoes got in amongst our horses and cut three of them out, chasing them into the wilderness. There was quite a fuss about it the morning after, but I was not overly concerned, the livestock not being my responsibility. That did not stop Mr Roberts coming to me and saying, 'Saddle up, McKenzie. You and I have to go out and search for those mounts.'

The two of us set out north-west, that being the direction the horses had taken. After about a mile the three sets of tracks diverged, two sets going north, the other set heading directly west. At first Roberts suggested we might split up, but I was no bushman and I told him we needed to stick together. I had heard of men out in that wilderness of red hills and yellow-ochre plains walking off into the bush to take a piss and never being heard of again. There was no way I was going to let Roberts abandon me in an environment in which — though I found it exciting and mysterious while in the company of others — I would discover hazards and dangers beyond my wildest fears.

'As you wish,' he replied, but without rancour. 'Let's go after these two first — it's probably the mare and her colt.'

So we spent the rest of that day following the tracks, but never quite coming up against the two runaways. We did indeed see the dingoes, if it was the same pack, and Roberts shot one of them, leaving the carcass for its erstwhile companions to fight over. That, Mr Roberts told me, would stop them hunting our lost horses for a while.

We spent the night in a hollow between two dome-shaped rocks that seemed to have shed their outer layers over time. It was an uncomfortable sleep, but we woke in the morning somewhat refreshed and ready to continue the search. That was, until we found we had lost the trail and had no idea which direction to take. We had no maps of course – there were none of this region – and our water supply was beginning to get very low. After a further period of trying to orientate ourselves we decided to make finding water our first priority, then to try to calculate where we might be in relation to the camp.

Neither one of us was panicking at this point, knowing that if we struck south-east we would eventually come across the telegraph line. A day of riding in what we thought was the right direction according to the position of the sun, without finding a set of poles with wire on them, began to arouse concern in my breast. It did not help our individual tempers to learn that neither of us had brought a compass. Roberts had believed he had one in his saddlebags (he was wrong) and I had thought that he, Roberts, had packed all the right things for our journey out into the wastelands. I suppose we each secretly blamed the other for a very stupid error of judgement. It was basic mistakes like this which ended up with men dying needlessly in the Australian wilderness.

That evening we lit a fire on a hill and hoped for someone to see it and come and find us. Our water was gone now. We had found none in the vicinity. My mouth felt like a sandpit and my tongue had started to swell in my throat. Eyes dried by a warm desert wind continually blowing into them, were gritty and sore. I had a nose that was blocked with bull dust and dried snot, which was so uncomfortable it was agony to breathe through it. My head hammered with pain and deep down I was as scared as I'd ever been, convinced I was going to die.

When the stars came out, I suddenly remembered something which brought a trickle of hope to my breast. Afeeza's gift! The brass instrument was in a pouch on my belt, along with my money and a silver hunter pocket watch with a photograph of Sally in the sprung cover.

'Here,' I said to Mr Roberts, holding up the device, 'do you understand one of these?'

He peered at the instrument which shone with a burnished light in the illumination from the flames of the fire.

'What is it?'

'It's called an astrolabe. I think the word must be Afghan. One of the cameleers gave it to me.'

'*Astro* is Greek, not Afghan. Let me see it.'

I handed over the brass device, saying, 'It's a compass of sorts, so I was told.'

Roberts studied the device closely. 'Zodiac,' he muttered.

'Yes, the night sky,' I said. 'A copy of the stars.'

Surely, Roberts, with his training a surveyor, would work out how to use this instrument?

'Yes,' he said after a long while, 'I can see how this might work. It functions as a star chart. See here, on the back of the thing? They've engraved a number of scales. Possibly a calendar for converting the sun's position of the day of the month to the sun's position on the ecliptic.'

It did sound as if Mr Roberts knew what he was talking about and the hope that had trickled into my chest began to flow more freely.

'Yes,' I said, not understanding half of what he was saying, 'I expect you're right.'

He held the instrument flat and looked along it. I think he was pointing it at a bright star we could see among the lesser stars in the blackness above. He played with the moveable parts, the discs and the pointers, for a while, before asking, 'Who was it gave you this, did you say?'

'A camel driver. Afeeza.'

'Ah, yes, Afeeza. Good man, though full of himself.'

THE IRON WIRE

Roberts then handed me back the astrolabe, while heaving a great sigh and staring out into the night desert that surrounded us.

'So,' I said, 'will it help us? Is it like a compass?'

'Like a compass? I believe so. But in answer to your main question, the answer is no.'

I was shocked. 'No?'

'No.'

'But,' I asked, helplessly, 'why not?'

His voice held a tone of infinite patience. 'Because, McKenzie, your astrolabe has a star map of the northern hemisphere. We, sadly, are in the southern hemisphere. I don't suppose those cameleers have an astrolabe of this sky,' he nodded upwards. 'though there're one or two constellations I recognise on the edge of the night. I'm no astronomer though. The 'Ghans probably use those things to find the direction of their holy city of Mecca, up there in the west of Arabia, the direction in which they must say their prayers. This is a new part of the world for them. I'm betting they're the first men from their region to cross the equator.'

I would have forced back the tears if I had had enough moisture in me to weep.

'Oh – of course.'

The older man placed a hand on my shoulder, as if I were his son, and said, 'Let's get some rest now. Tomorrow we may find the line and then we'll laugh at this, eh? You know McKenzie, I like you much better when you're not so puffed up with your self-importance as a telegraph operator.'

I nodded. 'Puffed up? I suppose I can be, sometimes. I come from humble beginnings Mr Roberts. It's easy to be modest when you come from a background where entering an elite profession, like surveying, is the normal expected path for man. My father worked on a big farm, he was responsible for the heavy horses – they call them horsemen in Suffolk – they're a bit like stockmen or drovers here. By rights I should be following a plough. I can't get over the fact that I now have skills which mean I can be a respected man.'

'I respect a man for his character, not his intellectual ability, or even for his skills, though I might *admire* the latter.'

I lay my head down after this exchange, angry that the astrolabe was a useless item in this part of the world. This is not say I blamed Afeeza. I'm sure the gift was given me for its value as a thing of beauty, not because he expected me to use it in earnest. It seemed unfair though, that I should have in my possession a device that might have saved my life in the Gobi, or the Sahara Desert, but which was simply an ornament in the Australian wilderness. No more use here than a painting or a statuette in someone's drawing room back in Europe.

Dawn brought no relief to the raging thirst we both felt and Roberts then suggested we split up to look for water.

'It stands to reason our chances of finding water increase if we look in different directions. Fire your gun when you find it,' he told me. 'I'll do the same. Keep firing every ten minutes until we meet up. Good luck, McKenzie. We'll come out of this all right, you'll see.'

But I didn't.

What I saw was hard-baked ground. I found flowering wattles, which must have got their water from somewhere, and honey myrtles and paperbarks, which are said to grow near swamps, though no swamps were visible. After two hours my horse was in agony, stumbling through lack of water. Eventually she sank to her knees and rolled over on her side. She'd had enough and I couldn't blame her. I couldn't shoot her because Roberts would think I was signalling to him, so I had to just leave her where she lay. I took what I needed from the saddlebag and carried on, on foot, praying that I'd find water soon or hear shots from Robert's rifle. My mind was full of visions of water. There were pictures of sparkling lakes and dancing waterfalls in my head which tormented me as all I could taste in my mouth was slick dust.

I walked on and on, muttering to myself, calling out in a hoarse voice for human contact. I have no idea how long I continued to roam aimlessly over the landscape, no longer admiring its mystery but cursing it for being what it was, a semi-arid place. I found dry creeks where I wanted wet ones. I discovered skulls of animals inhabited by lizards. I came across a place where there were hand-paintings on rocks: red palms with red fingers. It meant that human beings were somewhere near, even if they were savages with no regard for human life.

At noon I followed the example of my mare and fell down, and more or less stayed where I fell, rolling into a deep, rocky creek whose banks were lined by dwarf gum trees. In that position I went in and out of consciousness for God knows how long. At some time, vaguely, the sound of shots penetrated my brain, but I was not able to say for certain whether they were real or imagined. Once, I opened my eyes to see a face I knew staring down at me, wearing a twisted grin. That face belonged to Sholto Walker and I reached up and gripped his collar with my right hand. The grin never left his grizzled face as he forcibly peeled away my fingers and called to someone distant, 'No, no one over here.'

As he stood up again I slipped back into my dreamworld, weak and disoriented, unable to summon the energy to plead for help.

When I next opened my eyes, the lids as heavy as metal shutters, all I could see in a dim light was a horrible black mask with wide white eyes and large white teeth. Wild orange hair stood on end like spinifex grass on the skull of this creature, surrounding the face like the flames that surround the sun. The grim visage was only inches away from my own. I could smell foul breath coming from its mouth. I cried out in fear, thinking that I was indeed a captive in hell, now that death had taken me. The face retreated in apparent alarm and gibbered in some strange tongue. Other demons, standing behind this forward creature, made similar sounds. Then I felt a wet rag being forced between my lips, where it was wrung by strong hands and blessed water trickled down my parched throat.

I must have passed out again, because the next thing I was aware of was the smell of cooking. I was lying in the shade on a blanket of stiff hide, surrounded by black people. When they saw I was awake, one of them, a naked woman with long, hanging breasts, came and squatted by me and began to feed me with a warm liquid. I have never tasted so good a meal as that small bowl of meat soup. I have never smelt anything so delicious as that broth. The woman was murmuring all the time, as one might babble to a baby, each time she put a little more of that glorious essence into my mouth. Indeed, if I could have decided there and then to have a second mother, she would have been my first choice.

When I was able I took notice of my surroundings. I was in an Aboriginal village or camp of sorts, though whether permanent or temporary I had little idea. Studying their dwellings, which seemed to consist of sticks covered with bark, I would have been surprised to learn this was a place where they remained all year round. I'd been told the Aborigines were a nomadic people, the tribes roaming at will, and that they didn't farm the land in any way. Settlers I had talked to were contemptuous of the indigenous natives, telling me they were uncivilised and coarse, with no gentle manners, laws or organised society. 'The land's going for free,' one farmer told me, 'they don't use it.'

Few of the black people around me in this village had any clothes on and those that did wore the minimum. Most however, seemed have smeared their bodies with fats and ochre. I wasn't sure if this practice was for decoration or for warmth. The men all carried weapons: clubs, boomerangs, spears. One or two younger males paused by my resting spot to shout angrily at me in their own language, and shake a fist in my face, but they were quickly and easily moved on by older men who seemed to be intent on good hospitality. The children crowded round me a lot of the time, chattering, laughing and pointing, some of them trying to touch or pinch my skin. The woman who had fed me the soup appeared to have been given the task of looking after my health. She fussed over me and chased the youngsters away when they became too boisterous.

At first I found the smells hard to take, even after the open cess pits of the company's camps. It was probably because they were strange to me, rather than generally offensive. However, after a few days I got used to the odours, as one usually does, and eventually forgot they were there at all. I was fascinated by the daily life of these people. The men left the camp to hunt during the day. At least, I believed one could assume that, since they often returned with game. As well as half-cooked meat, plants and nuts were given me to eat, the names of which were not in my vocabulary. Even live larvae, insects and moths were put to my mouth by the fingers of my elderly nurse, who seemed keen for me to taste the same fare as the rest of the tribe. I tried to eat one or two of these, but sometimes retched and upset any onlookers.

Women tended the fires, boiled water and cooked, though some meats were eaten almost raw. Women appeared to do the majority of the manual work required around a camp. I have no idea whether their way of life was a happy one, or whether it was simply survival which shaped their daily toil. They certainly did not seem *miserable*, but then I was too estranged from their culture to even guess at a common emotional state. There was laughter, there were tears, there were fights and reconciliations, much the same as in European society.

Someone had stolen my revolver and the pouch containing my astrolabe, money and watch. However, I considered this theft quite worth my life, which these people had given me. I had been very close to death when they found me and without their hospitality and care I would without doubt be a corpse feeding the dingoes that had chased away our horses. They took me in, they looked after me and they fed and watered me, even though I was probably as foreign to them as an orang utan was to me, when I saw one in a cage on Singapore island.

As a tribe in the red centre of the continent, if they had come across white men before it would be a mere glancing blow, perhaps a view from a distance. Stuart or Ross passing through on horseback, or perhaps even the Company's men going up and down the trail. Or even me, on top of a pole. We would not be familiar to them, being bizarre creatures with skins the colour of witchetty grubs, beings who seemed intent on cutting down trees and stringing them together across the landscape, leaving them to the sun and wind. Perhaps they thought that our telegraph line was a religious symbol, an erection to the gods to whom we prayed? Or maybe they believed we were friends of the birds, providing the parrots and falcons with perches? Indeed, whatever they thought of the telegraph wire it would be impossible for those uncivilised bush people to guess its true purpose.

TEN

When I was able to walk around without assistance I indicated with gestures that I had to leave the Aboriginal village. From their expressions, sounds and gestures I gathered that the Aborigines themselves seemed to think that this was a good idea. Whatever else I was to them, I was a disruption to their lives. Some members of the tribe obviously thought it was a bad idea to have one of these strange new men in their camp. There were still one or two angry faces around and even those who had been kind to me seemed eager for me to go.

I thanked them as best I could, not knowing their language. One of them, a tall man with a shock of ochred hair – possibly the one who had found me in the wilderness – was obviously assigned to lead me back to my people. Just before I left my possessions were returned to me intact. I was desperate to show how grateful I was for the fact that they had saved my life and removed Sally's photograph from the pocketwatch, then presented my silver hunter to the head of the tribe. He grinned, holding it up by the chain so that it sparkled in the sunlight. The rest of the tribe made appropriate noises of wonder and gratitude. What they would do with this useless gift I didn't know, but I had to leave them something to show my appreciation. It would have been wrong to have given them the gun for obvious reasons. They had no use for the money I carried on me, which was not very much in any event. No, it had to be the watch and it was a beautiful object, even if it only served to hang on a stick and glitter for them. Then, a final idea came to me just as I was walking out of the village. I stepped back and took off my hat, placing it on the head of the woman who had nursed and cared for me. Her face was a picture of delight and there were murmurs of approval from the rest of her tribe.

As I followed the Aborigine over what must have been to him the equivalent of common land in England, I thought of Mr Roberts. Had he perished out in the bush? He had been in much the same state, much the same plight as myself. Perhaps he had managed to keep his mount and it had been his lifesaver? Maybe the search party had found him before he had expired? I hoped so, firstly because I would not wish the surveyor to lose his life, and secondly because I knew that, if they found I was alive while he was not, I would in some way be blamed for my sub-overseer's death. Walker would make sure of that, with insinuations and suggestions. People like to blame someone, to alleviate unwanted feelings of guilt, no matter that incidents and accidents might be the fault of nothing but the nature of the world. It seems to help make them feel better. If a man is struck by lightning there will be some who say he should have been warned by so-and-so to stand in a different place. So there were two strong reasons why I wanted to see Mr Roberts, up on his own two legs, when I walked into the Overland Telegraph Company's camp.

My tall black guide led me over the colourful plains and hills, until we reached a rise around noon. He pointed with his spear and in the distance I could see white men labouring, a wagon bearing a load of poles, two camels – both dromedaries – with their cameleers on their backs. I nodded to my guide and reached out my hand to shake his, but he merely looked bemused, failing to understand what I wanted him to do. So I simply left him standing there, watching my descent to the plain below. When I reached the bottom and looked up, he was gone.

I was feeling the influence of the sun after several hours without my hat and wanted to get in the shade. As I approached the work party someone gave a shout and pointed at me. They all halted in their various tasks and gawped. One of them still leaned on his spade – Tim Felix, the ex-schoolmaster – but then nothing seemed to put him out of kilter. Tim was always cool, calm and disinterested.

'G'day, gentlemen,' I said, in the best manner I could summon. 'I'm pleased to see you all hard at work.'

Tam gave a yelp of delight and rushed forward to pump my hand, but in the background I was aware of Sholto Walker, staring at me with a hard blank expression. Thankfully I could also see Mr Roberts, standing to the right of the gang of men, his expression revealing amazement.

'God man!' cried Tam. 'You're alive!'

'I can see it's a surprise to many,' I replied.

Mr Roberts stepped forward then. 'I'm astonished, but very glad to see you, McKenzie,' he said. 'We had given you up.'

'I'm happy to see you still alive too, sir,' I countered. 'I truly am. These past days I had no idea if…' At this point I was inexplicably and disastrously overcome with emotion. I began weeping, the drops streaming down my face, the words choking my throat. Ashamed of my tears, I turned away from the staring crowd and walked back a few paces, trying to dry the wetness on my cheeks with the sleeve of my shirt.

After a minute I felt a hand on my shoulder and Mr Roberts was there. He said in a low voice in my ear, 'I know, Alex, I know. It wells up from within. You can't stop it, so don't try. It's the relief. I'm very, very happy to see you alive. You can tell me your story later, but in the meantime I'll have Scully walk you back to camp. Report to Mr Harvey and I'll see you at supper.'

'Yes, sir, thank you, sir,' I blubbed.

'Go on with you, then.' He turned back to face the men. 'Scully. See that McKenzie gets to the camp. The rest of you get back to work now, show's over.'

Someone, Peterson, a deeply religious soul, cried out, '*"And he that was dead came forth!"* Lazarus! Henceforth I shall call thee Lazarus.'

'Quiet, you fool,' snapped the sub-overseer. 'Keep that kind of talk inside your head.'

Out of the corner of my eye I could see Tam, watching me walk away, a worried expression on his face. He was a good lad, that Scot. He really did think well of me.'

Walking beside me, Scully was clearly embarrassed until I had come to my normal self and then he said, 'We all of us thought you was dingo meat.'

'I very nearly was,' I told him.

I didn't want to tell Scully the whole story of my subsequent rescue before I had reported to Mr Harvey.

Mr Harvey almost dropped his precious theodolite when he saw me. He strode forward and shook my hand vigorously.

'But where have you been, McKenzie? We've sent a report down the line.'

I was suddenly afraid that such a message might by its own volition reach Sally's ears in England before it could be stopped.

'Did it say I was dead?'

'No, missing. Just missing. You're thinking of your parents, I suppose, getting a false report? I'll send one of the Afghans down the line to catch up with the report.'

'Not my parents. They're both dead. But – someone else.'

'You have a wife. And perhaps a family?'

'Not yet, sir, but I'm hopeful.'

'Ah, a sweetheart. Yes, very important to stop a report of your death reaching a sweetheart. They sometimes turn to the nearest sympathetic pair of arms…good God, what am I saying? I'm sorry, McKenzie, I'm babbling. I'm just so relieved to see you in one piece. How did you survive? Did you find water? When we discovered Surveyor Roberts, he was completely done in. Another few hours and we would have been making a coffin for him. We saved his horse too, but I expect yours has gone, yes?'

I nodded.

'Yes, yes of course. Well, and here you are, looking quite well after such a terrible ordeal. Good. Good. Now, sit down and tell me all that happened. Did you find water? I already asked that, didn't I? Well, did you?'

'I was taken in by Aborigines, sir. They found me after the search party passed me by.'

Harvey stared at me for a full two minutes, incomprehension written all over his face, before saying, 'What?'

'The search party, sent out to find me and Mr Roberts. I was lying in a dry creek, only half-conscious much of the time. I remember someone looking down at me and calling to the rest of the party. The words he used were, "There's no one here." Then he left me to die.'

'I don't understand. You're saying that the search party passed by the spot but failed to see you in the creek?'

'I'm saying a man saw me, but failed to inform the rest of the party that I was there.'

The surveyor's face hardened. 'The name of this man?'

'Walker.'

'This is a very serious accusation, McKenzie.'

'It's a very serious act, Mr Harvey. That man callously left me to die. He knew what he was doing.'

Harvey rubbed his face with his hands.

'You're absolutely certain about this?' he asked me in a firm voice. 'There can be no mistake?'

My head was aching. I asked for a drink of water. By the time Harvey gave it to me, doubts were already trickling through my brain. I knew I had to be completely honest in my answer. I disliked Sholto Walker intensely, almost as much as he seemed to loath me, and perhaps my abhorrence of him had caused my mind to invent the scene.

'No,' I said at last.

'No mistake?'

'No, I can't be *absolutely* certain. Naturally I was – what's the word – delirious, sir. But I don't think I was that far gone that I was imagining things. I'm pretty sure of that.'

A huge sigh escaped Mr Harvey's breast and I knew he was relieved to find an escape hatch from this awful situation.

'Well, you know, McKenzie, men in your state – the state you were in – do have false visions, hear false voices. Mirages. *Fata Morgana*. I'm aware, I'm told, that you and Walker do not see eye-to-eye. There is antagonism between you, right? Well then, you might well in your delirium have conjured up the sight of your enemy, turning his back on you, consigning you to death. The mind plays terrible tricks when it is under stress. Men see ghosts. Men swear that their dead fathers have risen from the grave and have confronted them with childhood errors.

'Listen,' he laid a hand on my arm, as I sat in the wicker chair he seemed to enjoy so much, 'Surveyor Roberts was out of his head when we found him. Raving. Completely wild. He was shouting about an eagle that was circling overhead, saying the Devil was about to descend and rip his soul from his body. The men were shocked by his state of mind, I can tell you, and if you were in the same condition while you lay in the creek, then surely your mind invoked something of the same ilk? Do you think that possible, McKenzie? Do you think you might have been so far gone that you were dreaming while awake? Of the man you hate?'

'I don't *hate* him, sir. He's done nothing to me in a physical sense. We just dislike each other.'

'A natural animosity?'

'I suppose so. He went for me right from the start, even while I was caring for him when he was in the same state as I have been.'

'You resented that – him attacking you, verbally.'

'Yes, I did.'

'He showed no gratitude for your services, for bringing him back to health, and he took an instant dislike to your character? I can understand how you might feel chagrined at such a thing. I have no idea what kind of man Walker is personally. He works well and as the supervisor here that's mainly what I'm interested in. Of course, if he disrupted the camp, generally, then I'd have to get rid of him. This camp is like a ship. If a man stirs up feelings of mutiny, then he needs to be got rid of. I would get rid of him like a shot from a cannon. But Walker isn't universally disliked. In fact the men seem to look up to him, somewhat. That may be galling to you, McKenzie, when you don't get on with him, but so far as running this operation, Walker presents no threat.'

'I can see that.'

'So, I'm asking you again, are you absolutely certain that you were completely in your right mind when you saw Walker leaning over you in your distressed state? Certain sure, beyond all doubt. These are men's lives we're talking about, because I would have to send him back to Adelaide under guard, you too, for you would need to accuse him in front of the authorities and make that accusation stick. Then, if they found him guilty, they would surely hang him.'

Suddenly, I saw all the difficulties. Walker's word against mine, a man who was half out of his head in a landscape famed for its strangenesses and weird visions. I could not see how I would be believed. Not only that, I would then miss the opportunity of being one of the first operators to work on the opening of the overland telegraph, an event in history which would make my career. The company would never send me back to E Section after bringing their operations into a bad light. The newspapers would relish the story and it was the kind of publicity the company was trying to avoid, being already lambasted by politicians and businessmen from other colonies in Australia, especially Queensland, who were furious that the South Australian Government had got the contract in preference to their proposed telegraph routes. The choice was taken away from me. I had too much to lose by prosecuting a man who was not worth the red dust under the soles of my feet.

'No, I can't be sure, Mr Harvey. I am forced to withdraw the accusation.'

Relief flooded into my boss's eyes and the supervisor took my one hand in both of his and held it there for a few moments.

'I'm glad,' he said. 'I'm very glad, McKenzie.'

I left the senior surveyor and took a short walk to a nearby hill to await the evening light. Not long after I reached this amber-hued lump on the central Australian topography the sky turned to indigo and darkness began to slide in over the vast landscape which I was coming to love. Even out here, in the red heart of a virgin wilderness, there were men who harboured evil against those of their own kind, along with a separate race of helpful people who had no reason to do good for intruders who might eventually destroy their way of life. All in one pot. Throw a handful of humans together and you get the whole range of variations that run through the nature of those two-legged aberrations.

The darkness above had been dusted with milled crystal. Staring up at the stars there was a yearning in my breast, chafing and raw.

ELEVEN

'So, you are the particular friend of our daughter, Mr McKenzie.'

I was in the parlour of Mr and Mrs Whiting's house in Southwark, drinking tea from a delicate china cup with violets captured under the glaze, and it was Sally's mother who had made the remark. Sally's father owned a shop that sold women's headgear and trimmings. I had already been corrected for using my own term, and told in a stern voice that it was a 'milliner's arcade' not a common hat shop. Sally was looking anxious, her eyes darting between me and her parents, probably wondering whether I was going to disgrace myself or that her hostile father might goad me into a retort we would all regret. Her mother sitting opposite me was a small demure lady with a sweet face, who did not seem at all unhappy that I was in her house.

I glanced quickly at Sally. 'I hope we are good friends, yes.'

'We're always concerned to meet our daughter's friends,' said Mr Whiting, a large man with a watch chain that hung from his waistcoat pocket down past his thigh. 'It's our duty as good parents.'

I knew already that I was being vetted.

'Of course. You wish to protect her from unsavoury characters. I am, I assure you, sir, not one of those. I value Sally's friendship. She has been kind to me, a newcomer to the capital.'

'And you're not a Scotchman, Mr McKenzie, despite your name? Not that I have any grievance against our northern neighbours.'

'A Scottish ancestry, on my father's side, but both my father and I were born in England.'

'And how did you meet our daughter – first meet?'

Sally would have already told her father and mother the story we had concocted to save her from censure by her parents.

'We were introduced by a mutual friend at the library. I was taking out a book and an assistant librarian, John Smithers hailed me. John and I had met once on one of my earlier visits to London. Miss Whiting was nearby and he made us known to one another. A most fortunate coincidence, John being out of his office that morning.'

Smithers had been primed and was ready for any questions should either Mr or Mrs Whiting ever meet him.

'What was the book about, Mr McKenzie?' asked Sally's father abruptly.

'What?'

'The book you were taking out? I'm interested in your choice of literature.'

'Oh –' my mind raced. I hadn't imagined this would come out. 'Oh yes, it was a biography, of Lord Nelson – yes, that was it, wasn't it Sally? You remember, you signed it out for me.'

'Yes,' said Sally, going alarmingly pink, 'I'm sure it was – a biography of Horatio Nelson.'

Fortunately Mr Whiting did not seem to notice his daughter's sudden discomfort. He continued to stare at me and then remarked, 'You know we are members of the Religious Society of Friends, Mr McKenzie – that is to say, Quakers, and therefore pacifists. We do not approve of war, nor indeed violence of any kind.'

I sipped my tea slowly, to give myself a few seconds grace.

'Yes, Sally has spoken of your religious views.'

'Ah, so now we slip down the conventional ladder of good manners to the more informal "Sally" and dispense with your previous "Miss Whiting"? Well, well – and you are aware Lord Nelson was a warrior. I am interested in your fascination with this admiral who raked the Spanish and French, and several other nations too, with red hot iron from the cannons of war, causing much bloodshed on the high seas.'

I took another sip of tea and spluttered as it went down the wrong way. Then Sally's mother intervened with a gentle smile on her face.

'Mr Whiting is teasing you, Mr McKenzie. Take no notice of him. He's not as intolerant as he sounds. Please have another sandwich. I baked the bread myself. I hope you like it?'

'It's – it's very good bread, Mrs Whiting.'

'Why not call her *Joan*?' said Mr Whiting. 'And perhaps you'd like to address me as Philip? Let's be cosy, shall we?'

'Now Philip, stop it,' said Mrs Whiting. 'He's known Sally long enough to call her by her given name.' She turned back to me, saying, 'Now, young man, how serious are you about our daughter? My husband has made you uncomfortable, but we actually would like to know the answer to this question. Don't tell me you haven't talked about it, between you, because I know when my daughter is taken with a young man – her eyes light up and the fondness when speaking your name is enough to give away her feelings – so, out with it young man. I don't mind what the answer is, I just would like to be fully informed.'

Her speech robbed me of my breath for a minute. I had never met such blunt forthright people before in my life. There she sat, looking as if butter would not melt in her mouth, and suddenly this diffident mother of my lady friend turned into a basilisk. Her sharp blue eyes bore into me and I placed the cup down on the small table between us with trembling fingers causing the teaspoon to rattle loudly in the delicate china saucer. Yes, it was true I had asked Sally to marry me, but I was hoping that I would have one or two more meetings with her parents, before I approached her father to ask his permission and blessing.

'Mr Whiting,' I began, 'Mrs Whiting, I love your daughter. She has no doubt told you of my background – I am from humble but worthy rural stock – and my plans for the future. It's my desire to travel to one of the Australian colonies to make my fortune. I'm now a trained telegraph operator and have a little education behind me. I hope to make good out there and then send for Sally for us to be married.'

'That's plain enough,' said Mr Whiting, leaning forward, his white hair bristling like the mane of a lion, 'but why not somewhere closer? The Americas? Canada? Surely a man of your profession could find work there just as easily? You will be taking our only child away from us to a land unreachable by ordinary people. A land where we send convicts, though as a Quaker I do not approve of this vile practice. It'll be a hard thing for us, if Sally leaves these shores for a place that takes four months or more to reach. What is your fascination with Australia, Mr McKenzie? Do you have relations there, on whom you can call for assistance and help in furthering your chosen career?'

'A cousin. He has a job for me. I know no one in America and I feel that that particular country, no longer a colony of course, is so well-established they will have their own young men eager for advancement in the telegraph industry. I believe my chances of success are greater in Australia or New Zealand which still need immigrants to forge themselves into completely separate nations. Like America, they will one day in the future break away from Britain and become their own countries. I want to be there, established, when that happens.'

The big man heaved a big sigh and looked at his wife, whose raised eyebrows obviously signalled her feelings. Mr Whiting turned back to me then and surprisingly uttered these words.

'It is with great reluctance that we give you two children our blessing. We believe that every individual should make their own path and if our daughter has chosen to do that with you, Mr McKenzie, then we would be wrong to stand in her way. We shall miss her greatly. A lot of tears will be shed on all sides because she's met a man with ambition, but – well, there you have it. I shall shake your hand.'

I reached out and took the much larger palm in my own.

'Alexander. My first name is Alexander.'

'Oh, we know that,' replied Mrs Whiting, the twinkle back in her eyes. 'We've known that a long time since.'

We continued with the tea party, but somehow I gathered that though these two older people had given their consent they were hoping, not without good foundation, that I would go off to my distant destination and that would be an end to it all. They were probably praying that separation might cause the relationship to falter and crack apart, or cause one of us to fall in love with someone more appropriate to the circumstances. They loved their only daughter deeply and did not want to lose her. To have objected to the union would not have worked. They were sensible and intelligent enough people to realise that trying to drive us apart would only end with strengthening the bond between us. Hell hath no fury like a woman scorned, but equally Heaven hath no determination like a woman in love.

The end might yet still come about as the Whitings had hoped, with Sally deciding that Australia was a place too far. It is no easy thing to bid a final farewell to the country of your birth, the land of your ancestors, your childhood home where your parents will reside for the rest of their lives, knowing that you will probably not return.

Sally might never leave the shores of Britain to be with me.

TWELVE

Not long after I had completed some line checks one day that was cooler than most had been, when a haulier's wagon arrived in camp. Joe Standeven was driving the wagon and he nodded at me before taking the pipe out of his mouth and spitting to leeward. Sitting next to Joe was a passenger wearing a bright yellow shirt. Such a flowery colour attracted insects and indeed he was covered with black and brown creatures, some of them winged, others wingless. They were mostly motionless, but here and there amongst the multitude one of them crawled, looking for God knows what, for the daffodil-hued material was just as bright in one spot as it was in another. How the bloke had managed to keep a shirt so clean in the billowing dust and dirt of the outback was a mystery.

I recognised the square-chested, stocky man instantly, though he had grown a short neatly-clipped beard over his previously shaven features. It was the then red-shirted chess player from D Section who had asked if he could accompany me to E when I took Bill Turmaine down to get his foot fixed or taken off. The reporter bloke. He'd managed to get here anyway.

He looked around him and saw me, then wagged a finger.

'You didn't wait for me, telegraph operator!'

I felt abashed. 'Couldn't find you. Looked, but you weren't around.'

He grinned, mirthlessly I thought. 'Where would I go? We're out in the bloody bush, mate.'

I shrugged and turned away. I wasn't going to get into an argument with a newcomer. I had work to do, disconnecting my batteries and tidying up the temporary shack. I heard him ask Joe where he could find Mr Harvey and Joe telling him he wasn't a bloody signpost and to look for himself. Joe was a cantankerous bloke who had little time for anyone. He did his job and that was where his duty ended. There being little profit in pleasantries, Joe Standeven had no time for them.

When I was ready to go I noticed a large barking spider climbing up the inside of the flap that served as a door to the shack, a huge sod the size of a gorilla's hand. I waited until it had crossed the gap between the top of the canvas and the ceiling. Those hairy buggers can scuttle like lightning when they want to and though I'm fine with them if they keep to themselves, I get a bit frantic if they're on my body or clothes.

You get used to spiders and to a certain extent snakes in the outback, but one creature I really detest is the scorpion. These spawn of Satan made me shudder with revulsion, having a tangle of legs, a hard shiny skin and an evil pair of pincers, not to mention the tail with the sting. They're slick and malevolent-looking, and mindless as any venomous creature. Fortunately, none of the scorpions out in the bush were killers, but they could make you pretty sick. I spent a hell of a lot of time shaking clothes, bedding and boots. The work was not in vain. Scorpions would drop out of my footwear or run out of a shirt sleeve as often as not. Once, I lifted my make-do pillow before I lay my head down to sleep and a small, ugly, colourless bugger emerged from beneath a seam. I yelled in fright and got short shrift from the others in the tent. That night I went through my bedding inch by inch, while polers and wiremen grumbled at me and told me to settle down or get the fuck outside.

I found out later that the reporter's name was Jack Ransome, and as I imagined, our two surveyors were not enamoured of his presence. I'm told he informed our bosses that he was here at the request of the company and although he understood their position they had no authority to turn him away. They were even more annoyed to hear this unwelcome statement. As Tim Felix, our tame ex-schoolmaster said, a newspaper story isn't interesting unless it's about something going wrong. We regarded the reporter as a predatory beast, waiting for us to make a mistake or some elemental disaster to arrive, so he could pounce and feed on it.

When this was put to him Jack Ransome explained to us, with a smile, that he wasn't that kind of journalist.

'I'm just going to write an article on the building of our own telegraph road,' he said. 'It's an amazing feat. History in the making. Future generations will look back on this enterprise and find all those aspects of men that are most honourable: courage, vision, hard labour under adverse conditions, many, many more. All those characteristics that have caused philosophers such as Abdala the Saracen to remark, "There is nothing to be seen more wonderful than Man!". Or Trismegistus to pronounce, "A great miracle, is Man!" I'm not going to interfere with your work. I'm simply here to observe and record. Sure, if you make mistakes, I'll put those in, but I'll also emphasise your bravery in conquering unknown territory and bringing civilisation to a wilderness seen only once before by a pair of European eyes.'

The learned content of this speech made Tim Felix's eyes widen. Tim realised he was no longer the only scholar in the camp. Those who went to Tim for erudite knowledge would probably seek a second opinion from this smiling man who wore dazzling shirts and (we were to find out) carried, day and night, a very expensive-looking revolver on his right hip and a battered chess set under his left arm.

At the campfire meeting that evening Mr Ransome was the cause of much speculation and interest.

'Is that the only new shirt you got?' asked John Scully. 'Why'd you want to go around lookin' like a wattle bush in bloom?'

This caused a deal of laughter, in which the victim himself willingly joined.

'Got a box full of 'em, mate. Look, when it comes to the outback, I admit to being cautious. I've read too many accounts of men leaving a group to have a quiet piss and never finding their way back to civilisation again. If I'm going to get lost, I want people to be able to notice me from a long way off. Is that so stupid? When I go behind a tree or rockpile, I want people to say "Jesus, look at that stupid idiot in the flash shirt – you can see him crapping from bloody miles away."'

This brought another round of laughter from the gang. It was clear this man was going to be popular, despite his profession. He had that friendly air about him. You couldn't help but like him. At the same time you knew he wouldn't take any serious shit from anyone. He was quite willing to laugh along with others, even when he was the brunt of the joke, but you felt if someone really did get under his skin and cause him discomfort, they would be in for a quick and nasty riposte.

Walker, unsurprisingly as far as I was concerned, was more interested in the gun than the man that carried it. The majority of the small arms in the camp were owned by the Overland Telegraph Company. Rifles and revolvers were issued by the storeman. Plain utility weapons. Nothing to excite a man who is interested in firearms. You signed them out and you signed them in, and authority was needed from the supervisor before that happened. Yes, there were one or two privately possessed rifles and pistols in the camp – Bates of course owned that notorious muzzle-loader with which he had accidentally shot Bill Turmaine – but they were few and far between. A fancy new revolver was an object of great curiosity not just to Walker, but to most of us, me included. I was a young man with a young man's passions too.

'Where'd you get the fancy cannon?' Walker asked the newcomer.

Jack Ransome patted the leather holster on his hip. 'This? A present from my boss. It's Austrian, so I'm told. An eleven millimetre Gasser Marine. Pretty, eh? Not that I can use it with any skill, but you never know out here.'

Walker slowly folded his arms over his chest and then he murmured, 'Eleven-point-three.'

Any chatter ceased and everyone stared at Sholto.

'What?' asked Jack Ransome.

'The calibre. It's not eleven, it's eleven-point-three.'

'Oh, so you know the gun.' Jack Ransome took it out of its holster and the steel glittered in the firelight. He pointed it menacingly at the moon, grinned, and placed it back in the holster. 'It's a new model. You obviously keep up on your weapons. Eleven-point-three, eh? Does the point three make any difference if a slug hits you in the chest? Is it going to kill you any quicker, or make you deader than you would be?'

He was still smiling at Walker, but there was something passing between them at that moment which was indefinable.

A half-smile came to Walker's face now.

'Look, I'm just puttin' you right, mate. That's a nice piece of artillery and you need to know it inside-out. Later on, when you write about the time you killed your first Abo in the outback, you'll need the facts to be absolutely down to the mark. Otherwise you'll get a lot of letters from blokes like me callin' you a liar and a fool because you ain't got the first clue about your side ordnance.'

Ransome looked down at the ground, then back up again to stare into Walker's eyes.

'That's right,' he said. 'You're quite right. A correspondent's facts have to be accurate, or the rest of his story might be called into question. I thank you, sir, for giving me that information. I'm certain you know what you're talking about and if ever I have the misfortune to use my weapon – be it on a black or white man – I'll know correct calibre to the precise decimal point and my editor will thank me for it.'

There were a few minutes of silence while everyone digested this reply and decided the reporter hadn't exactly backed down, but had simply fended off a remark that had been designed to rile him, the atmosphere dissipated into a number of separate conversations around the fire. I saw Tim Felix get up and go and sit by the new man, engaging him in an exchange which I knew would be too learned for me to follow. The pair of them were obviously soul mates and it did not surprise me to observe that before very long they were playing chess.

Walker came over and sat by me for a few minutes causing me to feel very uncomfortable, since he hadn't spoken to me since my resurrection.

'You know this bloke?' he asked me, breathing tobacco smoke into my face. 'Seen 'im before?'

'He was in D Section when I went down with Bill Turmaine.'

'Clever bastard, ain't he?'

'I suppose you have to be, if you're working for a newspaper.'

Walker's eyes narrowed as he studied Jack Ransome between the flames of the fire.

'Yeah. I s'pose. Well, he'd better not get too clever with me, or I'll shove his shiny brass cannon up his arse.'

With that, Sholto got up and went to talk to his cronies, leaving me wondering whether I was now in favour, now that this newcomer had arrived to put Walker's nose out of joint. However, much later in the evening I saw Ransome fold his board, gather his wooden chess pieces in their box, and go to

Walker's side. He sat down and began talking, and though I couldn't hear what was being said, it appeared that after a short while they had become the best of mates. Ransome even slapped Walker on the back and roared with laughter at something the tall man said. I went to bed feeling that the stars had been joggled out of place.

THIRTEEN

It turned out that Walker enjoyed the idea that he might appear in an article in the *South Australian Journal*. I should not have been surprised that he courted attention. He was that kind of man. He had ideas on everything, no matter what it was: the most efficient way to plant a telegraph pole; the proper way to pin the wire; the most proficient method of hunting kangaroos; the easiest way to get a girl into bed without promising to marry her; how to get rid of cockroaches, bed bugs, mosquitoes, flies, rodents; how to win at poker or any other gambling game, including two-up. Oh, he knew everything about everything and lectured you on the most obscure and archane subjects.

Some of the men were beginning to see through him, realising this Sholto Walker was a wiseacre. Others were either too afraid, too stupid or too apathetic to avoid him. He had one or two cronies who always paid him the kind of attention he seemed to need and it seemed Jack Ransome became one of those. While the correspondent did not cling on to Walker's coat tails he did stop and listen whenever Sholto accosted him. He would nod gravely, listen attentively to what was being said to him, then thank Walker for whatever advice was being given to him. If it was an opinion that Walker sought, about politics or social issues, more often than not Ransome would agree with Walker's point of view. If he did not, he offered up a not too dissimilar perspective which the big man digested and then somehow managed to make his own.

The days went by, the poles went in, the wire was pinned, I did the checks, and the work progressed with small incident. We heard that while A, B, C and D Sections were going well, the Northern Section was still in trouble. The country between Port Darwin and the Roper River had never fully been explored. The first sixty or so miles had been surveyed in 1869, but the other two-hundred or so were a complete mystery to the teams who were to sent out to pole it. And this was less than half the stretch of ground they had to cover to reach the point where we were expected to meet up with them. The land there was heavily wooded, being tropical rainforest, quite unlike the terrain we were crossing. The forest had to be cleared of both undergrowth and timber, before holes could be dug and telegraph poles planted.

The dry season in the north was only three months from coming to an end, which meant the problems with too little water would be superseded by too much water. It would indeed tumble from the sky in torrents. There was no happy medium. Once the wet started any struggle with the elements and the terrain itself would increase tenfold. I had heard that flies and mosquitoes in the rainforest were the size of swallows and shirts rotted on men's backs. It was said there were more living creatures in a man's bedroll than could be found in an ant hill or bee hive and certainly there was greater variety. In the wet season those insects and other small living things would increase in number, as they sought refuge from a truly biblical flood. Bob Patterson, now in charge in that region, had his hands full just keeping the men on the teams from throwing down tools and refusing to work in the terrible conditions.

We were lucky, not that you would guess it to hear the remarks in the tent and around the campfire. It's a certainty that men will complain about their lot even when they reach Paradise. It's in their nature to be dissatisfied and they seem to enjoy the art of pulling management to pieces and explaining how they would do things so much better. No boss, whether liked or hated, does it as well as it could be done. Rumours are rife and myths abound. The truth is nowhere to be seen. Often men wake up with a dream in their heads they believe to be real.

'Lazarus, did you hear about our pay being halved? Peterson told me they're not satisfied with the number of poles we're putting in and they're threatenin' us with cutting our money.' No one asks where Peterson's inside information has come from, but he enjoys the notoriety of being the bearer of bad news. 'I heard the supply wagon was attacked by blacks. There's nothin' coming through for a month and if we shoot anythin' to eat they're going to charge us for the ammunition we use. Cryin' shame, I say.' This from a man who has no direct contact whatsoever with the outside world at large, let alone the authorities in Adelaide. Information that comes to men in isolation presumably on the backs of eagles or carried by clouds and delivered by rain.

Such talk never ceases. Sometimes when the rumours get too alarming and the grumbles too loud, the bosses get us together and explain just what is fact and what is fiction, but the truth never hangs in the air for very long. Within a week there are new stories about impending disasters or affronts to honest workmen who are doing their best for the company, everyone convinced they are being betrayed by some clerk sitting on his fat arse down south in a nice comfortable office, drinking coffee and chatting to the females doing the filing. Indignation is never far below the surface and rises as in a whale coming to the surface of a calm sea to spout malicious gossip in all directions.

Two men who never seemed affected by the mood of the camp, whether it be good or bad, were Tim Felix and Jack

Ransome. Both were astute enough to recognise when the acid talk was the result of a mixture of isolation fever and labouring men's under-confidence. They let it pass over their heads, listening when others stopped them to tell of the latest offence against manual workers, but not offering any opinion or arguing the irrationality of the grievance. Perhaps they were concerned it would make them unpopular to offer a reasoned viewpoint, or maybe they were just bored, jaded by unfounded gossip.

I would sometimes sit and watch these two playing chess, and was therefore able to listen to more erudite conversation than could be heard around the campfires. I was now aware that although at twenty I had believed I knew everything that it was necessary to know in life, in fact I had been at that age an ignorant youth. It behoved me to learn more about things that had held little interest for my father the horseman, whose enthusiasm was reserved for the Suffolk Punch, Shire and Cumbrian heavy horses. Archaeology, history, geography, literature, art, architecture: all those subjects that my parents would have regarded as a waste of a man's time now fired my enthusiasm. Jack was not so much the scholar, though he was better educated than myself, but Tim seemed to have read every book that had ever been printed. The subjects that he held in his head were wondrous and multifarious, and much of the vocabulary I am using for this account I heard from his mouth.

Tim Felix had brought three or four battered books with him on this job which he let me read too. Learned books, which were helping me gain knowledge, pure knowledge, that might not be of use to me directly in life, but filled the empty pockets in my brain. It did not really matter to me that the blue whale was the largest mammal in the world, or that the molten rock at the core of our planet was called *magma*. These fragments of information were not going to advance my position in the profession of telegraphy one iota. Knowing these and many other facts gave me a feeling of confidence and superiority. It was not that I wanted to think I was higher than others, but that I was not lower. My ambition had taken me up to another level of society, where men of learning and education were rife, and I needed to be able to hold my own in their company without feeling as if I were drowning.

Tim was talking about the '...giants that once walked the earth, right here, in Australia.' My spine tingled at the thought, for I had been raised in a rural community where belief in fairies and giants had still not been shaken off.

'What's this?' I said, sitting down next to Jack, thinking we were talking about a race like the Maoris of New Zealand. 'Big men?'

Tim smiled at this. 'No, not men. Animals. Mammals.'

Now Jack looked up. 'Mammals? Not lizards? You just told me about giant lizards.'

'There were giant lizards here?' I cried. 'When?'

'Oh, millions of years ago, before you were born,' replied Tim, moving his knight to block an advance by Jack. 'They were called dinosaurs. Some of them were bigger than elephants. Have you not heard of dinosaurs?'

I hadn't, but I was ashamed to admit it. 'Oh, sort of. I think I can remember one of my schoolmasters mentioning them.'

'Yes, well after the dinosaurs were wiped out, along came some giant mammals.'

Jack said, 'Kangaroos?'

'Perhaps,' replied Tim, 'I don't know that for sure, but I do know there was a bird that was ten feet tall and weighed a thousand pounds. They call it the Thunderbird, though that's not its scientific name, which I don't know. Then there was a marsupial wolf and a marsupial lion, both giants, and a wombat that weighed more than three tons.'

'Marsupial,' I repeated. 'That means like the kangaroos – a pocket in front for the baby.'

'Correct, young man,' Tim said. 'A very useful pocket for the baby, which gives the infant constant protection.'

'How do you know about these animal giants?' asked Jack, retreating from Tim's knight.

'Read about it in a paper written by some archaeologist for the Royal Society in England. You can find such papers and pamphlets in libraries, if you look hard enough, or ask.'

'My fiancée's a librarian,' I said.

'Good for you. Good for her,' Tim said, now moving his queen. 'A very noble profession for either a man or a woman.'

Jack snorted. 'Hey look, I don't agree with women working, not outside the home anyway.'

'And if they're single women with no other means of support?' countered Tim.

'Well, I suppose that's all right, if they're maiden aunts or spinsters.'

'Or widows?' suggested Tim.

'Of course, widows.'

'Especially if they've got a brood of young?'

Jack was beginning to grind his teeth. 'Especially if they've got kids.'

'Which just leaves your hopeful virgins and your already marrieds.'

'Exactly. I just don't agree those two types should be in paid employment.'

Tim said mildly, 'You think that librarian is a suitable job for a grown man then? Looking after books?'

'Not as such. Look, there are men and there are men. Some blokes are pansy types who can't take their liquor and couldn't wield a pick-axe to save their lives. Let's face it, Tim, some men are not really men, they're women in all but…well, they've got the tackle, but that's about it. You couldn't find a tough muscle on them if you tried.'

'So, the profession should be kept for these pansies?'

'That's my honest opinion,' said Jack, stuffing his pipe into his mouth after this statement to indicate that the conversation was over.

I enjoyed watching these two going back and forth, witnessing their arguments, which usually ended with one of them stubbornly refusing to budge from a stated position.

Tim sighed. 'I think you're wrong, Jack,' he said.

The pipe came out swiftly. 'Look here, mate,' replied the reporter, 'I've only been wrong once in my life and that was when I thought I was wrong and I turned out to be right after all.'

I laughed out loud at this and Tim soon joined me. Jack was very pleased with himself and chuckled along with us. However, I still wanted to hear more about the giants.

'These creatures, did they live millions of years ago, like the – what were they – dinothings? The lizards?'

'As I understand it, they came after the dinosaurs, so it would be – oh, I don't know, maybe less than a million years ago. Something like that.'

'How do they know all this?' scoffed Jack, losing another pawn to Tim's rampaging queen. 'You tell me that.'

'They've found a pile of bones in a cave. Several caves. Lots of bones. Big ones, proving they were giants.'

'And they had dates stamped on them?'

'No, Jack,' said Tim, patiently. 'Check mate.'

Jack stared at the board. His king was trapped.

'You just tell these tales to distract me! That's what you do.'

'Not at all, Jack. To tell you the truth I don't know how they figure out how old the bones are. They probably just guess.'

Jack said, 'Couldn't be millions of years ago, because the world is only 4,000 years old. Says so in the Bible.'

'No it doesn't,' Tim countered. 'Some bishop said he worked it out from reading the Bible, but it's not there in print, not in black and white. It's just some pansy cleric sitting in a library making it all up.'

Jack looked shocked. 'You can't call a bishop a *pansy*. That's sacrilege.' He appealed to me. 'Don't you think so, McKenzie?'

Jack Ransome never called me by my given name, which grieved me a little, because it meant I was not a close friend.

'I don't know.'

A shadow then fell over my shoulder and onto the chess board. I looked up and Sholto Walker was looming over me. He had obviously heard the last few remarks because he entered the conversation.

'I think Ransome is right,' he said. 'You can't call a bishop names – it's blasphemy.'

Tim said, firmly, 'It's not sacrilege and it's not blasphemy – you're both using the wrong words. You can't just snatch words out of the air like that and use them without knowing their true meaning. Sacrilege is profaning anything holy and a bishop is not necessarily holy. He might be a bad bishop, wanting in all sorts of ways. Breaking into a church and stealing a wine chalice is sacrilege. Desecrating a church altar is sacrilege. Now, blasphemy is to speak impiously of God and bishops certainly aren't equal to God, or anything like it.'

'Well,' Jack said, 'it's wrong, anyway.'

Tim was now on his bandwagon.

'Now look, Jack – Sholto – just because a man has fought and weaselled his way into a bishop's mitre, doesn't make him a good bloke. He's no better than any of the gentry we came to these colonies to escape. Yes, we've still got one or two of them here, but they'll be gone soon, you mark my words. We'll do what the Americans did and make a bid for independence soon, then we'll be rid of them.'

Jack grunted, before saying, 'I got to admit, I'd like to see the backs of those bastard lords and earls. They're like some private club at top of the human race, looking down on the rest of us. I'd like to see them good and gone from here. They all watch out for each other – kings, generals, judges, lords and ladies. They come down like a ton of bricks on one of us working men when we do something wrong, but they let each other get away with murder.'

'I'd agree with that,' snarled Walker. 'Bunch o' bastards.'

I watched Tim carefully, knowing him better than the other two men. He always played the Devil's Advocate. Now that he had got Jack and Walker to agree that the privileged classes were a mob of self-seeking swines who looked after themselves and their kind, he was now thinking of offering an argument that proved they were not. I could see it in his expression and sure enough, out it came.

'Well, in the main yes, but then there was Admiral Byng.'

'Admiral Byng?' repeated Jack. 'Who was he?'

'Son of Sir George Byng, Viscount Torrington. Byng was admiral of the British fleet at the Battle of Minorca in 1756. He failed to do his utmost to stop Minorca falling into French hands, so they executed him.'

Jack was clearly shocked at this statement. We all were.

'Who did?'

'The British navy. The other admirals court-martialed him, found him guilty of not doing his best, and put him before a firing squad. Shot him to pieces.'

Even Walker found this hard to comprehend. 'What, a full-blown admiral, just not doin' his best, so they marched him up in front of a firin' squad and killed 'im?'

'Exactly,' said Tim, enjoying himself. 'Look, that same admiral probably hung a hundred men for not much more than stealing a piece of cheese when they were hungry, so why are you so disturbed by the idea that an admiral is shot for cowardice? I'll tell you one thing, it was the making of the British navy. Thereafter you didn't get admirals or any other officers – captains of ships of the line – ever retreating from a battle at sea, even if they were outgunned. The execution of John Byng did what it was expected to do. It told naval commanders that it would be better for them to go down with their ships rather than run away in the expectation of fighting another day.'

'I'll bet it did,' said Jack, thoughtfully. 'I'll bet it bloody did.'

I was left with the thought that men are strange creatures. Even though we despise those arrogant birth-right aristocrats and royals, we are shocked by the sudden death of one. A king can have any number of subjects executed or even murdered, but we are shaken and yes, sometimes even outraged, when that same king is marched to the block and beheaded. It is as if we actually believe in the myth that these people are there by divine right and that God himself will be outraged that his chosen one has been subjected to the laws of ordinary men.

A duke, a lord, even a king is, underneath all the pomp and fine clothes, just a plain, common man. Yet we are surprised and somewhat disconcerted when one of them is executed. Is it because we really want to believe there's a position in the hierarchy of men which can't be touched by ordinary life? Are we more concerned with keeping a secret dream intact, a deeply-embedded desire to have among us those who are superior beings, creatures untouchable by mundane laws?

FOURTEEN

I awoke the following morning feeling cold among the surrounding ironstone hills. Lumps of quartz were visible in some huge boulders of granite, glinting in the weak early sunlight, looking as if they had been inlaid by a craftsman in the way that mother-of-pearl is often set on a lady's ebony jewel box. The plain ahead was simply scrubland and large mounds of sand. You couldn't say, 'Oh, the Creator of the world did well here. What a magnificent landscape!' It was too jumbled and cluttered for that, the bush ragged and untidy, and the stonework hills and outcrops scattered higgledy-piggledy, with no set places or stations, looking as if they had been tossed there by giants.

There was a contradiction about the scene: at the same time as a I sensed a freshness in the air there was the knowledge that here we were treading on an ancient landscape, barely touched by human foot since the world had first begun. We might have been walking on the moon. That feeling persisted throughout the day, as I watched young Tam cutting down the wild trees and stripping them of their branches and bark, leaving the bone-white poles looking naked and vulnerable on a stack of its brothers and sisters. There was a strong feeling of timelessness about our lives in the red heart of this great continental island. Days came and went, drifting in and drifting out: hazy days with no real markers for the memory. We were in limbo, a great distance from civilised society, moving as if in a dream slowly, slowly, ever northwards. The end seemed a long way off, too far away to seriously think about.

I went out of camp with fifteen of the working crew, having some line checks to do later on in the morning, once they had increased the length of the wire. They were a ragged-looking set, all wearing worn shirts and baggy trousers, some with leather aprons tied at the waist, every single man-jack of them having a beard on his face and a brimmed hat on his head. Dirty for the most part, skin ingrained with desert dust. A good many of them had pipes in their mouths, mostly clay, but one or two with briars. You could not tell their ages, the beards disguising any youthfulness and their complexions as weather-beaten as any sailor's. They had individual hearts and minds, as do men everywhere, but they often gelled into a dreary-looking amorphous lump of humanity with thirty legs and thirty arms dragging itself over the ground.

Once they had started work, at their various tasks, they became separate creatures once more. The trees in this area were short and unsatisfactory, so the men had to bind two trunks together to make them tall enough for a single pole. The ends of these two were then bolted each-to-each securely with thick iron bands. After this had been done a hole was bored vertically down through the top of the pole so that an insulator pin could be inserted. Finally another iron band went round the head of the pole like a slave collar to prevent wear. These efforts were all well and good enough, but actually when the rain came the wetness carried the electric current over the surface of the insulator and down the wooden pole, thus losing a great deal of the power.

'Abos comin' in!' shouted one of the axemen, causing a racket among the parrots in the trees. 'Couple o' blacks, yonder by the creek.'

Work stopped. Men leaned on their tools, peering through narrowed eyes. Two natives were approaching our party cautiously, carrying some animal skins. They were young, not much more than boys really, and though one or two of our crew picked up their rifles the two youthful blacks did not seem to present much of a threat. The boys stopped when they were about a hundred yards away, seemingly too scared to approach any closer. They laid opossum hides on the ground and simply stood there. Clearly these were intended as gifts and I went forward slowly and casually, to pick them up. The skins had been well cleaned and were ready for crafting into a useful item.

'Whadda they want?' yelled Phil Trout. 'Tell 'em to bugger off.'

'You speak Abo, Trout?' I called back. 'Neither do I.'

'Well wave 'em away, goddammit.'

Mr Roberts was busy with something further back down the line and hadn't noticed that work had stopped. Axemen and polers were quite content to rest for a moment. It was small entertainment, but it was a respite from labouring. The wire-fitters, including Tim Felix, slid down their poles and ambled over. Tim went the extra hundred yards to stand by me, nodding and smiling at the two boys, then gesturing with the palms of his hands, raising them upwards as if to say, 'What do you want?'

There was no direct response to this, but after a while the boys simply sat down on the ground. The crew began their work again, watching the two Aborigines out of the corners of their eyes. Sure enough after a period one of the boys got up and walked over to where the equipment lay. He started rooting through bags and backpacks, curious as a squirrel. Since I was the only one not labouring away at a manual task I went to him and indicated that he should stop. He stared at me for a few moments, then continued to sort through the equipment. Finding a spare axe he picked it up and strolled towards his companion, who was now on his feet and seemed eager to leave. Walker then came running over to the boy and grabbed him by the throat.

'Drop the axe, blackie, or I'll break your jaw.'

The Aborigine looked terrified and, though he probably did not understand the words spoken to him, did let the axe fall.

Jim Gwilliams called out, 'Easy, Sholto – he don't mean no harm I'm sure.'

'Yes,' I said, 'let him go. You're scaring him silly.'

'I don't hold with blacks messin' with my stuff,' growled Walker. 'You might not care, but I do.'

'Good God, man,' I said, 'you wander into the camp with only rags on your back and now you talk about *your* stuff?' I was suddenly and inexplicably very angry. Why that should be so, I didn't know, because Walker was only voicing what most of the other men were thinking. I snarled at him further. 'Anything you own at the moment has been given to you, so let's not have any righteous talk about *your* stuff.'

I picked up the axe and gently nudged the young Aborigine boy with my shoulder, getting him to move out of Walker's range. The youth was rubbing his neck and staring at Walker with round eyes. However, after a second or two he did begin to leave, collecting his friend, or perhaps it was his brother, and they went off, taking their opossum skins with them.

'Don't you understand?' I asked Walker. 'They have absolutely no idea what private property is. Anything that's not being used, they see as free to take and use themselves.'

'That don't make it right,' said Walker, belligerently. 'It's still private property, whether they see that or not. I don't hold with all this talk about them havin' different ways to us which we've got to respect. I live by the law of the land and so should they. I don't believe they don't understand about stealin'. There ain't a country on earth where thievin' another man's goods ain't a crime. If I ripped that boomerang out of his belt, he'd soon enough yell at me, wouldn't he? And start creatin' a great fuss about it? What's the difference. You tell me, smart arse.'

I couldn't argue with this. I had no answers.

Mr Roberts now came marching up with an indignant look on his face.

'What is this, a holiday? Why aren't you working?'

'We had a visit from some blacks,' said Clancy the elder. 'No worries, boss. Just a short break.'

'Well it's getting longer by the minute. Let's get on with the work, men. We need to get those poles in. Wilson, what's the matter with you?'

The poler originally from Somerset was lying on his back down on the ground, staring up at the cloudless sky.

'Tired,' he answered.

'Get on your feet, man. Pick up that spade.'

'Can't. Too tired.'

We all exchanged puzzled looks. This was not like Wilson. He was a big lugubrious man, not given to playing games, especially with authority.

Roberts went over to him and kicked the sole of his boot, but not with any great force.

'Get up, Wilson.'

'No.'

The answer was in a low mournful tone.

The sub-supervisor then turned to the rest of us.

'Does anyone know what's wrong with him?'

We all shook our heads and stared at the prone figure.

'Is he sleeping? Bates, you share a tent with him. Is he not getting his sleep? I don't understand.'

Bates shrugged. 'Sleeps more'n the rest of us, if you ask me.'

'You, Bates – and Scully, get him back on his feet.'

Reluctantly the two men went forward and with great effort managed to get Wilson vertical. They then stepped away from him, leaving him swaying like a pole without a base. We all knew he would crash to the earth again if someone didn't go and hold him upright. I stepped forward and grabbed him. He didn't buckle at the knees, but remained as stiff as a board in my hands. Everyone else continued to stand there and seemed happy to witness what might happen next.

'Well, somebody do something?' I growled. 'I can't stay here all day.'

John Scully came forward and was about to help me, when he suddenly stopped and stared at Wilson's open mouth. After a minute Scully extended his forefinger and poked at Wilson's gums. Wilson's mouth began to bleed and a gasp went through the crowd.

'Ow,' muttered Wilson. 'Leave off.'

'What is it?' asked Roberts. 'Is he sick?'

Scully then lifted one of Wilson's trouser legs. Wilson's shins were covered in ugly bruises. Stam Meerdinck, a Dutch sailor who had jumped ship in Malaysia and had made his way down to Australia, now confirmed what Scully had suspected was the problem.

'Scurfy,' said Meerdinck. 'His sick, all right. His yolly sick.'

'Bloody hell,' cried the second surveyor, tearing off his hat and throwing it violently on the ground, 'have you not been eating what you've been given, Wilson? Shit and corruption. Damn your eyes and liver, you bloody stupid man.' He picked up his hat and jammed it on his head, yellow dust falling from the brim onto his eyelashes. 'McKenzie, take this fool back to camp and get some lemon juice in him. One man short again today. It's enough to make a fucking pastor swear.'

'How will I get him back?' I asked. 'I can't carry the bugger. He weighs a ton.'

'Use the handcart. Scully, Trout, get the bloody idiot into the handcart.'

They got the bloody idiot into the handcart and I began to wheel him over the rough ground back to the camp. It was no easy job, since there were rocks and ruts all over the trail. Wilson seemed to be enjoying the ride though, because he started chuckling.

'Hey, this is hard work,' I snapped. 'If you're so cheerful, you must be better. You can get out and walk.'

'He was mad, weren't he? Ol' Roberts was as mad as a box of frogs, weren't he? I ain't never seen him like that before. Off his head. See what he did with his hat? Madder'n a box of frogs.'

Once I got the giggling victim to camp I trundled him over to Cookie and left him to be dosed with diluted lemon juice or whatever there was there to combat the scurvy. I was only vaguely familiar with scurvy. I knew sailors got it through not eating green vegetables or any fruit, but I hadn't thought you could get it on dry land. It somehow seemed to be linked with ships and the ocean. I tried to remember if I had been eating and drinking all I'd been given. Obviously Wilson liked his meat, but hadn't been digesting the kind of food that warded off scurvy.

Now that I was back in camp, I intended to stay there. I needed to refresh my batteries and clean some of the other equipment, which was prone to collecting dust and dirt. Electrical devices do not take well to either dust or wetness. They need constant care and attention, which I was quite willing to give them. My keys, sounders, relays and other items were like treasures to me. I loved to see the brass and glass instruments shining on their rosewood bases: copper terminals burnished like old gold. A Morse relay, for example, is an intricate-looking piece of machinery, precision-made, with polished brass parts that do indeed look like treasures from a Pharaoh's tomb. The perfection is enough to lift a man's heart when he's feeling low.

Galvanometers, commutators, registers, repeaters, relays, sounders, keys. These were the jewelled instruments of the telegraph operator, his to handle fondly and to esteem in the way that a connoisseur would admire a work of art. His to shield jealously from the hands of others, from those not initiated members of the telegraph priesthood. His to work their secret and subtle ways, so that they sang their cryptic hymns to others of the brotherhood.

When I had finished with fussing over my tools of trade, I went and found Jack Ransome, who was writing in a notebook. He had on one of his bright yellow shirts, covered as usual in black and brown insects. How he could stand these creatures clinging to him, crawling all over him, while he wrote whatever it was he wrote, was a mystery to me.

He closed the notebook as I approached and said, 'Want a game of chess?'

'You know I'm not up to your standard. You would be Alexander the Great against the armies of the Indus. You would tromp all over me.'

'Ah, scholastic references. You've been talking to Tim.'

'I do my best to listen to him, though I don't always know what he's talking about. I don't understand what a man like him is doing here, digging holes in the ground when he could be teaching somewhere. It's not the money. Four shillings and sixpence a day? It's not the gold fields, is it? I could understand if he was digging for gold. You get university professors who do that. But four-foot holes for wooden poles?'

Jack shrugged. 'Maybe he'd had enough of dusty classrooms and prefers the dusty outdoors? I think he wants to use his body instead of his mind for a while. I reckon it's probably temporary. He'll go back to an academic life after this line is finished. Anyway, what are you doing back in camp? I thought you had line checks to do today?'

'Oh, I can do those tomorrow.'

I then told Jack about Wilson and his scurvy.

'Jesus. Scurvy? I thought only sailors got that.'

'So did I, but when you think about it, the disease doesn't come from salt water, it comes from not eating your greens.'

'I suppose. Will he get better?'

'I don't know. No one seems too worried.'

Next, I told Jack about the Aborigine boys and what had happened when they started to rifle through men's belongings.

'Yeah, the blacks are a curious bunch. Two youths, eh?' His eyes took on a faraway look for a moment. 'They make good trackers, if you catch 'em young enough.'

I thought this a strange remark from a journalist, but I didn't pursue the puzzle. Instead I asked him, 'Why young? I mean, the old fellahs are good at tracking too, surely? They need to be, to hunt game.'

'Yes, but it's a question of loyalties. If you get them young, they glue to you, stick to you thick and thin, no matter who you're hunting – black, white or purple.'

Not *what*, but *who*.

I think he realised then what he was saying and changed the subject abruptly, asking me if the poling was going well. I told him it was going as well as expected, but of course Mr Roberts and probably Mr Harvey might want it to go quicker. They were like all bosses on all projects and enterprises, they were never satisfied. If you got things done ten time faster, they would still urge you on to more speed. All things considered, we were doing very well.

'Jack,' I said, 'how come you only have that tiny little notebook?'

He stared at me for a while, knowing what I was thinking.

'You're too smart for your own good, Alex McKenzie. Just leave things be. It'll unravel, all in good time.'

FIFTEEN

I had been summoned to the home of Mr and Mrs Whiting by way of a note delivered to my lodgings in Blackfriars. The message was terse and to the point, almost amounting to an order. Clearly something was very wrong and my heart was beating fit to break through my ribcage when I arrived at the Whiting's front door. I was admitted by the maid and led to the parlour where I found Sally's parents sitting grim-faced in wing chairs, while Sally herself, pale and tear-streaked, sat at a side table with a sheet of paper spread in front of her.

'Good day to you, Mr and Mrs Whiting. Hello, Sally, my dearest – you look distressed. This seems to be quite a serious matter. Where shall I stand? In the firing line, I presume?'

My attempt at jocularity did nothing to lighten the heavy atmosphere that pervaded the room. You read of the poets telling you how the sky presses down on the earth on dreary days. Well, the ceiling almost met the floor in that room. Despite my attempt I myself felt oppressed and was filled with foreboding. The expressions on the features of those in the room were extremely dour. Mentally, I kept telling myself I had done nothing wrong and that any misunderstanding could be swiftly cleared up with a relevant explanation.

'Mr McKenzie,' said Mr Whiting, leaning forward, 'you have not been honest with us. In fact, you have been quite *dishonest*. I will not go so far as to say you have lied to us, but you have withheld something that you should have told us right from the beginning. There is no question of a marriage now, of course. Our daughter has asked that we speak with you before you go your ways and she is freed from her engagement.'

I looked at Mrs Whiting, hoping to see some support from her, since I believed she liked me well enough. All I encountered was a blank and barren stare in the direction of the floor.

'I don't know what you mean,' I said after an interval of silence. 'Would you mind telling me what I am accused of?'

Mr Whiting began to show anger. 'You still try to maintain this air of innocence, even though you must know what it is that has upset us? Shame on you, sir. Shame on you.'

'Oh, Father,' cried Sally. 'Stop these guessing games. Tell Alexander what it is that has angered you.' Sally now turned to me. 'Alexander, we understand your brother James McKenzie was convicted of a crime and transported to Australia. Is this true?'

My heart sank a little, but now I knew what it was that had disturbed them, I was better able to deal with it.

'Perfectly true, though I don't understand why this should cause so much disturbance amongst you?'

Mr Whiting's eyes widened in disbelief.

'You have a criminal for a brother – a man who has committed so heinous a crime that it requires him to be transported – and you believe this to be irrelevant to the circumstance of your engagement? You astonish me, sir, you really do. I am speechless.' His hands flew in the air for a moment to emphasise that fact. 'I knew from the moment you entered our lives there would be trouble. I knew it. I am rarely wrong about these matters. I have an instinct. Thirty years in business has taught me who to trust and who to steer clear of. I should have obeyed those instincts. But no, I have daughter who

I love to distraction and the desire for her happiness overpowered my common sense. Why do I not follow my intuition, which has so rarely led me in the wrong direction?'

This was a man who was speechless? But I dared not quip at this point, or I would have turned Sally against me forever. I could see she was distressed, but I didn't know whether that was because she was shocked by the news of my brother, or because her father was an obdurate man and clearly intent on getting rid of me. Her mother was saying nothing, simply staring down at the floor in front of her, clearly wishing this interview was over and I was gone from her house.

'Firstly, Mr and Mrs Whiting, let me say that if there has been a heinous crime committed, it was by the courts, not by my older brother. James did wrong, I admit, but he did not deserve the kind of punishment which has now turned him against mankind. Do you, sir, have any idea of what life in the countryside is like now? A rural existence? I think not. You are as you often tell me, a successful businessman, the owner of a London shop which is well customised. You can have no interest or knowledge of what life is like for a man in a Suffolk village, whose very existence depends upon the weather and the mood of the farmer...'

'What has all this to do with a crime?' Mr Whiting interrupted, loudly. 'You are prevaricating, sir.'

'No, I'm not beating about the bush, I'm trying to give you a picture of a farm labourer's life, which if you'll be patient will be explained soon enough. You people, here in the town – what do you do if it rains for a week? I'll tell you what you do, you stay indoors or you take an umbrella and consider it very inconvenient. Do you know what my brother the farm hand would do? He would starve.'

'Rubbish, sir. He would be paid his weekly wage.'

'Not so. Not so at all. A farm hand in Suffolk – and I imagine in the other shires as well – gets paid by the day. Two shillings a day to be precise. If it's raining, then the work can't be done and the men are turned away without pay. The longer the rain persists, the hungrier go the workers and their families. Naturally this includes children, young and old. My brother had the temerity to suggest to the farmer who employed him, that the hands be helped over the days of bad weather, especially in the winter when the work was scarce anyway. Thereafter the farmer refused to employ him at all, as did all other farmers in the district. Once you get known as a trouble-maker, you are branded and rejected.'

'The world does not need trouble-makers.'

'One man's trouble-maker is another man's reformer, Mr Whiting. In the end my brother gave way to his anger and set fire to a farmer's haystack at night. He was caught and sent to the assizes. He was found guilty and condemned to be transported to Australia.'

'Is that all he did?' cried Sally. 'How monstrous – to commit a man to transportation for burning a haystack.'

Mr Whiting frowned deeply. 'It sounds a very serious crime to me, daughter. Very serious. The cost alone – however, I suppose this is why you wish to go Australia, Mr McKenzie. I have wondered at this obsession for a long time. You wish to be with your brother the convict? And you expect my daughter to accept him too? Can you wonder at our disappointment in you? Your motives are very warped, Mr McKenzie, very warped. I should examine them, if I were you, very carefully.'

'Sally,' I said, turning to my lovely girl, 'I'm sorry I didn't tell you all this sooner. Your father is quite wrong. It's not my brother that draws me to Australia, but the knowledge that it's a land of opportunity. I have no desire to get back with James, though if he wants to see me when I get there, I shall certainly not turn him away. He's my brother, after all, and we are family. But I am really sorry I didn't tell you. I suppose your father's right in one respect. I probably didn't because I was ashamed of the fact that I had a brother who had been a convict. He's not in jail now. He was released a year ago. He doesn't write to me, or contact me at all, but I do hear about him through a cousin.'

'So,' Sally said, her unhappy look lifting a little, 'he's not a prisoner now?'

'No. I don't know what he is doing, but he's a free man.'

Mr Whiting now interrupted with, 'All that is of no consequence. I have forbidden Sally to marry you, sir. You may go your way now. We are finished with you.'

I whirled on him and I could see he was shocked. Perhaps he thought I was about to leap at him and attack him. At any rate, he pressed back into his chair and stared at me with frightened eyes.

'Forbid, sir?' I shouted. 'Forbid? Your daughter is of age and if she wishes to marry me, she can do so without your permission.'

He gasped, 'My daughter will do as I say.'

'Well, we'll leave that for Sally to decide, won't we?' I replied in a much quieter tone. 'Forgive me for shouting, Sally. He's your father and must deserve respect for his position as the head of your family, but I find this all very unpleasant. I've done nothing wrong. Nothing at all. I'm not responsible for my brother's misdemeanours. They are his affair, not mine. I love you very much and I shall be devastated if you decide against our marriage, but I will of course honour that decision if it's inevitable. I'm not going to ask you to reply now. I shall go and wait for you to send for me.' I turned to the parents, one red-faced and with blazing eyes, the other still staring hard at a spot on one of the carpets. 'Good day to you, Mrs Whiting. Mr Whiting, sir. I'm sorry to have disturbed your normally tranquil home and hope we might meet in a much more pleasant atmosphere in the future – but if not, please hold my final goodbye in reserve for that time.'

I left the house and went for a long walk along the Thames embankment, the north side, which took me past the Houses of Parliament on a blustery, grey, cold day where, as indeed the poets often say, the sky pressed down on the houses and the river. My heart felt as if it were made of lead and as if in concert with the day pressed down heavily upon my stomach. I was utterly miserable, certain in my mind that Sally would never get in touch with me again. Yes, she was of age, but there were few young women who would defy their fathers in these times, especially among that particular class of people.

I wondered about that piece of paper that had been open in front of her. Had that contained details of my brother's trial and subsequent transportation? Most likely I had a rival at the library, or amongst Sally's male acquaintances, who had dug around in the dirt and had come up with the details of my brother's crime. Yet she had not known the exact nature of the crime, or she would not have looked so surprised by the verdict of the courts. Well, that was water under the bridge now. I had to live with the fact that her family believed I had disgraced myself, though I hoped against heaven she didn't share in that belief.

Once back at my lodgings I tried to immerse myself in other matters. I read in the *Times* newspaper an account of a radical woman – a Miss Sophia Jex-Blake – who was determined to shock the nation by becoming the first woman doctor. She had indeed been accepted as a medical student following efforts by a certain Emily Davies and a Miss Elizabeth Garrett, who had attempted to open up the Oxford, Cambridge and London examination boards to women. "'I do not object to husbands, *per se*," Miss Jex-Blake told one of the *Times* reporters, "but I think there is more to women's fulfilment than marriage alone.'" Well, that article was good for my cause from one point of view, defying set norms, but bad from another, the seeking of fulfilment outside of marriage.

I sighed.

Women were beginning to organise themselves in various walks of life, but mainly in the area of suffrage. A member of parliament, John Stuart Mill, was in support of women obtaining the vote. While I could see no objection to a woman becoming a doctor, provided she was strong in body enough to cut through bones with a saw and strong enough in spirit not to faint at the sight of a patient's blood and innards spilling out, I was not so sure that they were politically minded enough to vote with sound impartial knowledge. Indeed, Sally and I had argued this point many times. Politics seemed to me at the time to remain a very male area of concern, since ruling a country required a man's good common sense and a solid knowledge of monetary issues, both of which – it seemed to me – most women did not have, or did not seem to have. However, Sally got very fiery when the subject was raised, so I had long since ceased offering my opinion on the subject.

I noted in a small paragraph at the bottom of the literary page, that Mr Wilkie Collins, friend of the author Charles Dickens, had written a mystery novel, *The Woman in White*. I had not heard the term, *mystery novel*, before, but I guessed it was one of those works that would be more of interest women readers. 'There you go,' I said to myself, 'women are different to men. They like different things. Politics is a man's domain and reading novels is a woman's.' It was certainly a good area for a man to make money in and it had me wondering if, one day, I might try to write a book of some kind myself, possibly about my love of telegraphy. Something on the lines of *The Compleat Angler*. I pondered the title. *The Absolute Telegrapher? The Unadulterated Operator?* Neither of those struck me as money-making. I would have to work on the idea.

Once I had finished reading the newspaper front to back I naturally fell back into a mood of despondency. I had surely lost the love of my life. I needed to get out to Australia as quickly as possible now and try to forget my lovely librarian with her dancing eyes and lilting voice. Surely, once I was embedded in the work of a telegraph operator I would have no time for mewling and musing on what might have been. I would shake off the doldrums and become a strong determined man, ambitious and striving to cast off a family background full of yokels and hayseeds. I was a man of science, a man of the 19th Century, a respected technician.

SIXTEEN

It had taken us several months to reach our starting point near Barrow Creek, what with loaded bullock wagons, horses and all the other encumbrances of travelling with a caravan over rough country. However, a fast camel can get to Adelaide and back in fifty days. Tim told me a camel could make seventy miles a day over reasonable ground, but the terrain between us and the south coast was not 'reasonable' and forty to fifty miles a day was as much as we could hope for. Afeeza had done the journey for us and had brought back newspapers and letters.

What joy! To receive mail from home and news from the rest of the world. I could not contain my happiness at seeing letters from Sally, her beautiful copperplate handwriting on the envelopes. I spent at least fifteen minutes just staring at my address written in her elegant hand, fearful of opening any letter lest it contain bad news. The last time I had seen her was when I parted from her on the quay at Portsmouth.

After my devastating interview with Sally's parents at the Whiting's house, I had immediately booked my passage to the colony of South Australia. In order to save money I offered myself as a supernumerary crew member, to be used as the captain thought fit. I was told that as someone who knew nothing about ships I would not be a great deal of use to them so I had to pay part of the fare. I prayed to God they would not send me up the masts to set the sails. My head is not good for heights and my feet are not good for narrow footholds. However, I need not have worried. They scorned men such as me and would not have soiled their yardarms with the feet of an 'ignorant land lubber'. I was told I would be working in the galley, which is their word for a kitchen, sailors having a separate language from those of us who prefer our *terra* to be *firma*.

It was a typical foggy evening at Portsmouth harbour. I walked from the Seamen's Mission, where I had spent two nights, towards the berth of the *Archibald Russel* a grain ship, a windjammer, whose destination was Spencer Gulf, South Australia. The captain's name was Herzogin, which sounded German to me, but then the sea is an international area providing work for many nationalities. Indeed, I had met some of the crew at the Seamen's Mission and they were from every part of the globe, including some from as far away as India, who called themselves 'lascars' for some reason.

As I approached the dock a figure came out of the mist. She was so bundled up with clothes I did not recognise her at first, but then when she threw back the hood of her cloak I saw the lovely features of my darling Sally. I let out a yell of surprise rather than joy, which startled her for a moment, but then she came to me and held out her hands.

'I came to wish you safe keeping on your voyage and good luck on your arrival in Australia.'

'You travelled all the way from London to the West Country?' I cried. 'Do your parents know you're here?'

'No, they do not – but I shall tell them. I shall also say that I intend joining you in South Australia, just as soon you send for me.' She bowed her head. 'Oh Alex, I'm so ashamed of myself. I'm ashamed of my parents too, for being so narrow. It was a shock, you know, to find out that you had a brother who had been transported. But we should not have let that influence our opinion of you as a separate person. I was upset you had not told me – which was wrong of you, if we were engaged to be married – there should be no secrets between an affianced couple.'

'It *was* wrong of me. I suppose I intended to tell you at some time, but we were so happy with each other I didn't want to muddy the water with the sordid side of my family history. James is not a bad man – at least, he was not on leaving these shores – and I do think our justice system is particularly harsh. My father offered to pay for the haystack, but the law would not allow it. Nor would the farmer, damn his black soul, excuse me, sweetheart. It leaves a very bad taste in the mouth, once you've come up against the establishment. I hope to find better in the land I'm going to, though I'm inclined to think I won't. The penalties for breaking the law there are probably just as severe and governors of colonies are not chosen for their sympathetic natures.'

'Well,' she said, kissing my nose, which was the only part of my face unbearded, 'you may leave knowing I mean to be true to you and our promise to one another. Do well, my love. Do well for both of us and send word as soon as you have employment so that we may face the future together. Write to me. Men are not good at letters, but do write to me, often, and never fail to tell me you love me to distraction.'

'I love you to distraction,' I said, and we both fell into each other's arms, and wet each other's collars.

Once on the boat – sorry, *ship* – I found myself under the power of a tyrannical cook who thought nothing of beating his assistants with a ladle to get them to work faster. The voyage was everything I feared. I was seasick close to death in the Bay of Biscay and would have given everything I owned to be back on shore at that point in time. By the time the ship reached Gibraltar the sickness had passed, but the cook made my life a total misery with his foul mouth and unbridled violence.

I knew if I rebelled against the cook I would be in even worse trouble, because ships are floating countries and the captains are kings. Worse than kings, because they seem to need no courts or juries to severely punish their subjects. They simply go ahead and do whatever they have a mind to do. I had been told by one of the crew that flogging had recently been abolished, '…but don't let that fool you, shipmate, it takes a long time to get captains to change their ways. They look on their traditions as entitlements and I wouldn't put it past any one of them to order the lash.' Our cook knew that if he went to the captain with complaints about us, he would be believed and we would be punished. Men such as I, landsmen, were regarded as lower than beasts.

The swiftly-sailing windjammer took only 100 days to reach South Australia and there I was set free. My heart was full of bitterness and a desire for revenge by that time and once I had left the ship I waited for the cook to go ashore. I followed him to an inn and entered after him. He saw me coming through the doorway. He grinned, nudged a companion, and then cried, 'Come and have a beer with us, squid-shit.'

I went to the table where he was sitting with other crew members and struck him a forceful blow on the face which sent him reeling backwards, crashing to the floor. Then I set myself, ready for his mates to pile into me. But they simply stared down at the cook with mild expressions, saying not a word, sipping their beer, seemingly uninterested in getting involved. The cook did indeed get to his feet and fought with me, but my anger was so fierce I left him a beaten pulp at the end. I expected to feel better, which I did at first, but later a sort of depression descended on my spirit.

Violence is a strange thing. To some men it means very little or even nothing. They can become involved in violence and not suffer any after effects, even when it's used against them. But they are few and far between, for most men suffer spiritual wounds, whether they have delivered violence, received it, or even just witnessed it. Wounds which last their lifetimes. Old men closing in on death brood on violent moments in their lives. Such incidents darken the soul and the heart.

Now I had letters in my hand and found a place to sit to be able to read them in private. There were men squatting or leaning all over camp. No work would get done until they had devoured their letters. One or two had none of course. Walker was one of those and he stared with contempt at those of us who did. Jack Ransome had several, which surprised me, him being a newcomer, but then it occurred to me that these were probably from his editors at the journal. Certainly he was not as euphoric as others on opening his mail. Yes, it had to be business.

All was well with Sally. She had not changed her mind and she said her parents were resigned to losing her. She was now waiting for a letter from me telling her it was time to board a ship. In fact I had already sent that letter, giving her a date when the work on the line was expected to be finished, so that I could get to Adelaide and meet her ship. I didn't want to be in the middle of a sub-continent when she arrived. I wanted to see her shining face as she stepped onto Australian soil.

'So,' said a voice above and behind me, 'you're not as white as you paint yourself, eh McKenzie?'

I turned and looked up, the harsh sunlight glare blinding me for a second, to see Sholto Walker standing there with a newspaper in his hand.

'What are you talking about?'

'This,' he said, squatting very close to me and tapping the newspaper, 'about this bloke called James McKenzie – the escaped convict.'

I very nearly gave myself away by blurting out something which would have confirmed my relationship to James, but managed to stop myself in time.

'McKenzie,' I replied as casually as I could, 'is a very common name.'

'So, you don't know him? Not a brother or a cousin, eh? Says here he's teamed up with a bunch of bushrangers. Liable to get captured or shot by the troopers soon. James McKenzie. That's what it says here, in the paper. Sure he's not one of your kinsmen? The picture looks very like.

'Very like what?'

'You, you stupid wombat.'

I said patiently, 'Don't call people stupid, Walker. Only stupid people do that.'

His face clouded over for a moment as he tried to sort out this sentence in his mind.

'One of these days, McKenzie, I'm goin' to break your back, so you better be ready for it.'

He started to walk away, but after a few paces he turned and gave me a malicious grin. 'I know he's your brother, or cousin or an uncle, McKenzie. Or maybe even your father? I saw it your face. You're not so lily-white, after all, eh? Just another bloody bloke working on the edge of the law. Not so different from the rest of us. So don't come the shining knight with me in future.' With that he did finally leave me alone.

So, here we had another man like Sally's father, implanting my character with the morals of my brother. Am I not a completely different individual? James is not even a twin, but a man five years older than me. Are our principles, our values, supposed to be deeply embedded in our physical make-up, so that if one McKenzie is a criminal, all McKenzies must therefore have criminality in their blood? If so, I utterly reject that philosophy. I could no more steal or cause harm to innocent people than cut off my own right hand.

Walker had left the newspaper . I picked it up and found the article he was talking about. It was indeed about my brother James.

> **Convicts Escape Work Party**
> Yesterday morning three convicts belonging to a work party escaped from a sheep farm north of Melbourne. Peter Kenworthy, William Bagley Frith and James Stuart McKenzie were on loan from Melbourne Gaol when they simply walked away from a tree felling task taking their tools with them. Stolen were: one large-sized American axe, two smaller axes both with new hafts, one tarpaulin nearly new, marked 'Critchets Dry Goods' in black ink, size twelve feet by twelve feet, with brass eyelets around the edge set at twelve inch intervals. The three convicts were last seen walking along Cook Road South towards Melbourne town. Kenworth, Frith and McKenzie are to be regarded as desperate and should not be approached by ordinary citizens, who are asked to contact their local policeman if the escaped men are seen.

My brother was not a dangerous man, but police and troopers hunting them would regard escaped prisoners as sport. I hoped to God that if he was found he gave himself up. One thing was almost certain, no one would report seeing them, the police being held in contempt in most colonies in Australia. I had not seen James in twenty years, he being ten years older than me, but he was still my brother.

So far as I knew James had not used violence against anyone, though I knew he had turned robber after serving his time for firing the haystack. Like many ex-convicts I think his time in prison had made him bitter and determined to get revenge on the society which had destroyed his life. Men who fester in jail have too much time to reflect on their lot and form clinkers of hate in their breasts for authority. Those sharp black pieces of burnt-out resentment towards mankind become impossible to dislodge and thereafter the carrier is forever lost.

I see now, much later in life, that perhaps this is what might have happened to Sholto Walker? Maybe he had experienced a similar history to that of my brother James? But such was my loathing of the man at the time I could not allow myself to fault others, rather than him – Sholto Walker – for the shallow ugly creature that stalked our camp in the guise of a human being. I wanted Walker to be a man born, not made evil. A malicious menacing thing that had come out the womb spawned by some foul agent of the dark regions of Hell. I wanted him to be a creature without a soul, a being with an unyielding heart of ironstone, devoid of compassion, unable to shed the misery of his own iniquity. This is how I saw him and this is how I wanted him to be.

I had long since ceased being distressed by James's situation, but it grieved me sorely that Sholto Walker was now aware of my family business. It gave him one more weapon to use against me during times when we, inevitably, got into an argument.

I went to find Afeeza. He was grooming his camel and shouting loudly at the boy who was making tea. The boy was bawling back using the same strident tones. Neither of them looked at each other or seemed to be listening at all. In fact they each appeared to be having an argument with some unseen presence in the air above their heads. They simply yelled and cursed, bellowed and swore, without leaving any gaps in their speech during which they might have been able to receive replies.

'Afeeza, thank you for my mail, my letters. You don't know how much joy it's given me. Also for the newspapers. You did well, a very fast run there and back.'

'Sikandar, my great friend,' cried Afeeza, his arms opening wide to receive my reluctant body, 'I am so look forward to see you again.'

As usual, and as with all the cameleers, Afeeza appeared every morning wearing spotless white clothing, a fact which always astonished the crews on the line. By evening his shift looked a little dusty of course, but how these Afghans managed to do their laundry in the conditions under which we toiled was a mystery. Perhaps they carried enough clothing to last the whole period of their stay?

I let him hug me, though as an Englishman born, I was not used to such intimacy with my male friends. I was heartily pleased to be released. Once he had squeezed the juice out of me we sat down with a kettle of tea to talk. He told me what he had heard a lot of talk in Adelaide about our enterprise, which seemed to be causing a great deal of furore in the other Australian colonies.

'Queensland people are hating us, for doing this thing,' he said, chewing on a strip of dried beef. 'They are telling everyone they should be making a line going down through their country.'

'Well ours is doing just fine,' I replied, 'so they'll have to put it out of their heads. Now, did you have a good time in Adelaide? I hope you didn't just work.'

'No, no, I met with two important brothers of our clan, Faiz Mahomet and his brother Tagh. They now are working – how is it, managering? – camel station at Hergott Springs. It is called Elder Smith and Company. This is good for me. When I am finished here, I will go to work for Faiz. He tells me he will buy this company for himself and his brother. Good, eh? My children will not starve, my wives will not starve, I will not starve. All will be well, after the line is finish.'

'How many wives do you have, Afeeza?'

'Four!' he held up the four touching fingers of his right hand, then parted them in the middle. 'Two and two.'

'Two and two?'

'Two wives in one place, two in another. In my country the wives do not always like each other, so I marry two sisters and another two sisters, from two separate families, so they do not fight all the time and send me complaints about each other. Sisters are fine. Sisters fight, but not about the husband. Sisters fight about who was the best favourite of their parents when they were seven years old. So, my friend Sikandar,' he said, 'and you are not having a wife, yet?'

'Not yet,' I replied, smiling, 'but soon, I hope.'

'I hope so too. Every man must have a wife. You must get children quickly, to look after you in old age. How many years are in you, Sikandar?'

'Twenty-five.'

'Ah, this is why I am so much wiser than you. I am thirty-six, an old man with an old man's wisdom.'

'That's not so very old, but four wives! You must have many children yourself.'

'Many, many children. Sometimes I do not know all the names and sometimes I think my neighbours sneak a child or two into my house, to feed it. But, I am a happy man. I have many sons and many daughters – and I have my Nasmah, who keeps me warm at night with her beautiful body, breathing with me, her heart beating in time with my own.'

'Nasmah. One of your wives?'

Afeeza looked shocked. 'My wives? No. God forbid. They are all on the other side of the ocean. What are you saying, Sikandar?'

I was puzzled. 'Then who?'

I thought, perhaps a mistress? though why any man would want a mistress when he had four wives was beyond me.

'My naga, my camel.'

I laughed. 'Oh, *her*. Yes, of course, you have her to look after you – but you're wrong, she's not very beautiful. Camels are quite ugly, to me anyway.'

'You do not see the beauty in my Nasmah? Shame on you, Sikandar. She needs to be seen as a charming creature, otherwise she will be spurned by men, even though she works very hard.'

'You know,' I said, looking at Nasmah, 'us Christians have a saint for everything. I was once told there is a Saint of Ugly Animals. Grotesque creatures that God made on a day when he dealt with absurd creations. I can't remember his name, but there is one. Just think of the blobfish, dugong, warthog, fruitbat, and the deep sea creatures like the angler fish that we can't even bear to look at, let alone touch – and the miserable, bad-tempered camel, of course. There has to be someone to love those creations and one of our saints has taken on the task.'

'Good, I am glad there is such a man, but – but I still believe my Nasmah to be a beautiful beast, whatever you say.'

'What does it mean? The name, Nasmah?'

'It means "fragrant breeze" in my language.'

At that very moment the lovely Nasmah, resting, legs under her belly just ten yards away, let out a loud, flapping, evil-smelling fart which wafted over us and had us both coughing for the next several minutes.

SEVENTEEN

Some mystic power has formed the natural architecture of the landscape out here in the wilderness. I never cease to be amazed at the rock formations, their shapes and immense size, and the spiritual atmosphere that surrounds them. There are giant boulders, smooth-looking and almost perfectly round. They lie like fallen red moons upon the dusty terrain. Despite their hugeness they seem to have a feminine quality about them, having come perhaps from the womb of the sky. Cinnabar sunsets bring out their deep rich colours, turning them into burgundy globes that stand together, dominating the desert. They dwarf the trees and any men who happen to be near them.

Then too, there are yellow-ochre ridges and dark-grey hills that leap up from the ground on the skyline. Some are like an ocean's wave, frozen in curling motion. They curve inwards and upwards, sweeping to a great height. Others appear as gigantic sallow pillars of stone which stand shoulder-to-shoulder, forming an impassable phalanx across a wide flatland. There are natural fortresses of feldspar and chalcedony, that guard mysterious shallow hollows full of water that shine like quicksilver. This is a land of stone gods: huge, brooding, silent gods. They seem to disapprove of strangers who cross their domains.

One of the most peculiar and somehow disturbing sights I ever saw out there in the red centre of this island world was when I was with Mr Roberts. We were riding ahead of the poling gang, seeking the best way across the terrain for the white, shaved trees which would carry our magic singing wire, when we came across a wide flatland covered in spaced-out stone markers that looked to me like huge, yellowy, rugged, heavily-weathered gravestones in an English churchyard.

'Are they tombstones?' I asked Mr Roberts in disbelief. 'Is this an Aboriginal graveyard?'

He smiled. 'No McKenzie. I don't know how the blacks deal with their dead, but this is not a sacred area. Those are magnetic termite mounds.'

'Termite mounds? You mean white ants?'

'If you want to call them that. Yes, they build those structures for their homes. Have you seen the termite cathedral mounds? They're even larger. Different termite, though.'

A cathedral mound I could envisage, but I asked, 'Why magnetic?'

'Magnetic or compass mounds. They are orientated north-south, so someone – I don't know who – gave them that name.'

'Why would insects do that? Do they have intelligence? Has it got anything to do with religion?'

I had some wild idea that termites had a god of some kind, whose domain lay in a certain direction. Immediately I'd said it, I knew I was being stupid, but it was too late to retract my question.

To give him his due, Mr Roberts did not laugh.

'I'm told it's got something to do with the weather. The prevailing wind or the heat of the sun at midday. If you think about it, the shape and orientation of those gravestone-shaped mounds avoids the sunlight at the hottest part of the day. We could learn a thing or two from the other living creatures of this world, McKenzie. They can do things we only dream of doing.

Birds fly, whales swim across oceans, ants build colonies and stick together to protect them…'

'We make colonies too.'

'Agreed,' he replied, 'but we sure as hell don't stick together – we fight amongst ourselves and ruin good projects.'

I knew he was thinking of the overland telegraph and the way the Queensland government had tried to scupper our enterprise. But who could blame them? The line was important. It would bring big business to the colony which controlled the traffic to and from Britain and America. Of course they wanted their own government to be the main power in the land so far as telegraph went. It was natural. It was business.

'This is true,' I agreed, 'but maybe ant colonies have powerful kings or dictators, who force them to stick together.'

Roberts didn't answer. I looked at him and found him staring at the skyline. I followed his gaze and saw that the horizon had suddenly developed an inky, dark-purple colour.

'Storm coming in,' said the sub-supervisor. 'We'd best get back, McKenzie.'

We raced the horses back to camp only to find a menacing atmosphere pervading. There were two groups of armed men facing each other. On one side were Mr Harvey, Jarvis the cadet, Jack Ransome and Tim Felix. On the other were the majority of the rest of the camp, with the cameleers and one or two others standing well to the side. A man called Burdon, normally a quiet and unassuming bloke, and the parasitic Trout were at the front of the workers, rifles in the crooks of their arms, the muzzles thankfully not pointing at a human being.

'I'm sorry, Mr Harvey,' Burdon was saying as we dismounted, 'we've got to have some justice here.'

I knew which side I had to be on, whatever the dispute, and both Mr Roberts and myself joined the smaller party.

'What's this all about?' said Roberts. 'You men – put those guns down. This is disgraceful behaviour.'

Though Mr Harvey was the chief surveyor here and the head supervisor, Roberts was a bigger man, with a more commanding presence about him. Much of the sub-supervisor's authority came from his tougher character, his strong voice and determined manner, while Harvey was the more academic of the two. That's not to say Harvey was a weak man. On the contrary, no supervisor of a gang of axemen and polers could survive if they were easily trodden on. But there was a hardness about Roberts that would make any man think twice about crossing him.

'It's them bastard Abos, Mr Roberts,' called Trout. 'They've gone and murdered a man. We're goin' to put that right.'

Roberts's eyes scanned the crowd and he shook his head.

'I don't see anyone missing.'

Burdon said, 'No, not here, sir. Up the line a bit. Up above Tennant Creek. A rider came through, heading south. He told us the blacks went'n killed the drover John Milner. Damn savages need to be taught they can't do that to civilised men without there's comeback.'

Harvey turned to Roberts. 'You remember the Milner brothers, who came through some time back? It seems one of them was killed in an Aborigine attack on their camp. Now our men seem intent on going out and shooting blacks wherever they find them.'

Roberts, as was his wont when he was angry, took off his hat and threw violently into the dust at his feet. This gesture seemed to be so universal amongst the surveyors it might have been part of their training.

'Where the hell do you get your brains from, Trout? Have you got any? And you, Burdon. I'm surprised at you. What good do you think you're going to do here, by shooting tribesmen who probably had nothing to do with any murder?'

Jack Ransome stepped forward. 'Mr Roberts is right. If someone's killed in Blakeney Street, you don't march down to Fitzwarren Street and start killing the people who live there, eh? Come on, men, put down the weapons. Get some sense into your heads.'

'There's got to be some justice, Ransome,' growled someone in the heart of the mob. 'Whose side are you on? You stay out of this.'

The voice sounded very much like Walker's to me.

Ransome said, 'I'm not on anyone's side. I'm for plain common sense. If we go out and start shooting blacks, it'll start a war out here in the middle of nowhere. All that hard work you've put in will come to nothing. Once they've killed everyone in camp the Abos will tear down the poles and burn them, destroy the equipment and melt down the wire to use as spearheads. We can't call on the army out here. It'll be weeks, months before they get here and by that time we'll be an untidy heap of bones. I don't know about you men, but I don't want to spend eternity with my bones locked to likes of Trout. You know how Trout never washes. If he stinks in this life, he'll stink worse in the next and knowing my luck I'll end up with his hoof in my chops.'

The mob laughed at this. In a camp where washing was a luxury, sometimes impossible through lack of water, Trout was the king of dirt and stale sweat. No one had ever seen him take off his clothes and scrub himself, even when water was plentiful. Thus he looked sheepish on hearing Jack Ransome's remarks, but didn't bother to protest. He was the butt of jokes about his personal hygiene all the time. Only when the man behind him laughed a bit too loud and shoved him in the back with the muzzle of a rifle did he turn and growl, 'Hey!'

Burdon, however, was still not happy at leaving the situation unresolved.

'Hey, look. What're you all laughing at?' he yelled. 'A good Christian man's dead, for God's sake, killed by heathens.'

Again, a quiet menace descended on the mob of men in front of us. Some of them were only armed with axes and clubs, but a few had guns. It was not hard to read their minds. They were weary souls who had not seen their loved ones and friends for many months now. Morale was very low. Tired, frustrated by the many problems we had to encounter – rocky ground, unsuitable trees, snakes, flies, mosquitoes, a scarcity of vegetables, many other worries, some small, some big – they were beginning to come to the end of their tethers. There were arguments and fights, feuds and grudges, and though the line was going as well as could be expected there was a dispirited air to the men. They were at war with the elements and though the environment was sometimes subdued, it was never beaten, and always came back to the fight.

Suddenly, a shot exploded amongst the men bearing firearms. In the deep silence of the afternoon it sounded as loud as a stick of dynamite going off. Several men visibly jumped and turned as if to run. I was as startled as anyone and my heart began beating wildly. I gulped down air. Within a minute though, most had guessed what had happened. Some fool's gun had accidentally gone off, the bullet burying itself in the earth. It turned out to be the American, John Scully, who waved an arm in the air and in a contrite tone, said, 'Sorry fellahs. Fingeritis.'

Again a strong ripple of laughter went through the work gang. Overhead the deep purple cloud had arrived. The storm which Mr Roberts and myself had run from had swept in. Rain came down as if from tipped barrels and the mob broke up, men running for their tents. Even Burdon seemed to have forgotten his fiery, righteous need for Christian justice. Before long the men were playing cards by the light of lamps, or re-reading their letters from home, or cleaning equipment both personal and company owned. I went with the two surveyors and Ransome and Tim Felix to the map tent where we all took a long breath and looked at each other significantly.

'That could have been nasty,' said Mr Harvey. 'Bob, you did well – and you, Ransome.'

I studied Jack Ransome's expression as he was being praised by Harvey. Inscrutable. Even bland. Here was a newspaper correspondent who was presumably good with a pen, or he would not have been sent out into the wilderness with one, but also very good at challenging unlawful behaviour. Jack Ransome had surely been in the military at some time, or some other strongly hierarchical organisation like the police or merchant navy. There was an unbendable authority in his bearing. But not just that. There was also a familiarity with violence, which he found easy to assess and seemed ready to use. I had no doubt that had there been shooting, his fancy revolver would not have stayed in its holster for more than a few seconds.

He caught me staring at him and I had to look away, embarrassed.

Mr Harvey continued with his praise.

'Thank you for standing with us, McKenzie, and Forster. And you especially Felix, you've got to go back in amongst the men. It won't be easy for you.'

'I'll manage,' said Tim. 'They look at me sideways, anyway, seeing as I've come from the schoolroom. They're not used to academics, so I don't have any bosom friends among them.'

'They treat you rough?'

'No, no, they just don't understand me.'

'Well now,' said Mr Harvey, leaning precariously on the edge of a trestle table which was likely to collapse, 'let me tell you what I've been told. Apparently the Milner brothers had driven their stock north of a place called Tennant Creek and Ralph Milner left his brother and another man in the camp while he went ahead to explore the terrain. John Milner was resting in the shade of a tree when a single black wandered into the camp, went straight for John Milner and clubbed him to death.' We all let out a collective shocked gasp as the image of the murder stamped itself on our minds. 'The other young man in the camp, Ashburn or Ashwoods, something like that – he drew a revolver and shot the native dead. That's as much as I know. Terrible thing to happen. You didn't meet them, Ransome, but the Milners were good men. Good stockmen. The kind of men that will make Australia a country people will want to live in.'

Mr Roberts said, 'Let's hope that's the end of it – I can do without any more trouble.'

'Trouble is,' said Jack Ransome, 'they're unpredictable, the blacks – they think different to us. Who knows, maybe it isn't the last attack? I don't trust 'em one inch. They'll thieve anything you leave lying around and they resent it when you try to take it back. Best to keep them well away from our working sites, with a show of force if necessary.'

'You can't shoot them,' I said. 'You can't do that.'

Jack turned to me. 'I wasn't suggesting that. You can show them you mean business without actually killing any of them. Fire over their heads. Yell at them. You can frighten people the way you frighten animals. How many big reds do we have bounding around the camp? None, because we discourage any 'roos by a show of force. That's all I'm saying, a *show* of force. No need to kill or wound any of them.'

The sudden storm was a brief, if violent affair. It left the camp a bit bedraggled, but it had cooled down the men. One might have thought that divinity had a hand in it, if one was that way inclined. Since those saved from slaughter were the Aborigines, perhaps it was one of their gods who had sent the storm? That made more sense than our own deity who actually seemed out of place here in the red centre where strange giant rocks and wide open spaces ruled the landscape.

When the group broke up I confronted Jack Ransome.

'What are you doing here, Jack?'

'Meaning?'

'Meaning I don't believe you work for a newspaper. Afeeza brought several editions of the *South Australian Journal*. I don't see any columns in there by a Jack Ransome. Then there's the sidearm and the way you step up to handle trouble. Other small things. Tell me who you really are, Jack.'

We were out in the open, walking across the camp site, following Tim Felix. Jack looked around, making sure there were no others within earshot.

'Leave it alone, Alex. Just keep your suspicions to yourself.'

'Or else what?'

He turned and stared into my eyes. 'Or you might get me killed.'

I stared back at him. 'You're a policeman!'

'Shut the fuck up,' he hissed in my ear after stepping close. 'Just shut the fuck up.' He then looked around, making sure no one had heard what I'd blurted out. 'Jesus, you have wombat turds for brains, McKenzie.'

'Yeah, it's because I'm so stupid I managed to work out who you really are.'

'All right, all right, but walk with me. Up to that ridge.'

I followed him over the rocky ground to a hillock overlooking the plain where Roberts and I had ridden to earlier. We found a place to sit. Up here there was no chance of anyone hearing our conversation. Jack seemed to have calmed down somewhat. He nodded at me and said, 'You're right, you're a clever little bastard, McKenzie. A bit too clever for your own good.'

'Now you see,' I said to him, 'no good newspaper man would use cliché's like that one. So, who are you?'

'I'm not going to tell you my real name, but I'm a corporal in the South Australian police. I'm after a man called Thomas Smith, a bushranger, a killer.'

'Captain Midnight.'

'If you want to romanticise a bloody thief and murderer, you could call him that, yes.'

'Well, that's what articles in the *South Australian Journal* call him.'

Jack Ransome smiled wryly. 'Touché.'

'So,' I said, my heart beating a little faster than usual, 'you're here to arrest Sholto Walker?'

Jack's next words stunned me.

'Not arrest the bastard, just follow him.'

'Follow him? Follow him where?'

A small dust devil formed a few yards away and swirled past us like a spinning top as Jack prepared to tell me everything.

'Sholto is not his real name. He's William Walker, one of Smith's cobbers. There was a robbery just outside Adelaide just about the time the telegraph company started on the line – Smith, Walker and another man, John Bolton were the thieves involved. After the robbery they rode north and then split up, going three different ways. Walker must have ended up getting lost and finally, after going through a number of sections on the line, wandered into your camp – we heard about him from one of the wagon drivers. I was assigned to come up here and just keep him tagged until he met up again with Smith. We want 'em all, of course, all three – but Smith is our main target. I don't know what Smith looks like, so I need Walker to lead me to him. Sooner or later Walker will try to meet up with Smith and Bolton again, and when he does I'll be there to arrest them all.'

'Just you?'

Jack smiled. 'I'm quite capable.'

'Hey, maybe the telegraph line will help you there – you can wire for assistance.'

'You'd like that, wouldn't you?'

'It would make a great story for the *Journal*.' I paused for a moment, then added, 'I can't believe I got the wrong part of the name. I thought he'd made up the name "Walker", but instead it was "Sholto" that he invented for himself. That doesn't make a lot of sense.'

'No, but I heard he staggered into camp near to death before you nursed him back to health. A man in that condition isn't going to be thinking too straight. There is a Sholto Walker, his cousin, so possibly that was the name that jumped into his head in a desperate moment. They have dozens of names, these bushrangers. Thomas Smith, apart from his Captain Midnight handle also calls himself variously "Thomas Law". "Thomas Henry", "Harry Wilson", "George Gibson" and "George White". Bushrangers are also actors, Alex, they like fooling people, thinking it makes them cleverer than the rest of society.

'Anyway, Alex, I want you to swear to secrecy on this. You know that's important, don't you?'

I nodded. 'Absolutely'.

'Good on yer. Shake my hand.'

I did as he asked and we went back down separately to the camp, having only been missed by Tim Felix, who was now on the receiving end of threats and curses from his erstwhile mates. They despised him for standing with the management on the Aborigine issue. The crew – cook, blacksmith, carpenter, linemen, axemen, polers – they all expected it of me, being a qualified operator, not part of the manual labour force. Tim Felix, for all his education and intellect, was basically a poler. The other members of the work force expected loyalty from him and they hadn't got it. It would be a while before Tim was accepted again, if he ever was on this particular project. He could look forward to finding kangaroo muck in his blankets, he would be shunned at meals, his kit would be scattered whenever he left it unattended. I knew Tim would make light of any abuse, but no man out here in the wilderness enjoys being shut out of camp society. It's mentally unhealthy.

I was not among those who treated Tim with disdain. I went looking for him and found him sitting alone on a rock staring out over the landscape. Smoke curled from his imported briar pipe, the column travelling almost straight upwards in the stillness of the outback air.

'I'm sorry you're getting the treatment, Tim – you don't deserve it.'

He looked up and shrugged. 'Nothin' to me.'

'You don't care what the men think of you?'

'That's the way of this world we live in, Alex. Deserve doesn't come into it. You either get given what you want or you go out and take it. A king, he gets it given on a plate. A poor bastard from the dregs of society, he either has to take it, or starve to death.'

I thought about this. 'He could work for it, the poor bastard I mean – most of us have to, don't we?'

I went and sat beside him, lighting my own pipe. We sat in silence for a while lost in our own thoughts. The quiet was broken by my companion.

'I've got a question for you, Alex. Two questions. Is the world a place of turmoil which men are hopelessly trying to put in order? Or is the world an orderly place which is being reduced to chaos by the actions of men?'

I glanced across at him. The sunlight was catching those parts of his beard which had been stained by pipe smoke and turning this feature a reddish-yellow, making him look like a bust I had seen in Sally's library, of the ancient Greek ruler, Agamemnon.

At this precise moment Tim Felix's head was fashioned from bronze.

'I'm not sure what you mean?' I admitted.

'It's a simple enough pair of questions, with only one answer of course. Men have been killing each other since the beginning of history – wars, feuds, murders. Nature has been killing them in equal numbers – shipwrecks, volcanic eruptions, earthquakes, floods. The savagery of the natural world itself is horrifying. There are creatures who eat their own mates after copulation and even those who devour their own young. The world is a mess, Alex. Just when the world seems to have settled down into a placid state, something flares up again. How many times have you heard the phrase, "This is the war to end all wars. Once this one is over, the world will be forever at peace."? Now either we're responsible for the chaos, or we're trying to overcome it. Which?'

'I think we're trying to bring order to – to chaos.'

'Now then, that's where we differ. I think we're causing the chaos and the world would be a better place without us.'

EIGHTEEN

As it happened, the fatal attack on John Milner was soon pushed into the backs of men's minds by a new development in camp. Some bloke shot a medium sized kangaroo (Tim Felix said it was actually a 'wallaroo', between a kangaroo and a wallaby in size) which was found to have a baby in its pouch. The joey in the jill's pocket was not quite ready to greet and shake paws with the great wide world, so one of the men – Abraham Bates – made a canvas bag and lined it with wool. He sewed straps to the bag which he attached to his chest. The joey was installed in its new man-made pouch and was thereafter carried around by a big-bellied, hulk of a man wherever he went.

It was of course given a name: Doughie, the baby roo having the appearance of a large lump of bread dough.

One of the mysteries of humankind is why grown men – rough, tough, beer-swilling, gang-working men – will go stupid over a baby animal. They who thought nothing of shooting the mother of Doughie would have lynched the bastard who hurt her offspring. (As Tim Felix put it, 'The vagaries and hypocrisies of the human race are manifold!') Everyone in camp wanted a peek at the joey at least once in every day. They enquired after the creature's health and well-being. They offered their own share of powdered milk to provide for the creature. They all wanted to hold it and feed it after a teat was fashioned from a piece of a kangaroo's windpipe and attached to a bottle. Paternal, nay, *maternal* instincts are buried deep inside all of us and it only takes the arrival of a helpless, motherless infant for them to emerge.

Ludicrously, Bates was permitted to work on the line with the joey slung around his chest, though after Doughie suffered a few close shaves from a sharp tool, Bates was given light duties.

One morning Tam Donald appeared in the doorway of the tent where I slept and I read his expression immediately.

'Oh no, Tam,' I groaned. 'Not again?'

'Aye,' he said, excitedly, 'but this time it's different, Alex. It's no the same…'

'Will you never learn? You can't beat the Clancys.'

'Aye, not at cutting down the trees, but this is throwing, Alex. Throwing the axe. I'm gude at this, really gude. The Clancy brothers'll nay ken it, but I'm likely to win this one. You'll support me, o' course, bein' mah best pal and all that?'

I sighed. 'Of course, Tam.'

'Ye'll put a wager on me winnin'?'

'I'll put a bet on you, Tam, yes. But how does it work? Do you have a target?'

'It'll be just one o' the gums, but we'll start with only two turns of the axe in the air. Then, if all the axes stick in the trunk, then we'll go to three turns. And then, if the…'

'How many turns can you do, Tam? What's your best?'

'I can do five, no every time, ye ken. Two an' three turns, I'll do it wi'out thinking. Four, maybe miss a strike here and there. Five, well, one out of every three throws. But, see Alex, I've practised this all my life. There wasnae much else to do back home in Scotland. So I'm really gude at it. The Clancys, I've never seen them throw at all.'

And they haven't seen you throw, either, I thought, and yet you profess to be 'really gude at it'. But I didn't say this to Tam, who needed all his confidence if he was to win against this daunting pair of Victorian axemen. After all, Tam and I were citizens of the only Australian colony to be settled by free men, the others all being penal colonies. Thus it followed to a South Australian's way of thinking that Queenslanders, Victorians, New South Welshmen and Tasmanians were all convicts or ex-convicts and therefore naturally inferior people.

We had recently found an area of hot springs, so those of us who considered cleanliness close to Godliness rose early and went down to the stinking, steaming waters. We stripped naked to bathe. I had enough soap to clean my body, which I scrubbed vigorously standing waist deep in the pool, but very little left for my clothes. However, I did as I had seen others done and beat my soggy shirts and trousers with a heavy stone, hoping to smash the dirt out of them. There were those who didn't join us, who believed that dirt protected them from all sorts of things like ailments and the cold. I considered this pretty selfish since they were immune to their own stench but tent-sharers had to suffer it.

Tucker Burdon was one of the unwashed, but though he never let water soil his skin personally, he seemed fascinated by the ablutions of others and always came down to the waterholes to watch. He sat on the bank and stared at us with an expression I have only ever seen on babies a few months out of the womb: a mixture of deep curiosity and wonder at the world around it. What actually goes on inside a baby's mind, or indeed that of a Tucker Burdon, must remain a mystery, but it seems to me that those who wear that particular look are lost in a kind of mental struggle to come to terms with some strange new experience.

Abraham Bates also failed to enter the warm, steamy, sulphuric pools. Having recently become a doting mother he had little time on his hands for frivolous activities such as washing. He too sat and watched the bathers while he stroked the head of his mewling infant. Eventually the noise of men larking around caused the little wallaroo to poke his head above the parapet and stare. Its big round eyes brought a fresh murmur of admiration from those men who were missing their families. Cries of 'Eh, Doughie, you comin' for a swim, mate?' and 'Little 'un, come on cobber, get your paws wet. It's as warm as a toast.'

Sholto Walker was one of those who did go in to wash. In fact he was fastidious about his appearance, scrubbing himself almost pink and raw, especially between the toes, in his ears, under his arms and around the groin region. One of the other men was brusquely asked to scrape Walker's back with a sandstone. Burdon was the man and though I could see by his face he didn't like the task, the request came as an order and probably rather than create a confrontation Burdon did as he was told. While this was being done I happened to look up and was amazed to see the number of long white scars like scratch marks on Walker's back. He turned suddenly, catching me looking, and his lip curled.

'What're you lookin' at, mate?' he growled.

'The scars – on your back.'

'Lash,' he said, carelessly. 'Tried the navy for a while.'

'Were you press ganged?'

'Nah. Volunteered. Didn't work out. I didn't like them and they didn't like me. The cat's a vicious tool. I caught one of the bastards that gave it to me later, in a bar, and beat him near to death.' His eyes had narrowed and by his faraway tone he was clearly talking to some enemy in his distant past. 'You don't get on the wrong side of Sholto Walker and walk away with nothin' to show for it.'

We left it at that, but I was not convinced about his wounds being the result of shipboard punishment. The penal colonies also administered corporal punishment in the form of flogging with the cat. It was indeed a 'vicious tool'. I had witnessed punishment once, at Moreton Bay, and the rituals made it all the more an ugly spectacle. The man wielding the lash would pause every so often to deliberately separate the knotted thongs of cord, staining his fingers with the victim's blood. Then the punisher would take a long satisfying draught of water, before squaring his shoulders and continuing the flogging. Given that the whole procedure was accompanied by drum rolls, probably for the benefit of the onlookers, it seemed to a young man who had grown up in a peaceful, rural part of England a very barbaric form of dispensing justice. It was used in my old country though, and many, many others, and was certainly preferable to hanging by the neck on the end of a rope.

So, later in the day, most of us with our skins shining, we gathered for the contest between the Clancy boys and Tam Donald. Tam was wearing his kilt of green and blue tartan: a sure sign he was of a serious mind. The only other item of clothing on him was a faded tartan waistcoat which he had told me once belonged to his grandfather and had been passed down to him. The Clancy brothers wore thick wool shirts, nankeen trousers and hats with floppy brims. As usual the Clancys were grinning and larking around. They were a very popular pair in the camp, never complaining, always bearing sunny dispositions. Tough too, hard as steel axe heads, as Walker had found out when he got into a fight with Frank Clancy. Frank was a good deal shorter in height than Walker, but he made up for it with his furious, storm-driven attacks.

Frank's (and indeed Freddy's) idea of fighting was a ferocious hail of punches and kicks on his opponent that only ceased when Frank was utterly exhausted. By that time his adversary was usually lying semi-conscious in the dust. Walker did manage to fend off this barrage with his longer reach, but could hardly find a gap to get in the odd return hit. There was no winner that time, both men ending up with multiple bruises, but I noticed Walker never challenged either of the boys again. Other less proud men were subjugated to the will of Sholto Walker, either with threats or physical force, but not the Clancys.

'Did Walker put you up to this?' I whispered to Tam, as he was doing his flexing exercises on the competition ground.

'Naw,' said Tam.

'Well, here you go again.'

He started doing press-ups, using a log for the handhold, until one of the passing men winced and said, 'Jesus Tam, put some knickers on next time you do that, will you mate?'

I bet a whole gold sovereign on Tam winning, kissing the hard-earned money goodbye. I noticed Mr Harvey and Mr Roberts were also present. They were men like us and appreciated a little entertainment out here in the ochre wastelands. The two surveyors would never have attended a two-up gathering, disapproved of by the company bosses, but this was different. This was a contest of strength and skill between real men, much like the Scottish highland games, or a game of rugby football in England. I would like to have known on which man they wagered their money, but was too shy to ask. Perhaps they just bet with each other, not wishing to involve themselves with the working men.

The axe-throwing did indeed start just a few paces away from the chosen gum tree, with Freddy Clancy throwing first. All three axes thudded into the trunk and no one was eliminated during that round. In the next round, three turns of the axe, Freddy's tool hit the trunk at a slight angle which caused it to skid away and fall to the ground, thus eliminating him. Tam's axe head thudded surely and cleanly into the wood. I suddenly began to get a little excited for him, though indeed the better of the two brothers was still in the competition. The remaining pair now moved back a pace to perform four turns of the heavy implement, a feat which looked as difficult as it appeared magnificent.

'Come on, Tam!' yelled Joe Standeven, the wagon driver having arrived in camp the evening before. 'Show 'em who's boss!'

Afeeza and the other cameleers were enjoying the spectacle as much as anyone and I noticed that money changed hands rapidly between each of the rounds. Clearly the Afghans did not just bet on the eventual outcome, but on the various stages too. Their eyes were bright and registered their feverish excitement with the contest.

I went to Afeeza and said, 'You told me your religion forbade you to gamble.'

'Yes,' he said, 'it does, it usually does. But the prophet said that with bows and arrows, it is permitted to wager.'

'Ah, you did tell me that, but this is not archery, Afeeza.'

He shrugged. 'What is the difference? Sharp weapons go through the air and stick in targets.' Even as he was speaking to me his eyes were keenly studying Frank and Tam, and he turned away from me to gabber to one of the other cameleers, coins swiftly changing hands. 'This I have already told you, is permitted in the Koran.'

'You also told me,' I persisted, 'that only the contestants are allowed to wager, not the spectators.'

Afeeza gave me a stern look. 'Who are you to tell me what the prophet wishes me to do? Go away, Sikandar Jah, and leave an honest man to his simple pastime.'

I knew that somehow Afeeza would have found a way, his own wily way, to justify his flouting of the rules of his religion. Somehow he would reason that he *was* a competitor here today. I was extremely curious about this, because I knew he took Islam very seriously and he would not like to be accused of breaking its laws.

'So,' I insisted, not going away as ordered, 'how are you managing to do this, my friend?'

His face suddenly took on a look of shining innocence.

'Last night,' he said, 'I sharpened the axe of Mr Donald. We are men of the same team. He told me so. He is the thrower, but I am the assistant, making sure the axe beds in the wood securely. Without me there would be no true contest. A blunt axe might fall from the tree, into the dust, and all would be lost for Mr Donald. Together we make sure that his axe strikes true and he wins the contest.'

I was impressed. 'Yes,' I said, but pointing to the other Afghans who were again pressing money into his palm, 'but what about these men?'

'They sharpen the axes of the first Mr Clancy and also the second Mr Clancy.'

I laughed, shook my head, and went back to where Frank and Tam were making ready to do their four-turn throws. Tam was making a fuss about Jack Ransome, who was as usual wearing one of his bright shirts, a red one.

'Will ye no stand at the back o' me, Mr Ransome,' grumbled Tam. 'I'm blinded, so I am, by that signal flag you're wearin'.'

The crowd laughed at this, but they laughed even louder when Jack retorted in a mock Scottish accent, 'Can ye not wear that skirt o' yours again, Mr Donald – the white of those knock-knees is making mah head spin.'

Tam looked as if he was going to go into the sulks at this, but eventually everyone calmed down and the contest continued.

Frank went first. The blade flashed in the sunlight as the haft of the axe spun once, twice, thrice, four times in the air. Honed metal bit into gum with a satisfying *thunk*. A ragged cheer went up among those men who had bet the way of the Clancy boys.

Tam stepped forward, making sure his toe was behind the line in the dust. Unlike his opponent this time Tam didn't just step up to the mark and do a standing throw: he swung the heavy axe several times like a windmill on his right side and then released it. It looked fraught with danger, that technique, and there was a general expectation that the axe would fly off somewhere completely away from the target. One or two men even stepped back in fear of being decapitated. However, the implement swished through the air in a similar pattern to that which Frank's had done and miraculously struck the gum square in the middle of the trunk, making the whole tree shudder and quiver.

'Yes, Tam, yes!' I cried, full of admiration for the young man. 'That's a hell of throw, mate.'

'It ain't over yet,' said Walker, in a tone which suggested I should shut up. 'Someone's got to miss yet.'

Tim Felix said, 'Alex was just expressing his excitement, Sholto.'

Walker made no reply to this, but instead turned and muttered something to Jack Ransome, who in turn passed it on to Stam Meerdinck. The three of them burst out laughing. I wondered if they were having fun at my expense, or maybe Tim Felix's. It struck me forcibly that Jack Ransome was playing a very dangerous game, keeping Walker on a string. Despite being a desperate man, Walker was no fool.

'Five?' suggested Tam to Frank.

'Nah, mate. Four's enough for both of us, you know that. We'll stick at four until one of us misses.'

The throwing continued for two more attempts after that first round of four spins by each man. On the fourth set of throws Frank Clancy's axe hit a thick wad of peeling bark and the edge of the blade skidded off the trunk to plunge to the ground. A groan came from the watchers, many of them having bet on a Clancy to win since all other competitions of a similar nature had been the brothers' for the taking. The pair had seemed invincible, but in fact it was a capricious skill, throwing axes, and the unpredictable had to happen on occasion.

Tam now trudged up to the dust line, his kilt swinging with the exaggerated movement of his hips. The walk indicated to me that Tam was not feeling confident. This was the gait he slipped into when he was nervous and unsure of himself. However, I was probably the only man there who recognised the trait. Everyone else held their breath. They watched as the Scot whirled his axe in that peculiar method he employed over a certain distance, saw it whirl through the air in a dangerously quick spin. It was the butt end of the haft which actually struck the trunk, but the momentum of the turn took the head up towards the waiting timber and the edge of the axe buried itself firmly in the wood.

There was a period of silence as the audience struggled to collect their faculties and come to terms with what they had seen. Many of them had trouble believing the outcome. Surely an axe that strikes its target handle first could not end up stuck in solid lumber? Yet there it was, not even hanging there, but embedded securely in the innocent trunk of an outback tree. Tam was standing aside with a sort of bemused expression on his face, as if he too could not believe the outcome.

Frank Clancy stepped forward and grasped Tam's hand, shaking it vigorously.

'Best man won,' said Frank. 'Good on yer, mate.' Then he turned to the gaping audience. 'Who bet on me? Sorry, mates, not this time.'

Freddy also went to Tam and shook his hand.

'Next time, eh Jock? You know us Aussies can't stand being beaten. We'll get you next time.'

'Aye, I've no doubt you'll try hard enough,' replied Tam, suddenly realising he was the winner. He pumped his opponent's hand with great energy. 'Aye indeed, but I'll be waitin' on you. The Scots dinna like being beaten either, so it'll be a gude match, so it will.'

Men were paying men, money passing reluctantly from hand to hand, especially among the cameleers. Afeeza looked triumphant. I was feeling pretty good too as I collected my winnings from the American John Scully. Not that I was in the black with him. He had won so much money off me in the past it would be a long time before I would be back where I started when we began the hike to Barrow Creek.

I glanced at Walker, expecting to see fury on his face, but he took his defeat surprisingly well. I had absolutely no doubt that he had bet on the Clancys, but there was no anger in his demeanour t losing. He too went with others to shake Tam's hand, which annoyed me intensely. The young Scot was still convinced that Walker was a genuine, sincere friend who was full of goodness and light. I wished I could tell Tam what Jack Ransome had told me, but I was sworn to secrecy, for good reason.

NINETEEN

On the 10th of October, '71, Section A reached completion. The news came up the line and we whooped with joy. When you work on something day after day, cutting down trees, fashioning poles, sticking them in the earth, time stands still, everything seems to move as if in a slow dream and you wonder if this will be your lot until the end of eternity. You wonder if you will ever be part of normal society again or have to stare out forever over the red-and-yellow, seemingly infinite landscape which has been your waking hours since you said goodbye to civilisation. You wonder if the rest of your life will be spent among eucalyptus trees and spinifex grass, with echidnas and kangaroos for playmates.

So, one part of the line was finished and we had not got far to go and we learned that B, C and D should be ready in a month, or two at the most. Stone telegraph stations had been and were being built on the way, at The Peake, Charlotte Waters, Alice Springs (named after Mr Todd's wife) and Barrow Creek. Wooden stations also at Tennant Creek, Powell Springs, Daly Waters and the Katherine. It was my hope that if I did not get a job at either end of the line, at Palmerston or Adelaide, I would be taken on to man one of the stations on the line. I wasn't sure how Sally would feel about starting her married life in the heart of this continent, but I had to progress in my career from some starting point.

The news from the north was not good. Five ships had been chartered: *Omeo, Himalaya, Golden Fleece, Laju* and *Antipodes* as well as the Government schooner, the *Gulnare*. Everything had to go by sea to Port Darwin and on the last voyage carrying stock and equipment, over 100 bullocks out of the 500 had died. The horses too, had suffered deaths and sickness, apart from being untamed and not ready for the harness. Robert Patterson, the leader of the Northern Section, was faced with the huge problem of getting men and equipment close to the head of the Roper River, before the wet came to slow him down. In fact, five days before Section A was finished, an overloaded *Gulnare* set out hoping to go up the Roper and thus save a trudge across land, only to be caught in a heavy tide under a lee shore and wrecked on a reef.

The line going south from Port Darwin had now passed the Katherine and was on its way to the King: some twenty-five miles or so of currently dry country lay between the two rivers. But they were still a long, long way from meeting up with us and their stores were dangerously low, their equipment falling to pieces and their stock sick and dying. Mr Harvey was in despair over the Northern Section's problems, wondering if we would have to push on and on until we had closed the gap ourselves. Though the work was welcome for its income, being stuck in the middle of nowhere with the same people around you causes tension which leads to friction. Real hatreds set in over trivial matters, such as the way a man eats his food, or how he never washes his socks, or even how he breathes noisily through his nostrils. Sharing tent, work, meals and air with the same men, day in, night out, can lead to thoughts of killing those whose habits are sending you insane.

Even such a simple thing as a pulsing vein in the forehead of a man who has absolutely no control over his own blood pressure, might drive a fellow worker crazy, or the grinding of another's teeth.

'What the fuck *is* that thing in your skull?' shrieked George Trout one morning, slamming his tools down on the ground in aggravation. 'All the time, blurp, blurp, blurp. Never stopping. Who can work with you? I try not to look, but it's always there, pumpin' like a bullfrog's throat. I can't stand looking at it any more. I can't stand it, I tell you. Someone give me a knife. I'm goin' to cut the bloody thing out.'

As always, when he got agitated, Trout's cheap false teeth took on a life of their own and clacked wildly in his jaws.

A bemused and hurt Gwilliams touched the place on his head where he thought Trout was pointing, wondering what was the matter. He obviously felt nothing and came to the conclusion that Trout was going mad. The anger visibly rose in him as he considered the man standing before him. Gwilliam's eyes widened, the whites expanding and the pupils shrinking to fierce black dots inside the blue irises.

'Someone cart this bloody monkey off to Bedlam,' Gwilliams snarled savagely. 'Lock the bastard away with the other loonies. He's driving me up the wall with the way his teeth clatter and click all the time in his stupid gob. Someone put the poor sod out of his misery.'

A fight then ensued, with Trout trying unsuccessfully to burst the vein in Gwilliams' forehead with his thumbnail and concluding with Gwilliams wrenching the false teeth out of Trout's mouth and throwing them as far out into the desert sands as he could manage.

Just a day later, there was a spade fight between Walker and Burdon. These battles with implements were spontaneous affairs that blew up in the heat and dust of the day and as they were often during work time they naturally found men with weapons in their hands. There had been two other such fights in Section E during the construction of the line, both ending without any serious injury to the combatants. Despite the rage on both sides, there was an understanding that only the flat of the blade should be used and swinging at the head was taboo. Burdon twice managed to strike Walker on the shoulders, causing nasty weals to appear on Walker's skin. Walker's attempts at retaliation were defended vigorously, Burdon being an expert at parrying blows.

Such fights did not last long, since wielding a heavy spade was an exhausting exercise. Finally, both men were leaning on the tools, sweat pouring from them, licking the dust from their lips.

'Enough?' suggested Burdon, his chest heaving and his breathing rapid.

Most would have sworn Walker nodded his head in agreement, but the moment Burdon took his eyes off his opponent, straightened his body and loosened his grip on his spade, Walker suddenly swung at Burdon's legs. Metal rang out like a gong as the flat of the blade struck Burdon's kneecap. Burdon went down like a felled gum. He screamed in agony, writhing on the ground as Walker raised the spade again, this time like an axe, and would have brought the blade down edge first on Burdon's head had not Scully lunged forward and knocked Walker off his feet.

Walker was quickly back up and this time intending to attack Scully, but Mr Roberts had appeared.

Roberts shouted, 'Stop that!' and drew a pistol from his holster. 'Put it down, Walker.'

Walker's murderous eyes were on fire and he took a short step towards Mr Roberts. Tim Felix stepped in front of him and stared directly into his face. All the madness fled from Walker's features at this moment as he returned the ex-schoolmaster's stare. It was almost as if he was indeed a small boy suddenly confronted by unassailable authority which had brought him to his senses. The way the rage of children can be immediately checked by the sudden presence of an adult. This is how it appeared to me, as I stood on the fringe of the crowd. Indeed, Walker then dropped the spade and strode off, towards the water point. There he took a basin of cold water and poured it over his head.

Burdon was carried still groaning and snivelling to his tent, where someone tended to the wound. He did not walk again for several days. Mr Roberts and Mr Harvey took Sholto Walker aside, out of earshot of the rest of us, but who knows what was said to him? Walker returned looking less than chagrined. He did visit and try to apologise to Burdon, who told him to go and fuck himself. Had he not caused enough trouble already I had no doubt Walker might have laid into Burdon again at this point, but the accompanying Tim Felix told him in a quiet voice to let things alone. Again, Walker surprisingly followed the ex-schoolteacher's advice. I found the dynamics of the situation mysterious, but did not have the intellect to unravel the motives and forces involved in these enigmatic exchanges. Very soon I just mentally shrugged them from my mind, having far more other concerns than the whimsies of working men.

No one actually murdered his fellow man on our section of the line, but we were often only a hairsbreadth away from such an act. Even good friends fell out, some never speaking to each other again. Tim Felix told me this was a normal state of affairs on such expeditions.

'Imagine being on one of Columbus's ships,' he said, 'sailing off into the unknown with a bunch of strangers in a small wooden box. No one can get away from anyone else, the space being so limited that you can never be out of earshot of anyone's voice. They must have come to hate their leader's guts in a very short time. At least we've got plenty of space around us – more than the mind can cope with at times – so we're reasonably lucky in comparison with Christopher's mob.'

Nevertheless, I still wondered at the time whether we would make it to the end without destroying each other. One of the main problems was the mental stress of not being given a date when we would complete the line. There's a certain expectation of when a piece of work will finish and men will strive to meet that expectation, but if they are asked to continue on without any real end in sight, they will rebel. There had already been strikes and desertions in and from the Northern Section. It seemed clear to me that we would be poling until those in the north met with us in the south and the wire was joined.

One point of real anxiety amongst the men, though it was never spoken of openly, was the fact that we were steadily working towards the area where John Milner had been killed by Aborigines. Jack Ransome remembered reading an extract of John McDouall Stuart's explorations and informed us that Stuart too had been in a confrontation, probably with the same tribe. The area had already been named 'Attack Creek' and we were all wondering whether we might indeed have to defend the camp against hostile natives when we got there. Those like Walker and Jack Ransome declared they would be more than ready to meet an attack and were probably looking forward to such an event. Those like me who might have to stay in the region for a lot longer than others, at one of the telegraph stations, were hoping that all would be peaceful.

However, before we reached Attack Creek, men were allocated to completing the building of the relay station at Tennant Creek. I stayed with Spanish Joe (who was not Spanish at all, but had an olive complexion), William Wilson and one or two others, to supervise finishing the construction. Nails, screws and other necessary equipment had been brought up by camel and we erected two single-storey buildings and some outhouses.

The main buildings had porches and were quite smart in appearance. Some blacks came to watch us while we worked, but they appeared to be merely inquisitive rather than unfriendly.

I enjoyed the time away from the tension that was developing between Jack Ransome and Sholto Walker: a state which involved me too, since I was aware of the situation. Walker was beginning to suspect that Jack Ransome was not the man he professed to be. He was also still antagonistic towards me, the man who had saved his life, and of late took every opportunity to belittle me in front of the other men. Those who did not like me, probably for what I was – a man with a professional skill and therefore above myself – enjoyed the sport. Those who considered themselves my friends told me to ignore the taunting, saying I would only feed Sholto Walker's ego by retaliating.

Nevertheless, I had now stood so much ridicule I was ready to challenge Walker to a fist fight. Many of the men were beginning to wonder if I was a coward or not. Walker was bigger than me, but despite now being a man with a profession I had, after all, been raised on a farm and had the body strength of a farm boy. I had lifted heavy sheaves and piled hay ricks, dug ditches, ploughed fields of heavy loam, turfed roofs, constructed barns, and many other tasks that had built up my body strength over my youth. Walker was making the mistake of thinking me a puny office worker, unaware of my origins. There was a good chance that I could take him, if it did come to a fight in the end. As it was, I basked in the relief of not having him around: a pleasant experience.

'Let's go hunting,' suggested Spanish Joe one morning as we neared the completion of the compound. 'Let's go and shoot somethin' that's not easy to shoot. How about we make it a competition? Waddya say to having a pop at some hare wallabies?'

Hare wallabies are smallish creatures around fourteen to sixteen inches long that look something like a cross between an English hare and a ship rat. We went out one morning when the sky was full of cloud puffs, as if a steam engine had thundered through the outback and left its trail in the blue, and shot some hare wallabies. I felt like one of those aristocratic landowners back in Britain, out on one of their grouse shoots, except we had no gun handlers, dogs or beaters.

There had been one dog in the camp until we reached Charlotte Waters in the far south, where an unknown snake had bitten him. Rufous, so named for his rust-coloured coat, would have died thrashing around in agony in the bush if someone hadn't found him and put him out of his misery with a single shot to the brain. The trouble with most hounds is they're inquisitive creatures and they won't be told to let things alone. They're unaware of the danger of foreign creatures like serpents, which being smaller than hunting dogs, are believed by those canines to be lesser creatures and therefore regarded as playthings.

We laid out the morning's shoot on the ground by the newly erected relay station buildings. Spanish Joe had triumphed of course. He was a crackshot with a rifle. Surprising to the other three shooters, I had come second with my haul. The trouble with most men out in the bush is they rarely look into another's early history. All they saw in me was someone who had found himself an expertise that would tie him to a desk for the rest of his working days. Had they bothered to ask me, I could have told them that I had been shooting on farmland since the age of ten – rabbits, hares, crows, rooks, rats, pigeons – and over the years had developed a sharpshooter's eye. True, I was out of practice, but my inbred skill with a firearm more than compensated for my lack of form.

We kept some of the game for the pot and left the rest out on the edge of the bush for the Aborigines to take. It did no harm to cultivate a good feeling between them and those who would eventually occupy the telegraph station. Indeed, I might have been one of the operators who were assigned to this particular station. The game disappeared within a few hours, hopefully not down the bottomless throats of dingoes.

While we were building the station a haulier brought up some more mail. Among it was a parcel for me which I opened with excited, trembling fingers. It was a new Morse key. The company supplied Morse keys for its operators of course, but just as there are company rifles and pistols, there are also privately owned small arms. Operators like me want to own their own key, to carry it with them from job to job. It's like a king's sceptre, a symbol of my office as a telegraph operator. In later years, when hopefully I became more important, possibly even the chairman of a company (my ambition fostering wild dreams) it would serve as a paperweight on my desk, to remind me of from where and from how far I had come in my working life.

I unwrapped my treasure, and there it was, a camelback KoB – or Key on Board – a key and a sounder on a block of polished and then varnished cedar wood. Made by Charles Williams of Boston, the brass key was to my eyes absolutely beautiful. The arm of the key had a hump shape in the middle, giving the instrument its 'camelback' epithet. I was enchanted with it. With this magic device I would send messages across continents and oceans, between merchants, businessmen, lovers, hunters, explorers, satraps, princes, oligarchs, sheiks, sultans, maharajahs, sea captains, officials, generals, politicians, presidents, archbishops and courtroom judges. My key was a narrow brass gateway between the high and mighty of the whole world. They would come to me, a lowly but proficient messenger, to send their requests and demands, their offers and rejections, along the singing wires of telegraph road. My key would start and end wars, bring kings to their knees, raise peasants to dictatorships, bring lovers to the same boudoir, free colonies of their masters.

'Whaddya got there, mate?'

It was Spanish Joe, observing me from the doorway of the tent.

'Oh, nothing,' I said. 'A Christmas gift to myself.'

He saw the glint of polished brass as I rewrapped the key.

'Ah, a man's toy, eh? Not as soft as a woman, but then not as fickle. Just like my old Springfield rifle.' He tapped the breech of the weapon in the crook of his arm and sighed and a swimming look entered his eyes as he recalled some past experience. 'There's nothing like lyin' next to a floozy in a warm bed, but there's also somethin' really special about the kick of a trapdoor Springfield nestling in yer shoulder, eh?'

'I – I've never lain with a woman – not yet,' I confessed.

'Well mate, that thing you've got tucked under your arm might seem to be the ultimate in Christmas gifts at the minute, but I guarantee there'll come a time when you'd be happy to exchange a dozen of 'em for one night with a musky maiden with a dusky skin.'

She did not have a dusky skin, nor did she smell of musk, but I think I was already willing to give up my precious brass key, essential to the future well-being of brotherhoods and nations, should it ever be necessary in order to get Sally Whiting beside me in the marriage bed. The world can go to Hell in a basket so long as Sally's in it with me.

Once we had done all we could do at the telegraph station, we returned to the line camp once more.

TWENTY

Our crew at Section E had reached our original destination at Tennant Creek in early November, but Mr Harvey now had instructions to continue working northwards until we met with those coming south. Thus we were still on the line and it was Christmas Eve.

There was a feeling of deep sorrow in the camp which was almost tangible. A yuletide of sadness flowed slowly back and forth in the air, through the smoke of the fires, its waves breaking heavily on the shoulders of the men as they contemplated celebrating the season of great joy without their loved ones. Merry Christmas and a happy new year? Not in one of the loneliest places in the world, among snakes and lizards, scorpions and spiders. No carols could turn those semi-arid wastes into a place of delight. No stories of babies immaculately conceived and born in a stable could lift the spirits of men who suffered almost a handful of grit in the plum pudding. No marvellous tales of itinerant kings (albeit the sky was crammed with stunningly-bright stars) or of token shepherds could illuminate their souls. Only the low moaning of the camels when they were hungry provided any flavour of the birth of the wonderful boy-child.

We had a baby of course, though hardly a baby any longer, since Doughie was out of the pouch and bouncing around the camp. He must have been about seven months old when we shot his mother, because he came out of Abraham Bates's bag about two months after that. Now he just wandered around the camp, still going back into the bag to sleep and still drinking from his bottle, hardly ever letting his mother Abraham out of his sight. Indeed, for the last several weeks we had been calling Abraham 'Ma Bates', which he didn't seem to mind. There are those among us who are happy to be famous for anything, no matter what it is, so long as they are greeted and acknowledged wherever they go.

I found Doughie slightly eerie. He often turned up in some place he was not supposed to be, quietly, without a herald, simply to stare: in the sleeping tent, or at the back of the kitchen, or even the toilet area. Once, I was working in a battery lean-to, replenishing the copper sulphate, when I turned and saw a shape in the half-darkness which made me almost leap through the roof. Two eyes were staring at me with such intensity I felt sure they belonged to some malevolent creature of the red centre, a beast that could now be taken off the mythical list and placed on the actual. It was of course, Doughie, ever curious, who had followed me into the wooden-framed canvas lean-to and simply stood silently and stared, his nostrils twitching at the strange acerbic smell that came from the batteries. I yelled at the same time as I jumped and he bounded out a second later, probably looking for his mother to comfort him.

Anyway, try as we might we could not see this plumbob of a youngster as a replacement for the infant Jesus. Christmas was therefore devoid of most of the trappings of our most celebrated festival, though Tim Felix had anticipated the event and had brought along a story by Charles Dickens. Tim read it by the light of an oil lamp. It was called *A Christmas Carol* and a chilling yet edifying tale it was too, though several of the men scoffed at the sentimental ending. John Scully produced his fiddle from his kit and played the tunes of some carols. We sang *Once in Royal David's City*, *See Amid the Winter's Snow* and *O Little Town of Bethlehem*. Then John played a haunting, sorrowful tune in a minor key, full of yearning and sweet anguish, and several men started weeping. He was told rather sternly by Mr Harvey to find a more jolly song and so he started up with *The Palace Garden Polka*, which had been very popular in my dad's time and was still a big favourite at the barn dances in Suffolk .

Though we found a bush which in a poor light served as our festive Christmas tree, we had no crackers to bang with the plum duff that the cook had produced out of nothing. Mostly we sat around the fire and talked. Stam Meerdinck told us stories about *Sinter Klaas*, who brought the children gifts in Holland. I was confused by his description of this character because in Suffolk we had a similar individual, normally dressed in green, who heralded the coming of spring and the end of winter. These two creatures seemed to be of the same stock, though for completely separate festivals.

John Scully asked about the meal we might have at home on Christmas day and I told him it was usually a family affair.

'What would you eat?' he asked.

'My family? Usually rabbit, but I can remember having beef when we were well off. The farmer my father worked for, his family would have goose, but we couldn't afford that kind of fare.'

'Well,' he said, 'bullock's rump ain't so far away from beef, if you chew it well enough. That's what we've got. One of the older ladies was slaughtered this morning, being not able to pull her weight any longer.'

It was indeed a chewy dinner, though to give the cook his due, he put mutton and 'roo meat on the menu too. It was hardly a feast, but it did a job.

Christmas in the bush was not Christmas, but it was a good two-day break from the routine of hacking down trees, pinning wire and lugging batteries from one place to another. Afeeza and the cameleers were not in the camp at the time, so we didn't know whether they would have joined in with the festivities or not. Probably not, since they have their own events to celebrate at various times of the year. On one of them, I know, they don't eat anything for a whole month from each sunrise to sunset, which doesn't strike me as much of a celebration, but that's up to those that have it. What surprised me was the festival moved around because Afeeza's people used a thirteen month year – lunar months, I supposed – so it moved around year on year, much like our Easter. Well, not exactly like Easter, which hangs around, because their fasting month creeps forward, moon by moon, as the years go by.

Several things of consequence had happened of late. The main occurrence was the completion of the undersea telegraph cable, which crossed oceans and touched lands, which had arrived in Port Darwin. The British-Australian Telegraph Company cable came to us from Batavia in Java via Singapore, joining India, Aden, Egypt, Malta and Gibraltar, before connecting our new land with the old homeland, England. Now Australia was in direct communication with Britain. It was a magnificent and mind-numbing thought. Communication with anywhere in the world was here to stay and men like me were the core of the system. I felt both humbled by the magnificence of the event and intensely proud that I was to be an essential part of it all. If you had told me I would be needed as the next king of England, I would have rejected the position. What and who are kings next to men at the heart of progress and science? They are but symbols, while telegraph operators are indispensable.

For us though, the men on the line, there were still massive problems. Sections B and D were finished, it was true, but the

Northern Section was still in very deep trouble. The line between Adelaide and The Peake, over 600 miles, was already open and working. Ironically however, there were still 600 miles of nothing but poleless sand and rock between the northern group and us, Section E of the central division. They were deep in the wet up there, bogged down, choked by mud, and thoroughly dispirited from all accounts. We, on the other hand, moved steadily northwards, hoping our compatriots would stick to the work and be there to meet us when we arrived at our journey's end.

On Boxing Day, a very apt day for relaxation, Mr Harvey and Mr Roberts rode out together, to explore the trail ahead. Walker took advantage of their absence and the short festival holiday to challenge me to a fight out of sight and earshot of our bosses. Walker announced that he was going to beat me to a pulp, since in his words, he could not stand men who thought they were better than others and puffed themselves up like they were something special. He announced he was going to knock the 'toff' out of me and make me grovel and beg for his mercy, which, he said, was not in his make-up since he was born without a thread of sentiment in his body.

Jack Ransome came to me directly.

'I can stop this, if you want me to.'

I shook my head. 'Walker's been itching to fight me, ever since I nursed life back into him when he was dying of thirst. Best get it over with. He seems to resent the fact that without my assistance he might have departed this world. He left me to die once, you know, when I was out in the bush and needed the same kind of help. I don't understand the man. Why does he hate me? I never gave him cause.'

'His soul is twisted,' Jack said, helping me off with my coat. 'All the good nature and pity has been wrung out of it. There's not a drop left to curb his vicious nature. You did give him cause to hate you. He owes you his life and men like Walker can't stand being beholden to anyone. If it was money, he'd have paid you back as quickly as he was able and would have spat on the coins before handing them over.'

'But he had the chance to pay me back, in the bush.'

Jack smiled, wryly. 'Sure, but he made a decision at the time to get you out of his sight and mind for good, and now that adds fuel to the bitterness he feels towards you. He owes you twice over. I can tell you now, that even if you beat him here today, it won't end with that. He'll still be out to get even with you for making him indebted to you.'

Walker was standing among a group of his mates, tall and lean. Then he stripped off to the waist and I saw those scars again, which he said he had gained at a flogging. Clearly he was no stranger to pain. He oiled his upper body next, his chest and shoulders and arms, with a substance that smelled rank to me. His face and neck, down to the vee left by his open-throated shirt, had been reddened and coarsened by the harsh Australian sun. The rest of his chest and back were as white and hard as cordwood, and to be honest, faintly repulsive by their pallor.

'Come on, shit-face,' he said, 'it's time to take a beating.'

I removed my shirt and stood ready. I used no oil, hoping that it would not get to a wrestling struggle. I intended getting under his longer reach when he came at me and trying to fell him before he could get his hands on me. I had taken the time to wrap my knuckles in bandages though, aware that many bare-knuckle boxers break their fingers on an opponent's bone and gristle. I'm of average height, with a squarish upper body, arms muscled by the use of farm tools and reasonably powerful legs. As a boy of fourteen I used to walk ten miles to work and back again in the evening, so my thighs were solid enough and my calves thick and strong.

The men formed a wide circle and we two entered the ring. I saw Walker now staring at me strangely and I knew what he was thinking. I'm sure he had expected a puny stature to emerge from my shirt, one used to desk work and breathing office air. He was clearly surprised by my physique. However, unknown to him or anyone else at this meet, I had no real experience at fighting. Men who work on a farm have little time for such hobbies as pugilism. We would labour from dawn to dusk and a boxing match in the dark is no fun for spectators. Yes, there were bouts on the village green, from time to time, but these were often between gentlemen with nothing better to do. Farmer's or squire's sons, or even upper class gentlemen who liked to engage in the noble art bound by rules laid down in the Marquess of Queensbury's rules. The working men, out in the fields or in the barns, were scornful of such time wasting.

He came in at me crouching low, shoulders hunched, his eyes like slits above his bony cheeks. A left fist flashed out and caught me just below the right eye, knocking my head backwards, but before he had withdrawn his arm I was under it and hit him hard, twice, in the hollow below his rib cage, hearing his breath 'ooof' out of him. We both back-pedalled then, out of each other's reach, now aware of the force of our opponent's blows. His were indeed hard, painful blows. The sort of striking force one might get from a swinging branch of a tree. However, I knew my punches were like the thump of a wooden hammer when they struck his solar plexus and that's where I intended to hurt him.

The first couple of blows exchanged, Walker now came in a like a windmill, intending to mow me down before I could counter. This kind of attack was physically draining on the assailant. It was the kind of assault that either worked in a minute, or failed completely and had been used by the Clancy Walker had already fought. It surprised me that he was copying a technique which had failed when employed against him, but then Walker was a creature of impulse with little reasoning power. I knew if I could ward off some, hopefully most of his blows, he would tire very rapidly. This I did, fending off his fists with my forearms, not attempting to counter until his flailing ceased. Then I went in again, under his longer reach, and struck him four times in the chest below the heart.

He staggered back, his eyes registering pain and anger. Amazingly he came in again, using the same tactics of a rain of fists, showering blows on my head and shoulders, hoping to mill me down to the ground where he could then stamp me into the dust. I withstood the storm as before, countering with more punches, but this time to the belly.

'Foul!' he shouted, breathlessly. He appealed to the spectators. 'You all saw that? Below the waist. He hit me in my privates.'

'Lying bastard,' I snarled. 'Can't take it, eh?'

This absolutely incensed him and I was amazed at the speed and ferocity of the next attack, very similar to his last, but this time clearly using every ounce of energy in his body. I only managed to escape being hammered to the earth by stepping hard on the instep of his foot. He yelled 'Foul' again and backed away breathing rapidly and heavily, throwing straight-left punches at me as I tried to come in again, managing to keep me from repeating my earlier successes on his ribs. Then suddenly he pounced forward with the speed of a leopard, and grabbed me in his arms, forcing me to the ground with his tall frame.

'Got you, you fucker,' he wheezed. 'I'm a fuckin' python, I am. I'm going to squeeze the fuckin' life out of you.'

And indeed, he was a constrictor, his arms wrapped around my torso, trying to work themselves up to my throat. I knew if he got me in a neck lock I would have great trouble in getting free, so I squirmed and wriggled and twisted as much as I was able, frantically even, to make myself as difficult as possible to hold in a lock. Once or twice his groin was within reach of my knee and I did my best to punish him there, but somehow he managed to turn so that I caught his inner thigh. We struggled there for a good several minutes, both tiring over the period, but finally he managed to get an arm around my throat. I kicked out, tried to slip underneath his grip, but his arm was well and truly locked there and I began choking. Men must now have moved forward at this point to get Walker to let me go for I could feel fingers trying to prise themselves between my throat and his arm. There were shouts of, 'You're killing him, Sholto – let it go now – let him breathe, mate.' But Walker was having none of this soft talk. He did indeed want to kill me.

Their intervention favoured me though. Walker's arm relaxed a fraction and I managed to hook my chin under it to relieve the pressure on my throat. The position allowed me to sink my teeth into his flesh and I bit into forearm down to the bone. He screamed like a woman on fire, thrashing off the two men who had come to help me. Again he began raining punches at my head. He was over me now, his knees on my chest, as he smashed down at my brow and on the sides above my ears with his ivory-hard fists. The shape of his body above me was illuminated by the sunlight, giving the edges of it an ethereal glow, as if he were some fierce avenging angel intent on destroying a terrible demon.

With the last of my strength I struck at his exposed windpipe, my punch slamming full into his Adam's apple. The hail of fists on my head ceased. Walker's eyes bulged and he coughed in a strangled manner, rolling away and clutching his neck. He writhed in the dust for a good several minutes, gagging and fighting for breath, while a group of men stared down at him with a helpless look in their eyes. I staggered to my feet, shrugged off Jack Ransome, and went to kick Walker. The others pulled me away, pushed me off. I fell down again, exhausted, sitting on my bottom in the dust, looking up at a smiling Jack Ransome. He gave me a wink and then went to the assistance of

Sholto Walker, saying, 'I think he fouled you there, Sholto. I'm sure I saw a foul.'

Unfortunately Walker didn't expire that day, considering his nefarious role in my future, though I think he came close to it. The bruise on his throat was evident for a long while afterwards. My punch had indeed caused damage, for every time he inhaled over the next four or five days a whistling sound came through his nostrils. I hoped now that he would leave me be, since if he was angry at me for saving his life, this was now negated by the fact that I had tried to destroy him. Surely one wiped out the other: the bad turn overlaying the good, thus squaring it and smoothing it all out? That was my thinking. Of course I didn't ask Walker if that was the way he saw it, because I knew his poor common intellect would not allow him to analyse the nature of his hatred.

Walker made sure he had nothing to do with me after that, neither antagonising me, nor offering to make appeasement. He simply ignored me, treated me as if I were invisible, passing me on his way elsewhere without a glance. As far as I was concerned this was an improvement, though it was a concern with regard to what he was thinking. Did he still hate me? Probably. Was he planning some sort of revenge? Doubtless. What could I do about it? Nothing, since I was now a ghost in his eyes. He refused to speak to me, looked right through me, and never mentioned my name again. I couldn't influence the situation in any way, so I didn't try.

Normally when you have a victor and vanquished in a camp fight, or street fight, the winner is lionised by the spectators. They fawn on him and slap his back, telling him what a great man he is. Not in this case. Walker was still greatly feared and not many men wanted to be seen congratulating the bloke who had beaten him, however fair and square. I think others recognised the nature of the beast we called Sholto Walker. He was one of those whose violent disposition is just a hair's-breadth away from madness. You knew, looking into his eyes, that he could kill a man without conscience and without consideration of the law. The deed might put him in the hangman's noose, but that would be no sop to the victim, lying dead on the ground. It was best to have men like Walker believe you were on their side and against his enemies.

When they looked at me, however, I could tell that though they might be pleased by what had occurred, and admiring of what I had done, they knew I was not a dormant lunatic, the darkness in my soul veiled only by a necessary need to keep my derangement in check for the sake of my freedom. That was how Walker appeared and the men would rather snub me, knowing that I was relatively harmless, than rouse the enmity of a man who was quite capable of cutting their throats while they slept. I do not know why it is, but dangerous men like Walker are rarely checked in their stride by others of sane reasoning until they have committed the most heinous of crimes and stand glowering on the gallows.

One man who did come to me was Jack Ransome.

'Are you all right?' he asked. 'Any damage?'

'No – no worries,' I replied.

'You know he'll be out to get you now.'

'He always was. I don't know why. I've never done anything to purposely antagonise him. He just seemed to take an instant dislike to me.'

'We've talked about this before. Don't worry about it. But watch him. You know he can't be trusted. He might not do anything directly, but you can be sure if you get caught out by him he'll make the most of it.'

'I'll watch it. When are you going to make your move?'

Jack sighed. 'I wish I could do it now, but I can't. I'm hoping he'll lead me to Tom Smith. I want Smith more than I want

Walker. I'd like to think I can get them both, with a little guile and cunning.'

'You need to watch it too.'

He smiled. 'Yep, but Walker has an ego the size of an emu's egg. Told him I want to do an article on him, once the line has been built and the work's over. Told him he's the sort of man my readers would admire for the way he survived being lost in the outback. Told him his experiences were incredible enough to make him famous in places like Melbourne and Sydney. He swallowed every word. You should have seen his eyes glint. "Will there be money in it?" he asked me. "Oh, I'm sure my editor will come up with something if the story's interesting enough – which I'm certain is true," I told him. Swallowed very word. Massive ego. Bigger than yours and mine put together and we don't do so bad in that arena. We both think we're the cat's whiskers, eh?'

I smiled at him. 'I guess so.'

'You *know* so. Anyway, stay away from that son of a whore as best you can. He'll get his, don't you worry. I'll see to that.'

TWENTY-ONE

It was evening and I was sitting with Tim, Jack and Tam at our own fire, while others were hunched over theirs. We didn't need the fires for warmth. Noon temperatures were around 95 degrees Fahrenheit and even the night temperatures were around 75 degrees. But the fires provided a focal point for men who could stare into the flames and lose themselves in their dreams. We sat on logs that had been cut down while the sweat leaked from our skins as through porous cloth. There had been a light rain about three days previously, but this had almost sizzled on hitting the hot ground, turning to vapour within minutes.

Jack was cleaning his beautiful revolver. I watched as he emptied the magazine chambers of their bullets, then polished each round with a clean handkerchief before replacing them. It was true that dust got into everything out there in the wilderness, but Jack Ransome was a particularly fussy man. He still wore his bright shirts, though somewhat creased and crumpled now. Everything about him was neatness and order though. I'm sure if a flat iron had been available he would have turned those shirts into something fit to wear to a ball. Certainly he cleaned his boots every single night and was the only man in camp who shaved and cut his hair. The rest of us had thick bushy beards and long straggly locks that tucked under our hats. The men put his obsession with neatness down to his supposed profession as a writer. Well they were half right, but it was down to his profession as a policeman, not a reporter. I wondered if the need to be smart had been instilled in him during his training and was so ingrained it was impossible to ignore.

We had been sitting in silence for at least an hour. Men thrown together for months on end have little to say in during an even, having emptied themselves of conversation over the course of the day.

Tam suddenly drew back from the fire quickly and pointed to a rock near Tim Felix's shoulder.

'Spider!'

Tim turned his head and indeed there was a large eight-legged monster not far from his left cheek. However, even as we stared at the black creature it was gone the next instant having been snatched from its stone perch by a passing bat. The spider was now in the fanged jaws of a night time predator and being crunched to death. Instinctively we all looked upwards into the night, actually without any hope of seeing the bat that had swooped through the light of our fire. Up above the stars blazed in their million-millions, the bats lost somewhere in the bits of blackness that separated those far distant suns.

Tim went back to his book, which he was having to hold close to a lamp near his head. Perhaps it had been the lamp that had attracted the spider, for there were moths and other insects swirling around the glass that covered the flame. Jack continued to oil his revolver with the utmost care and attention. Tam turned to me and asked me a question.

'We're nearly finished here, are we no Alex?'

'Yep. I think we are.'

'What are you going to do when it's all done, Alex.'

I stared at my young friend. 'You know what I'm going to do – I shall be on one of the telegraph stations – Barrow Creek or Tennant Creek most probably.'

His face suddenly took on an expression of anguish in the firelight.

'Aye, but what am *I* going to do?'

Tim looked up and at Tam, probably because of the nature of the young Scot's tone.

'Well,' I replied, 'that's up to you, Tam. There'll be a need for linesmen and maintenance men still. They're already talking about replacing some of the wooden poles with iron ones sent from Britain, since the termites and woodrot have since played havoc with the ones we've put in. Have you applied to Mr Harvey in that respect?'

'Aye, ah have, but he says the list is full.'

'Ah. Well, there's plenty of work elsewhere. This country is young, Tam. They need strong men to build it. You should have no trouble in getting work elsewhere.'

We then got down to the real reason for his questions.

'I don't want to die with a spade in my hand, Alex. I want to amount to somethin'. Will you no teach me that Morse? Will you no teach me how to do operating, man? I would like to be one of yon operators working in a telegraph station. I'd like it fine.'

It was painful for me to see Tam so needful. I had indeed been showing him the rudiments of operating a telegraph, giving him the codes for the letters and figures which he had painstakingly written down in a scruffy notebook that Jack had given him and explained how the batteries worked, how interrupting the current on the line produced the dots and dashes for the characters. But it was only surface stuff and Tam was not the best of students. He tried hard but information had trouble sticking to his brain.

Tim came to my rescue.

'It's not as easy as all that, Tam. Alex had to train under qualified instructors in a workshop with the right equipment designed to instil knowledge into the students. He can't pass on that knowledge just like that, especially since he's not a trained teacher.'

'Och, you're just saying that because you're a teacher yourself, are you no?'

The inference was that Tim was trying to bolster his own profession by making it sound as if it needed more skill than Tam was prepared to accept it required. This naturally annoyed Tim.

'You think it's easy to teach, do you?'

'Well, it disna seem all that *hard*.'

Tim shook his head. 'Those people who sit on one side of the classroom always seem to think that being on the other side is a walk in the park. Try it sometime, Tam. In fact, do it now.' Tim placed down his book and folded his arms, while Jack looked up from his gun cleaning now that the conversation had got interesting. 'Right, go on Tam. Teach me something,' said Tim. 'Anything at all.'

Tam looked flustered and embarrassed. He hung his head, his blond hair in danger of catching fire.

'Och, I don't know anythin' I could teach.'

'What did you do in Scotland, Tam?' asked Tim.

'Worked the farm.'

'So, tell me how to plough a field.'

Tam brightened now, a smile coming to his broad face.

'Aye, I can do that. See, you stand behind the plough and walk the horse…'

'Horse? There's a horse involved? What kind of a horse?'

Tam frowned. 'Weel, a heavy horse, of course – you wouldna use a riding horse for the ploughing.'

'Ah, well I did not know that. I do not know anything about ploughing, so you'll have to explain it all in detail. How does the heavy horse become attached to the plough? Let's start with that. I'm completely ignorant don't forget. I hardly know what a horse looks like, let alone anything else.'

'Och, you're just bein' awkward, Tim.'

'No, no, I want you to tell me how it all works. I have no idea. No idea at all. I've been busy trying to stuff knowledge into the heads of young people all my life, in dusty schoolrooms with dirty windows. I know what a slate looks like and a piece of chalk, but I've never even seen a plough except in picture books.'

Tam's eyes widened. 'Really? Well...' and he stumbled forward, trying to explain how to harness a heavy horse to a plough and getting into a great tangle, since Tim did not seem to know the names of any of the bits of tack, nor how they connected to one another. Nor did Tim Felix the schoolteacher know the names of a the various parts of a horse. This, before Tam had even started on the mechanics of a plough. Eventually, after trying to batter Tim with information, he gave up and almost looked as if he were about to start crying. Tim took pity on him.

'See, Tam, it's not that easy. Alex here would need a great deal of time and the right conditions to turn you into a telegraph operator – and even then, Mr Harvey and the company bosses wouldn't accept it. You have to go to the right people to get qualified.'

So then the poor lad went back to his original plea.

'Well then, what am I to do when it's all over?'

Jack Ransome said quietly. 'You come to me, Tam – we could do with good honest men where I come from.'

Both Tim and Tam looked taken aback at this statement and stared quizzically at Jack.

Tam said, 'I canna work on a newspaper, Jack. I canna write good for a starter. I can copy stuff, like Alex does, but I canna think of stuff to make up a story.'

Jack blinked, probably realising now what he had said, but he recovered fairly quickly.

'It's not all about writing, Tam. There's the printing presses to maintain and service. That sort of thing. Just you come to me afterwards and I'll get you trained in a profession you'll enjoy.'

'Och, that's braw of you, Jack. I appreciate that. I'd like to work with Alex, here, but if I canna do that…'

'You just apply to me, when the time comes. We won't be leaving here just yet, anyway. Not until the line's up and running.'

Two days after this reflective evening around the camp fires, the line was open as far as Alice Springs. Adelaide could now communicate with the centre of Australia. There was not a lot of traffic as people might imagine, the red centre being occupied at this point in time by a handful of telegraph men, Aborigines and kangaroos. Two of these groups were totally oblivious of sending telegrams to each other or anyone else. However, there was now talk that the company were going to use a pony express to bridge the gap between us and the southernmost point of the Northern Section. We needed now to connect with Alice Springs. That would not take long, once we found out where the line was down. Mr Roberts sent out men to look for any breaks. Jack Ransome and I rode with them. I had made all the connections at our camp before going out, so I could test the line from any point between there and Alice.

One evening we were sleeping around the wagon when we heard the sound of thunder and the ground shook beneath us.

Jack looked at me quizzically, his tin mug full of coffee halfway to his lips. 'Earthquake?' he said.

John Scully, the American, shook his head.

'That's no earthquake.' He looked back down the trail. 'That feels like a cattle drive to me.'

We all stood up and stared south. A dust cloud was billowing up from among and between the rocks and trees. Then some dark shapes appeared, at first moving quite fast, then slowing to walking pace. Some taller shapes appeared. Eventually, in the evening light and through the veil of dust, the scene congealed into a herd of horses driven by riders. Two drovers flanked the steeds, one of them black, and a third brought up the rear. They came to the clearing where we were camped and Bates shouted, 'Hey, watch our gear, you buggers!'

'Sorry, mate,' said the black rider. 'We 'aven't got 'em on string, eh? They got legs what take 'em where they wanna go.'

'You get some respect in your voice, Abo,' said Bates. 'This is a white fellah, you're talkin' to.'

'Yeah? Under all that dirt, eh? Couldn't tell what colour you was, boss. You could be green, purple or yeller, I'm thinkin'.'

The other rider, a white man, laughed at this. So did our party, which enraged Bates for a few minutes. He went lathering off at the black, then at us, and ended up stomping away into the bush to cool off.

The three drovers settled the horses for the night, then came and sat with us around the camp fire. We gave them some steaming hot coffee, for which they seemed grateful, and a flour damper or two to fill their stomachs. You would expect men riding out in the wilderness, where human contact was rare, to open up and fill the evening air with talk, but it's never like that. What seems to happen is a man goes down inside himself for a while, shying away from immediate communication, happy to be in company, but not able to open up. However, as the evening drew on, they began to talk. It seemed they were heading north, to Palmerston, to start a stud farm.

'You might sell a few of those mounts on the way,' I told the owner of the herd. 'The Company is talking about forming a pony express between the northern section and our lot.'

'Well,' he said, 'they'll have to give us a good price – it's been a hard drive to here. We've lost several on the way. I expect we'll lose a few more before we get to the top end. We sold one or two to your mates down the trail. You're nearly through, eh? The government in Adelaide is tellin' everyone you'll be up and running by March.'

We looked at each other, the telegraph men, knowing this was a very optimistic date.

'March is doubtful. Maybe a couple of months more. Coming up through the centre has been relatively easy compared with the crews coming down from the top. They've had it a lot tougher than we have, though it hasn't been easy for these blokes either,' I indicated the polers and wiremen sitting around the fire.

The drover nodded at me. 'You the boss-man, are you?'

'No,' I said, as a few looks were directed at me, 'just a telegraph operator – I help out now and again with the hard work.'

At this point Abraham Bates came back and sat down opposite me, then, looking around the ring of men, said, 'What's the bloody savage doin', sitting with civilised men.' Bates knew that his views were shared by several other men around the fire. Most of the crew thought the Aborigines were inferior human beings, if human at all.

The drover leader stared hard at Bates.

'You shut your bloody mouth, gallah. He's as civilised as any one of the rest of us and twice as civilised as you. You're the bloody barbarian here.'

Bates jumped up. 'You want a punch on the snout?'

The drover rose to his feet. He was around six-feet-two, maybe three, with broad shoulders and big hands: an older man than most of us, being about thirty-five years of age with a skin as gritty and rough as spall from sandstone. He had dark, almost black eyes that glinted in the flames from the fire. Buried in the black beard was a scarred upper lip that twisted the corner of his mouth. There was dust in his dark curly hair which hung in ringlets which might have been worn by a French king. It also flecked his black beard, giving it a whitish tinge. You could tell at a glance that he was a hard man, having a life packed with tough problems and decisions. He was not the sort of bloke I would want to fight.

'You goin' to give it to me?'

Bates blinked rapidly. 'You can't come in here and just let your black sit amongst decent men.'

'I don't see anyone else complaining.' The drover turned to Jack Ransome. 'Who is this arsehole anyway? He's got the brains of a chook.'

'Oh, you must've heard of Abraham Bates,' said Jack, lightly, 'the fellah who makes a speciality of shooting men in the feet.'

'He does that? When they're standing up, or lying down?'

'Either. It's no sweat to Abe Bates how they position their bodies – he shoots their heels off anyway. He's very good at it. I should watch yours, if I were you. He doesn't often miss.'

The drover had guessed two sentences back, that they were taking the rise out of Bates, and he nodded, sombrely.

'I'll wear my old boots then, while I'm around him. No sense in gettin' holes in my best ones.'

'Bates,' I said, interrupting the entertainment, 'if sitting near a black man offends you, go and sit at your own fire.'

'You against me too, eh?' He glared at me, suddenly seeing me as an easier target than the tall drover: a way of saving his pride. 'I'll knock your head off, for a start.'

'No you won't. You'll sit down and shut up,' snarled the drover. 'I've had just about a belly full of you, sonny. Now do as you're told.'

Bates stood there for another minute, then sat down and stared into the fire while others completely ignored him. He might have had men who agreed with his views on Aborigines, but they weren't going to say so. The drover too resumed his seat and began chatting to Jack Ransome about horses. Jack seemed to know quite a bit about the subject and it left me wondering if he had been a roughrider for the police. By the time we were all ready to turn in, Bates had cooled down and was listening intently to John Scully about the latter's exploits in the war between the American states.

'I was at the First Battle of Manassas,' Scully was saying, 'which some call Bull Run. I was fourteen years of age with a gun taller than I was. I could hardly lift it up to my shoulder at the end of the day, it got so heavy in my skinny young arms. I must've fired it twenty times. Had a bruise on my shoulder the size of your fist. But I probably hit nothin' at all. Fired it in the general direction of the enemy, was all.'

'You was in the Union army?' asked Bates.

'Naw, listen to my accent, fellah. I was with the South. My family come from South Carolina. We was the first state to secede from the Union.' His eyes narrowed. 'I tell you I saw some things on that first day that would have you violently discharge the supper you just ate was I to describe 'em in detail. Legs and arms blowed off. Guts decorating the branches of trees. Growed men screaming for their mothers. Fourteen. Fourteen. I'd not seen a dead mouse at that age and at the end of the battle the ditches were crammed with dead men. My dad owned a dress store and I ran away to find the glory they was all talkin' about. Shit, if I saw glory it was the ugliest thing I'd ever laid eyes on.'

'I was at the Crimea,' Bates said, 'fighting for queen and country, so don't tell me about dead men. Battle of Inkerman. We fought in the fog and didn't know friend from foe. Officers all disappeared into the mist and we was just left to fend for ourselves with no orders nor any sort of leader. I lost my best mate on that day. Shot through the eye by a Ruskie ball from three feet away. Took out the back of his head. I only got away alive by fallin' down and pretendin' dead.'

'Wasn't that a bit cowardly?' I asked, as I passed the pair. 'Pretending you were dead.'

'You wasn't there!' yelled Bates, venting the pent up fury which had been in his breast since the earlier exchanges. 'You don't know what war is like, McKenzie.'

'How the hell do you know I wasn't there?'

'What regiment was you in?'

I snorted. 'None. You're right, I wasn't there, but you didn't know that.'

'I could've guessed,' he sneered.

Something occurred to me.

'You were at the Crimean war. So was Walker. At least he says he was. Have you talked with him about it?'

'Walker? He weren't there. He told me. He only said that to make hisself look good when I shot Bill Turmaine by accident. Walker was just gettin' at you, McKenzie. He don't like you. He don't like you one bit. He told me he's goin' to kill you one of these days. Said it straight out. "I'm goin' to kill that bastard McKenzie one of these days." You'd better watch your back, McKenzie. Walker's out to get you.'

This seemed a source of satisfaction to Bates, but I said nothing in reply, affecting a careless attitude in front of this ignorant man.

The next morning I went to look at the horses. They were beautiful beasts, a stockman's dream, I would have thought. They milled around under the trees, sniffing the air, some looking hopefully at the wagon where I imagined their feed was kept. There was and had been grass in various locations on the way, but we were in a desert area with little greenery to be seen. Some tough, spiky clumps of spinifex here and there, but nothing substantial enough for a whole herd of horses.

While I was leaning on a rock, watching the animals, the Aborigine drover ambled up and began stroking their silky noses, murmuring to them in a low voice, no doubt telling them all was right with the world. The black man smelled so strongly of horses himself, I wondered if they thought he was one of them. He moved through their mass slowly, stroking flanks and heads, murmuring, murmuring, occasionally tapping one sharply but not forcefully on the nose with his thick forefinger: a beast I imagine who had not been good the previous day's drive and was being severely punished for its mischief or misdemeanours.

'G'day,' I said. 'Sleep well?'

He looked up at me from under the brim of his sweat-stained and filthy hat. 'Yep, thank you, boss. Slep' good. You?'

I had slept badly, but replied, 'Fine. You moving on today?'

'Think so, boss.'

'Well, good luck.'

At that point, Jack Ransome arrived at my side.

'Fancy a walk, mate?' he asked. He nodded towards a ridge. 'Let's go and see what's left of the sunrise.'

We climbed the rocky ridge until we stood on its prehistoric back and stared out over the vast expanse of wilderness. The deep coarse mineral colours of the landscape were unbelievably beautiful: burnt umbers and siennas, indigoes, yellow ochres, cobalt blues, tuscan earths. The quick shadows of the early morning sun raced over the backs of domed rocks and craggy crops, tipping the ragged trees with bright points of light and picking out the dark crosses that were eagles gliding on the backs of thermals it was creating. There is nothing to be witnessed like the outback for rich earthen hues that stir your soul. The Aborigines had been immersed in this wide basinful of dyed stone since the world had begun and they moved across it with the grace of birds.

'This land is old, isn't it?' said Jack, staring out over the plains that stretched out below us, seemingly infinite. 'Ancient. It must have been the first thing God made before he went on to make the rest of the world. Look at it. He didn't even bother to finish it. Rocks and dust, and a few trees, not much more. But so much of it. Look at it. What a country. You can't get it all inside your heart – it's too big. I was born here, McKenzie. This is my homeland. I don't even know that place you've come from, but I can't think it's better than this.'

'It's greener,' I offered.

'Is it though? Well, that's somethin'. But the top end's pretty green too.'

'A different kind of green. Not so soft and lush.'

He let out a huge sigh. 'Well, I'm not that struck on greenery anyway. I'm a town man. But I love *this* place. You can breathe out here. Deep breaths full of warm air. They say you can fit England into a tiny pocket of Australia. I wouldn't want to live on an island not much bigger than Van Diemen's Land. Van Diemen's all right, of course,' he said quickly, probably feeling he was being disloyal to Australia's child-island, 'but only because this place is reachable.'

'Tasmania,' I corrected him. 'It's called Tasmania now.'

'I call it what my dad called it.'

We were quiet for a while, just taking in the morning that was beginning to turn the mellow scene to a blazing glare.

Then Jack asked, 'Do you believe all that stuff that Tim talks about – big lizards at the dawn of time?'

I shrugged. 'He reads a lot,' I said. 'He's a teacher.'

'Yeah, but mate – big lizards? Big as elephants. Bigger, Tim says. Giants.'

'You've never seen an elephant.'

'I've seen pictures. If God made those lizards – and the other big animals he talks about – giant wolves and lions – why aren't they here now? What could kill off giants like that? Other way around. They'd kill everything else off, wouldn't they? Doesn't make sense. I don't think God made creatures that would just lay down and die before we came along. He would want us to be masters over them, just the same as we are over everything else on the Earth. Masters of all we survey. And that bloke, Darwin. What's he on about, eh? Apes? Us? They need to put him in Bedlam, that bloke. He's as loony as a kookaburra.'

I didn't argue with him, mainly because I was confused myself. I'd grown up like most people believing that God made us. When I asked my mother how God had done it, she told me that He had an oven and baked us out of clay, then breathed life into our bodies. When I read about Indians in India, and Negroes in Africa, she then said that an Indian was left in the oven a bit too long and had browned, and a Negro had been left in longer and had been burned black as charcoal. As a child I had believed this account of our origins, and even in school our lady teacher told us that Mr Darwin was a liar and should be hanged for saying that people were no different to monkeys. Later, in London, I met a young scholar from Oxford University who tried to explain Darwin's idea that raw creatures developed into others. I respected that young man, but I also respected our vicar, who thought the idea 'monstrous' so was left, as I am today, with two conflicting accounts in my head.

'Somebody must think Darwin is an all right bloke, because they named the port after him,' I offered, but Jack wasn't listening to me. 'Cook, or Flinders – somebody,' I finished, lamely.

'Australia's probably the biggest place on Earth,' said Jack, with great satisfaction.

I must admit at that moment, in the outback, it looked it, but I said, 'Africa's as big. And America's supposed to be bigger.'

'America,' snorted Jack. 'Scully says that, but look what a bloody liar he is sometimes. Africa? I don't know. It has elephants, which as we've talked about, are bloody big blokes.'

'There's a man called Livingstone who's lost in the middle of darkest Africa,' I mused. 'I've just read it in one of the newspapers Afeeza brought.'

'Well if it's anythin' like this place, he's going to have a hard job finding his way out,' Jack replied. 'What did he want to go in there for in the first place?'

'He was looking for a river, I think. Where it started.'

'What the fuck for? Some buggers haven't got the sense they were born with. What the bloody hell does it matter where a river starts? Now, building a telegraph, that's something else.'

Jack brushed himself down. A cloud of living creatures billowed round him. He was wearing one of his bright yellow shirts and it was already covered in small black insects that he had disturbed. We stayed for a short while longer, then made our way back down to the camp, where the smell of breakfast was wafting up to our nostrils. I had found our talk interesting and informative, from the point of view of getting to know Jack Ransome better. I felt he was a good, straight-forward man, which is more than you can say of most policemen anywhere.

TWENTY-TWO

We moved on through February, into March, and thence to April, poling, wiring, testing. Work had bogged down and ceased on the northern section for a while, but by mid-April had restarted and was even so surging towards our weary crew. Our men had had enough. They had been crossing the wilderness of the red centre for well over a year and their orifices were caked with its dust. They might have been primal men for the way they looked, creatures who had crawled out of caves. The outback had left its mark on their faces and on their souls. Their spirits bore the indelible stains of working with the same people for too long in isolation and harsh conditions. Shoulders were slumped, heads hung low, limbs were lugged around as heavy burdens.

I was euphoric however. Afeeza had brought letters and among them was one from Sally. She had boarded a ship for Australia. It was the *Sheerness Sands*, a sailing ship and even now it must have been cutting its way across the Indian Ocean towards its destination. What a gift from the postal service! I went around with a stupid smile on my face which must have irritated all those others who were clumping around, with the claws of depression buried deep in their hearts and minds. I couldn't wait to see the love of my life, to fold her into my arms again, to hear her sweet voice and laughter in my ears. For too long now I had been in the company of wild men with spirits as dark as pitch.

'Bugger off, Doughie,' I said, as the wallaroo came to the entrance of the tent and stared at me. He hopped closer, staring down at the letter in my hand. 'You can't eat it,' I told him. 'It'd clog your guts. Go on, bugger off somewhere else. Go and find your ma.'

Much like a trained dog, the creature did as he was told. Doughie had been good for the camp, a distraction. Men who had begun to hate one another could be fond of a misty-eyed animal which appeared to reciprocate. The men did indeed find each other's company unbearable at this point in time, though I knew that once it was all over, and they were back in polite society again, they would probably get together in inns and talk over the great time they had together building the overland telegraph, and how they missed the great camaraderie.

A harassed-looking Jack Ransome suddenly appeared in the doorway of the tent.

'You have to get a message out quick,' he said. 'Send the following to Adelaide police: *Thomas Smith and Thomas Walker have stolen horses and are riding south towards Tennant Creek. Am in pursuit. Will keep you informed when able.*'

'Walker? Gone?' I cried. 'Smith? Where did he come from.'

'I can't spend too much time now, but our Tim Felix turned out to be your Captain Midnight. I've got to get after them, McKenzie. I'm taking young Tam with me.'

I then saw through the opening Tam Donald holding the reins of two horses and talking quietly to Mr Roberts.

'Tam's going with you?'

'Get the message out, Alex.'

It was the first and only time he used my Christian name.

'All right. But...'

'But what?' he snapped, impatiently.

'Tim Felix? Are you sure he's Tom Smith?'

'They rode out together, him and Walker. It has to be him.'

'Maybe it's another bushranger – not Smith? Or–' as a better scenario came to me, '–maybe Walker has kidnapped Tim Felix, taken him as a hostage?'

'In which case, does it matter? I still have to go after them. Look, Walker is one of Smith's men. It seems likely that the two of them have got back together. I think it's Smith, but if it isn't, I still have to ride after them and arrest them. They wounded a man – one of the drovers – when they were stealing the horses. They fooled us, Alex. Fooled the hell out of us. I'd be the first to say I never saw through Tim Felix. His disguise was perfect. The man's a born actor. He just chose the wrong profession, 'cause we'll get him in the end, you can put your money on that. I'll see the bastard hang if it's the last thing I ever do.'

I stuffed Sally's letter into my shirt pocket and went to the shack where the equipment was stored. My first really important message! My heart was pounding with a mixed feeling of elation and fear. Fear for the well-being of my two friends and joy at being able to do what I had been trained to do. I made contact with the operator at Tennant Creek, where I also would be stationed in a few weeks' time. I tapped out the message and after dealing with one or two requests for verifications, received an acknowledgement. Not only was the message on its way to the authorities in Adelaide, and would be with them in the blink of an eye, but Tennant Creek was also warned and would be on the lookout for the two bushrangers. The world had changed. Information on murderers and thieves could be instantly broadcast to the authorities and there was nowhere they could hide that would bury them in distance and time.

Tim Felix? I leaned back in my chair, trying to come to terms with this amazing information. Tim, a bushranger? Captain Midnight, no less. It was surely a mistake? Tim was a schoolteacher, a scholar, a man who loved books. Intelligent, somewhat meek and gentle, and seemingly wise. Could such a man also be a vicious criminal? How so? Yet, perhaps my prejudices are inclined towards the good? I went over and over my conversations and dealings with Tim Felix in my head, trying to find some small indication in his behaviour or demeanour which might lead me to think he was a cold-blooded killer. I could find nothing. Not a single clue. How strange is human nature that it is wont to form malefactors in the guise of parsons.

Roberts came towards me, looking stunned.

'I can't believe it,' he said to me, kicking the dirt off his right boot at the same time, 'Felix and Walker?'

'I can believe it of Walker,' I replied, 'but Tim Felix always seemed to me to be a gentle man.'

'Well, perhaps it's a mistake?'

I said nothing in reply to this. I could imagine how Roberts felt and how Mr Harvey would feel, to have had two killers in the camp all these weeks and months. They had to be angry, with themselves for not recognising the fact, but also with the bushrangers, for making them look fools. There would of course be a certain amount of relief that nothing had occurred to interrupt the progress of the work.

I heard the sound of the distant operator trying to get in touch with me and I excused myself and went back inside the shack. Indeed, I then took a message which expressed the incredulity of those down in Tennant Creek, that we had harboured two bushrangers. The message asked for details and I knew that, because the senders had had no direct contact with the two men, they were curious about them. There would be no condemnation, I was sure of that. Bushrangers were romantic figures to many Australians and if not regarded heroes, close to it.

I replied rather pompously that I couldn't pass on information which might prejudice future convictions and warned Stan Spillman that these criminals were dangerous and not to be trusted on any account. I knew the name of my colleague on the key at the other end without him telling me who he was. A Morse operator's way of sending those dots and dashes, and the gaps between, is as revealing as his voice. You get to recognise the pattern of the sender's keying and so his identity is evident to any of his regular colleagues on the receiving end of the line.

When I joined the other men around the fires that evening, the talk was all about the two bushrangers and Jack Ransome.

'I guessed he was a trooper of some kind,' said George Trout, airily, 'you could tell by those fancy shirts he wore.'

No one told this idiot man what a fool he made of himself.

Tucker Burdon stated, 'I don't care what anyone says, I'll never believe it of Tim Felix. He was a good bloke. He taught me how to play chess.'

And so the conversations ran, the believers and the non-believers, and those who had guessed long ago, and those who would never have guessed in a million years, and the clues that had made some suspicious, and the clues that had passed over the heads of others. All evening it went on, becoming more outrageous as the night grew older. Even our leaders, those wise and measured section head surveyors, were willing to inject an opinion just as wild as any other. You could have collected surmises and filled a sugar sack with them. It did at least give the camp something other than poles or galvanised wire to talk about.

Not long after this we reached Tomkinson Creek, where Mr Todd shook hands with Mr Harvey. Charles Todd was of course the Superintendent of Telegraphs, the man in charge of the whole enterprise, who had personally joined with the Northern Section to see his dream through. There remained a gap between the Northern Section and us, but this was temporarily joined by a pony express service, so that it could be announced that the line was finally open for traffic.

I became a busy man, with riders going back and forth carrying the messages which I had to send or receive. There was a need for more operators to assist me in this work, which became overwhelming. I think the pony express allowed Mr Todd to tell the government that the line was now open. History had been made and heroes had fulfilled their role. We had actually carried out an astonishing feat, now being connected directly to London and New York. It took all my faculties to comprehend such a wonder of science. A message, if not instantly could within a short while be passed from a businessman sitting at a desk in South Australia to a merchant in his office in the United Kingdom. The globe had suddenly shrunk from a massive sphere to one which could be stepped over.

And we had done that. *We* had done it. We, the surveyors, bushmen, polers, axemen, wiremen, operators, hauliers, drovers, cameleers and stockmen, others. Of course it had needed men of vision, like Charles Todd, to get it all going and governments to provide the money, but it had been workmen and labourers, the exploratory bushmen and pathfinders, who had made it happen. We had cut the trees, dug the holes, pinned the wire, and all the while facing storms and possible hostile tribes (at least one murder), suffering thirst (at least one death) and disease (one at least, from scurvy), living in terrible fly-infested insect-ridden conditions, getting lost (and yet another fatality), getting eaten by wild beasts (the saltie croc who had taken one of our compatriots in the north) in a vast dreamlike wilderness, facing mortality from poisonous reptiles and accidents, living with the stink of unsanitary conditions, in temperatures that blistered men's souls.

We, we had done it.

Yet, now that it was there, up and running, successfully completed, there would be banquets for the high and mighty to which we would not be invited. They would go in their fine clothes to town halls and the houses of the rich and toast themselves, calling each other great fellows for having achieved a miracle of engineering. They would pat each other on the back and kiss their wives on their cheeks, and puff out their chests in pride while we carried on, making sure the thing worked, keeping it maintained, sending their messages of congratulation between government officials and company chairmen.

I am minded of a poem in which a 14th Century stonemason is pushed to the back of the crowd while witnessing the inauguration of the cathedral he and his fellow stonemasons built, while the bishop and the mayor, and princes and prelates and generals are standing in their warm boots at the front, receiving all the accolades. How that stonemason's eyes travel up and down the spire, along the length of the magnificent cathedral as he mutters to himself, 'I bloody did that.'

That first day I was busy taking and sending messages. I dined on mutton and flat bread in the evening and felt like a king. Who was happier than me? Not a living soul on the earth. My beloved was on her way to my side, I had been promised a senior post in the Tennant Creek telegraph station and all was right with the world.

The very next day three more telegraph operators arrived. Andrew Garvey, I knew, but the two younger men were fresh faces to me. We all shook hands and then delighted in falling into trade talk and jargon. One of the men had a Morse key he himself had made in a workshop in Port Darwin, which had instead of an up-and-down movement, an arm which he could push from side-to-side. He had some sort of modification he had invented himself which allowed him to send dits on one side and dahs on the other. I had never seen the like and we marvelled over his ingenuity. He was one of the younger men and he took great pleasure in being lionised by his contemporaries.

I realised at that moment that there would be many new developments, improvements on the standard equipment, which would begin to appear in various corners of the telegraph world. Once you have the basic designs, there are those who will delight in modifying and improving the fundamental devices.

'How was it?' asked Andrew, when he managed to get me alone. 'Working on the project, I mean. I wish I could have been part of it. You have no idea how lucky you are to have been chosen to follow the erection of the wire.'

'I think I do have an idea,' I replied. 'I'm very proud.'

'So you should be. You must tell me all about your adventures when we have some time. I'm coming to Tennant Creek with you. I understand you've been appointed Stationmaster there? I heard Mr Harvey spoke very highly of you to Mr Todd. That must be very gratifying, but of course they need to reward you for your good work during the project. Quite rightly so. I am happy to be one of your acquaintances. I am looking forward to us working together in harmony.'

Andrew Garvey was a serious man, with a grave way of talking, and it was difficult not to echo the same gravity when replying.

'I very much appreciate your words, Andrew, and I'm sure we shall make good working colleagues.'

In fact right at that moment I felt I could work with all three of the men who had been sent to join me. Perhaps it would not always be the case: a telegraph station out in the middle of nowhere is a little like a ship and I would have to share many hours with my colleagues, maybe not getting a respite from their company for a long period. When you work very closely together, are thrown upon one another like a ship's crew, unable to escape the personal habits and behavioural tics of your fellows, they are likely to drive you mad after a while. These three blokes seemed fine at the moment, but I knew that in the end we would all get on one another's nerves in some way. The trick was to develop a shield around oneself and not let out or allow in any bad temperaments. It was the only way to survive being isolated with men you would not choose as friends or even allow as acquaintances in the world outside.

TWENTY-THREE

When it was time to leave the camp and go south to our telegraph station at Tennant Creek I chose to go without my three colleagues. Or rather, they chose to go separately from me. Afeeza had offered to take me on a camel, which he rightly said would be much swifter than going by bullock wagon. Andrew Garvey and the two younger telegraphers did not like the idea of sitting on a 'stinking camel' a long way up from the ground and indeed someone had to accompany the equipment going in the same direction. Thus I ended up being the only one who was prepared to sit up on a dromedary and sway back and forth as it walked.

'One of those beasts bit me once,' complained Andrew Garvey, 'on the neck. It was a most painful experience and one I do not wish to repeat. The wound required several stitches and an ointment that stung like a dozen bees. I don't think camels like me very much. Yes, and another spat a wad of chewed fodder into my face. No, no, not for me, thank you, all the same. I'll join you at the station and trust to my driver to get me there in one piece, rather than in pieces.'

The other two men were of the same mind.

Once we had started out, I felt like one of the Magi, a king of all I surveyed. Rocking to-and-fro on the one-humped ship of the desert I was high enough to see miles around me. The dried-blood and stale-mustard coloured landscape undulated away on all sides like the waves of a frozen sea with the occasional outcrop of rocks imitating storm-battered lighthouses. Indeed I could imagine myself back at the birth of the Christ-child, offering my beautiful brass Morse key as a gift more rare than gold (which it would have been in those far off times).

Riding a camel is an experience not to be missed by any man. I hoped Afeeza and his string of dromedaries would be around when Sally arrived so that I could get her up on one of these lustrous-eyed beauties, no matter that they were rank to the nostrils, especially on a hot, steamy day with the sun burning theirs coats. Yes they had foul habits, yes they were stubborn sometimes and vicious too, but when they were in a docile, willing mood there was no transport to beat them. Afeeza loved all three camels he owned and spoke of them more fondly than he spoke of his wives. He slept amongst them, smelled like them, talked to them as one might talk to one's own children. For the most part they were obedient to his commands and only kicked up a fuss on rare occasions, taking out their wrath on others rather than their master.

'The stars are much in splendour tonight.'

We were camped in a hollow overlooked by some black-footed rock-wallabies who were gathered on a ridge staring down at the fire. I had not been looking at the stars, but at the silver wire overhead, marvelling at the fact that it was at that very moment carrying messages back and forth across continents. This slim streak of metal that now ran from Adelaide to Port Darwin hummed with words that would undoubtedly change people's lives. The singing wire, some called it. Certainly it sang in the wind, but it also sang with internal songs, its hymns carried from end to end by the flow of electricity. What a miracle of science and progress! What an astounding leap forward for the world of men! Such an invention took my breath away. God himself must have been shaking his head in wonder, thinking, 'Those creatures I created are now creating great marvels themselves. I gave them voices so that they could talk to one another over a few yards and now they've improved on my work and can talk over thousands of miles.' It was an amazing achievement and I was part of the phenomenon.

'Look how they blaze in the sky.'

Afeeza was in poetic mood and this was not the first utterance of the kind. Indeed, he was right, in the heavens was a rash of stars as white as surf breaking down one of Australia's long beaches.

'You are Omar Khayyam tonight, Afeeza,' I said.

He snorted derisively. 'Do not speak to me of that man. He is a boil on a camel's arse. I spit.' And indeed, he did spit with great force and volume, amazing me with the amount of viscous fluid that left his lips and shot out into the darkness.

I had recently been reading Omar Khayyam's 'Rubaiyat' poem translated by a Mr Fitzgerald, the copy given to me by the notorious Captain Midnight in his guise as the schoolmaster Tim Felix. The words had impressed me and I had learned one or two stanzas which I tended to quote when the mood was on me, but I had forgotten for some reason that Afeeza and his cameleer compatriots did not approve of the Eastern poet for some reason. They would not tell me why Omar was not in favour, but they cursed him whenever I mentioned his name.

I quickly changed the subject.

'Do you think,' I said, nodding at the silhouettes of the wallabies, 'that they know we are eating one of their brothers?'

Wallaby meat was roasting on a spit over our fire.

'They know and in the night they will come and beat us to death with their big feet.'

'You're not serious?'

'Of course not, Sikandar. They are stupid creatures.'

I knew that, but I had not been sure Afeeza did. He believed in ghosts, demons and fairies, so why wouldn't he believe that animals could feel anger and revenge? How complex are the minds of men. It seemed very odd to me that a man like Afeeza, full of courage, full of practical knowledge on how to survive in the wilderness, should be frightened of mythical beings and would even deviate from an easy path, taking a much more dangerous and difficult route, in order to avoid an area where such non-existent creatures might be said to dwell.

'Are you going to make us some bread, to go with our meat?' I asked.

'Ah,' his bulky form rose in the firelight, 'I shall heat the stones and prepare the bread.'

It was flat bread of course, not one that would rise, but I loved the texture and taste of it. Afeeza had a special skill of cooking such bread until it was just right, not underdone yet not burned. His hands, when he worked the flour, seemed to have a magical quality. I had asked him to teach me the art, but he seemed reluctant to pass on his ability.

We ate and drank in the starlight that lit the hills around us. The colour having drained from the rocks and earth once the sun had gone down left the wilderness a strange grey bleak place that seemed so dreary it filled my spirit with a sense of dread. I knew this was fanciful and had no real grounding in reason, but when you are virtually alone in a landscape that is so far from civilisation, your deeper fears of the supernatural emerge. I had retreated in my mind to the kind of man that roamed the world before tools were invented. In every rock, every shadow, every skeletal tree, a soul had welled into being with the setting of the sun, and these were now regarding me. I could not look at any corner of our surroundings without seeing a shape that might start up from its position and walk towards me. The worst part of this feeling was the fact that I could not discuss it with Afeeza, who could be spooked at the merest suggestion of inanimate objects having life.

We made the discovery when we were three days out.

The pestful flies were driving me to such a high state of irritability with their continual efforts to get moisture from my eyes, mouth and nose, that I was distracted almost to insanity. They were small blowflies more terrible for their persistence than their numbers. You flicked them off with a switch and they were back again within a split second. It was because I was so engrossed with attempts at ridding myself of these relentless buggers that I almost missed seeing him.

I did however catch a flash of colour on a hill to the east, despite being employed. It was not one of the muted ochre hues which was ingrained in the red centre, but much brighter. Brushing away flies for the hundredth time I followed the shining wire which looped from pole to pole with my eyes. I found myself straining my eyes in the dazzling sunlight to study what I thought was a flag or banner high on a rounded hill. Then, as we drew closer I recognised the flashy red shirt that I had seen worn so many times before. Jack Ransome, the policeman, was sitting on top of the low hill, his back against one of our telegraph poles. He was watching us approach, his eyes hidden under the brim of his hat.

'Sikandar!' cried Afeeza, from behind me.

'I know,' I replied. 'He must be sick or something.'

We both took our camels up the slope to the top of the hill, Afeeza leading the riderless beast by a loose rein. Still as we approached there was no movement from Jack. His hands were linked in his lap in a sort of peaceful pose, as if he were waiting patiently to be called in for something like a job interview or doctor's appointment. I knew he was dead even before I saw the bullet wounds in his head. The body was covered in insects and his bootless feet had been gnawed at by some carnivorous creature. After getting my camel to kneel in order to let me dismount, the smell hit my nostrils and I retched a couple of times.

'Gone,' said Afeeza, unnecessarily.

Poor old Jack. He had worried so much about being lost in the wastelands of the red centre he had never been without a brightly coloured shirt on his back. Well it had served its purpose. We had found him all right, but too late.

The murderers had propped him up in a sitting position and had presumably placed his hat on his head. There were two savage-looking holes in his face: one below the right eye, the other above it in the forehead. The back of his skull revealed a misshapen cavity the size of a man's fist. His handgun was missing, presumably in the possession of the killer or killers. Of course I believed I knew who had done this to him and they would be far away by now, probably on their way down to Adelaide or up to Palmerston. It was possible that this act had been perpetrated by the local Aborigines. They may have obtained firearms from somewhere. But given the circumstances I believed it to be Smith and Walker, who had no doubt lain in wait for their pursuer.

'Who did this thing?' asked Afeeza, in a matter-of-fact tone. I guessed he had seen worse in his time.

I told him my suspicions.

'We must bury him,' Afeeza said. 'He stink very bad and the dingo-dogs smell him from far off. And the birds have eat him, I think, just a little bit. Maybe crow-birds? I don't know. Anyway, we get him in the ground where he can be safe. Worms, yes, but not dogs. It is not good to feed the dingo-dogs on people. They get use to it and like it too much. Pretty soon you find them sniffing you while you sleep, eh?'

There are no vultures in Australia, not that I have heard, but I knew wedge-tailed eagles would eat carrion. Even as this thought came to me I looked up instinctively to see one of these beautiful raptors circling, gliding on the warm air above us. Had this been the bird that had fed on Jack Ransome's feet? More likely it was a dingo, or a rodent. I didn't like the thought of such a magnificent creature as a wedge-tail tearing at rotting human flesh. It was not a pleasant image.

We found a soft patch of earth and began digging a hole. Afeeza was a reluctant worker when it came to this kind of job and I had to bite my tongue several times, having the urge to complain about his slackness. He lifted very little earth on each shovel and his movements were slow and laboured with many pauses between to simply stare at the horizon or drink some water. Each activity took him an extraordinary amount of time before he lifted his shovel again. I think he believed this kind of toil was beneath the dignity of a cameleer. I had heard about 'untouchables' when I stopped in India on the voyage to Australia. It had me wondering if this was the kind of work they did. If it was, then Afeeza was indeed making a great effort, for most Indians of caste would not even contemplate doing an untouchable's work. Yet, was I right? Did Musselmans like Afeeza have castes or was it only Hindus? It was all very confusing to a young man born in an English cottage on the other side of the world.

Even before it was half-finished the sweat was pouring down my back, soaking my shirt, and running from my hat-band down my face. I had dug holes for poles when men were sick and now I was digging a hole to take the body of a friend. And he had become a friend, Jack Ransome, even though he was a policeman.

'I think it's deep enough,' I said, sucking in hot air for breath. 'Let's lay him to rest.'

'Not deep enough,' grunted my companion. 'They will dig him out – the dogs and others.'

'Then we must both work harder,' I replied, pointedly. 'My strength is being sapped.'

It made no difference to Afeeza's work rate. It was still slow, still many shovel-spits behind mine. In the end I moved most of the dirt.

When the grave was finally ready we placed the body in it wrapped in a blanket. Then we piled rocks on the mound to deter any grave-robbing animals. Jack Ransome, the policeman in the guise of a newspaper reporter, had arrested his last criminal. I said a few words over his tomb. I can't remember now what they were, because I was a little in shock. It had occurred to me while we were patting down the hump and sticking a cross made of broken branches on it that the two bushrangers might still be in the vicinity. They had killed one man, a custodian of the law, they would not hesitate to kill any others who threatened their liberty. I scanned the horizon looking for signs of horsemen. There were none that I could see, but that didn't mean they weren't there. Heat hazes hide a great deal in desert places.

'We'll sleep with loaded rifles tonight,' I said to Afeeza, who was always armed to the teeth anyway.

He put his hand on the hilt of his broad-bladed curved dagger.

'I will open their throats, if they come,' he assured me. 'I have meet men like these two dogs many times before.'

Once we had camped for the night, we spoke at length about the killing. I explained to Afeeza that Jack Ransome was a policeman and that the other two men were lawless killers. He did not seem overly impressed by either revelation. He told me he had came from a region in Balochistan where such things were common. In fact, I don't believe he thought any worse of Walker and Smith, mainly because, as he mentioned casually, Jack Ransome's wounds were bravely in the front and not in his back. Afeeza was from a place where only the strongest and most ruthless men survived and what I regarded as an unspeakable act he simply saw as normal behaviour in a place where survival depends on either having dependable friends or eliminating enemies.

'We have to keep a good lookout for these men,' I warned Afeeza. 'I hope they've gone, but we can't be sure.'

Afeeza pointed to the side of his head. 'My ears are sharp,' then to his nostrils, 'but my nose is sharper. I shall hear them. I shall smell them. Even if they come in darkness, Sikandar, they shall die like lizards with their bellies and throats slit. This I promise to you, my friend.'

I believed him.

The thought that had obviously been bothering me ever since we had found the body, now fixed itself in my mind and refused to be ignored. Tam Donald had left the northern camp accompanying Jack Ransome. So where was my young Scottish friend? Had the murderers killed him too? If so, where was the body? Surely it should be sitting next to Jack? Or had they kidnapped him, taken him as a hostage? I could not imagine Tam going with them without putting up a fight. Was he then injured, wounded in some way, and therefore possibly dying? And what could I do about it, if he were in the hands of the two bushrangers? Nothing, at the moment. I needed to get to the telegraph station so that I could send a message and get the right people searching for him. I was following a shining galvanised iron wire, pole by pole, to the station, that was true, but I had no equipment with me – apart from my personal key – to use to tap into the wire.

Still, over the next few days I studied the wide and distant horizons around us, seeking any sign of dark figures on the plains. My camel gave me greater height than riding on a wagon or horse and I felt this was a blessed advantage. No longer was I a king, a magus, but now a nomad with terrible enemies in the wilderness. How had I, a horseman's son from a gentle rural upbringing in a peaceful English county come to this? This was a desperate life, threatened not only by death from thirst, or loss of direction, or hunger, but from violent men who killed for a living. My rifle was in my hands the whole time, though ironically I was reluctant to use it to get meat for our dinners in case the shot should be heard. I was also afraid for Andrew and the telegraphers in the wagon heading for Tennant Creek, in case they should come up against the two killers. Those city men were no match for a brace of bushrangers without consciences. The driver might put up a fight, but I doubted the three telegraphers would even know what to do with a gun.

I spent my hours swaying on the back of my dromedary, thinking about Jack's end. Had he fought it out with the bushrangers, exchanging threat for threat, shot for shot? He was not the kind of man who would roll over at the least opposition. Or had they seen him coming, expected him, waited in ambush and shot him down before he even had a chance to confront his quarry? In the end had the hunter become the hunted? Or perhaps they waited until he went to sleep and crept up on him in the middle of the night, firing down into his face. In my mind's eye I could see Walker doing this terrible act, but not Tim Felix. Walker would do it with a sneer on his face and make a joke afterwards, but Tim – Tim Felix, possibly Tom Smith – he was an intelligent Christian man with, I believed, a soul and therefore a conscience. Surely such a man would have woken Jack Ransome and challenged him to a duel? I could not reconcile my knowledge of Tim Felix with a cold-blooded killer of men. Only his ruthlessness at chess gave any clue to his real profession.

'How far are we away?' I asked Afeeza one morning. 'Two days?'

'Maybe three, Sikandar.'

'I don't think they're around, are they?'

He looked genuinely puzzled. 'Who is around?'

'The men who killed Jack Ransome.'

Afeeza drew in a deep breath and shrugged. Clearly he had not even thought of Walker and Smith for several days. 'I think they are gone away – far away. Long, long gone. Men who kill a policeman know they will be hunted like animals. I am sorry for their lives. They will be caught and they will be hanged and God will tear their souls to pieces with his teeth and nails. They will suffer for all time a terrible fate.'

It was true, I reminded myself. The police are usually assiduous enough when it came to hunting down murderers, but if the victim is one of their own, they will step up their enthusiasm to the highest pitch, will leave no stone unturned, will work to exhaustion to catch such a malefactor. Murder a policeman and you have a pack of savage blood-thirsty detectives on your trail for the rest of your life. His kind will take no rest until you are captured and executed, or slain in the taking. However, I did not feel sorry for them in any way. I hoped they would die a terror-stricken painful death for what they did to Jack Ransome. Yes, Jack had been a policeman, a profession not universally liked, but I had known him simply as a man, and had thought him a good one.

We reached Tennant Creek without further incident. The building work I had helped to start seemed now established. Someone on the porch saw us coming and came out in the sun to greet us, a man about my own age, perhaps younger. He looked clean and healthy under his broad-brimmed hat and his face was shaven. I got my dromedary to kneel and then slid off his back. The man thrust a hand towards me.

'John Gardner,' he said, 'Assistant Stationmaster.'

'Alex McKenzie.'

He smiled, broadly, 'Ah, our Stationmaster. Welcome to Tennant Creek Telegraph Station Mr McKenzie. But you've already been here, eh? You helped to lay the foundations.'

TWENTY-FOUR

The station was already almost fully staffed. It just wanted me and the three telegraphers who were following. There were even two wives and a child who had come up from Adelaide with the telegraph operators. Water was available, pumped from a nearby spring. John Gardner showed me to my quarters, which were basic and bare, but more luxurious than I had been used to. Afeeza went off somewhere out the back of the buildings looking for another cameleer who had come from the south. The place looked busy and thriving. There were two hauliers unloading more equipment, supplies and building materials out front, while inside – through the open doorways – I could see a telegrapher sitting at his key, hard at work. Clearly my daydream of traffic flowing, as I had followed the wire down to the creek, were no longer flights of fancy.

Afeeza brought the rest of my goods to me a short while after I had washed and changed my clothes. Then we had a meal together before I was shown over the station by John Gardner. I then called all the staff together in the telegraph office, including the two women, and asked those present if they had seen anything of two – or three – men on horseback. I described all three: Walker, Smith and Tam. I was hoping someone would say the trio had indeed passed through on their way down to Adelaide and – aware that Tam would probably be travelling with the threat of violence and death hanging over him – that the third man was strangely quiet and reticent.

Pete Goody, one of the operators, shook his head.

'The only blokes who've been through here, have been Afghans and hauliers.' He looked to the others in the room for confirmation, which he got with heads nodding, then added, 'Why, boss?'

'A man's been killed – murdered – out on the trail. Another one's missing. There're two bushrangers out there, deadly killers. We must keep a sharp eye open for them. The two men I described first. The third man is the missing one. He may have been kidnapped by the two killers.'

One of the women let out a little cry and put the knuckles of her right hand into her mouth. The others all stared at me in disbelief, even the duty operator. In the background the equipment was clicking and clacking away furiously, ignored for the moment.

John Gardner said, 'Bushrangers? Out here? What the hell are they doing out in the middle of nowhere?'

'Hiding, initially. Running from the law. They were being pursued by an Adelaide policeman by the name of Jack Ransome...'

'Ah.' The operator on duty at that time spun round on his stool. He was a gangly man whose name I hadn't yet been given. 'We've passed messages on for him, haven't we Pete? They're wondering where he is.'

'Dead,' I said, dramatically. 'That's where.'

'Yeah,' replied his colleague. 'Murdered though?' He whistled. 'You'd expect it might come from blacks, but bushrangers?'

'I know what I'm talking about,' I told them, in case there was some doubt still hanging in the air, 'I've spent the best part of the last year with all three men. It's been a strange experience, travelling with killers and detectives, being in the middle of it all.

Anyway, keep your eyes skinned. Now, I have to get a message to Adelaide telling them what's happened. Can you let me near the key, fellah?'

'You just give it to me, boss,' said the gangly operator, clearly not going to move. 'I'll get it out – and we ought to tell Port Darwin too.'

I hesitated for a moment, not liking the idea that I couldn't send my own messages. But this man was on duty and it was his shift I was interrupting. The others went about their business elsewhere, only John Gardner staying with me. The operator returned to his work and I sat at a table in the corner writing out my message, which I then duly gave to the gangly bloke who now told me his name was Phil Skinner. Skinner sent the message with an 'urgent' tag on it, but not long afterwards Jack Ransome's superiors in Adelaide were rattling messages down the line to me, asking me more questions and taking over the line completely. Since only one of us could be sending or receiving at any one time, I ordered Skinner to go and get a coffee while I dealt with the traffic.

Once the flurry of messages was over, I handed back the key to Skinner and sat back to contemplate. I decided there was not a lot more I could do. I had passed on all the information I had to the authorities and now it was up to them to catch the bushrangers. My job, my responsibility, now lay with the station. I had to become familiar with the geography, not only of my immediate surrounds, but also further afield. Among the staff I had spoken to were two wiremen who would, I was pretty sure, be constantly going out to repair breaks in the wire. Poles would need replacing from time to time, when the termites got them, and there would be lightning strikes, shorts due to rainwater, cuts due to interference from Aborigines, a whole basket of problems. It was now my job to keep this station running smoothly. I hoped I was up to it. My man-handling skills had never been tested. I'd never been in charge of any staff before this day. I felt a weight on my shoulders and a flutter of panic in my gut. This would either be the making or breaking of me.

I spent the rest of the day walking around, inspecting the perimeter of our station, climbing rises to get a feel for the area, and then sorting out my kit before going to see John again.

'I'm sure you've been working things fine, John, without me – but I want to get my hands on now. Sit with me and we'll work out a new roster for the men which includes me.'

There was no way I was going to simply 'manage' the station. I needed to keep up, even improve, my skill at Morse. John was however surprised.

'You don't have to go on shift,' he said. 'You'll have enough to do – administrative stuff and generally managing the place.'

'I need to, John, to stay sane. Look where we are. Out in the red centre of a huge country, almost a continent in itself. If I isolate myself from the outside world, I'll certainly go barmy. Anyway, I don't want to lose my touch. I might not stay as the manager, if I don't do the job well enough, and have to go back to operating.' I paused before continuing. 'This is not going to be easy, you know. I'm sure you've already had clashes between the people here. Human beings do not do well when thrown together in a small bunch who sit on each other's shoulders day in, day out. We'll all get on each other's nerves, there'll certainly be trouble at times between the wives, and between married couples, and Lordhopefullynot, woman trouble between two men.

'No, this is not going to be easy, not by a long chalk. It'll be a struggle to keep the tension from overwhelming us. We need to sort out some activities between the two of us – entertainment and activities to keep the troops happy, so to speak. Sing-songs, music, plays, dances – not formal stuff, you understand, but a fiddle and a jig – the sort of thing we did on the ship. During the day men not on duty can go out shooting, or even better, trying to log the wildlife, if we've got anyone who's interested in that kind of thing. I certainly am. We've got a unique opportunity here, to study – what? – rocks and minerals, birds, mammals, insects, weather patterns, you name it, we don't know much about it. I hope we've got someone here who's interested and bright enough to lead us in something like that...' John was looking very sceptical.

'What?' I said. 'You don't agree?'

'Sorry, boss...'

Boss. That sounded very strange to my ears. I'm not sure I was ready for it.

'Alex. My name's Alex.'

'Sorry Alex, but I think you're worrying about nothing. The men are quite happy, simply working and doing their own thing.'

I sighed. 'They are at the moment. This is all new to them. But I've just spent a year with a bigger bunch than this and we were all at each other's throats by the end of the project. Believe me, this will only work if we *make* it work. The worst part of this job will be getting along with one another without trouble flaring. I know what I'm talking about, John. You'll probably have a station of your own pretty soon – the Company must think a lot of you to make you my assistant. John, if you just leave things to trundle along, they'll fester inside and then break out into open sores. You need to stay on top of the general feeling of the camp – sorry, station – and be sensitive to any undercurrents. Look, even now you and I are in disagreement. If I simply did things my way and ignore what you're saying, without giving you an explanation, you'd go away and spend the next few days brooding on my imperiousness. Right?'

He shrugged. 'Maybe – even though I don't use words like that – imperiousness.'

'Too pretentious?'

'I don't use words like that, either.'

I grinned and made a wry face. 'Sorry, I've spent a great deal of time with a man who does – unhappily a very devious man. He uses words like that a lot and he's taught me to use them. I thought his name was Tim Felix and that he was a schoolteacher, but I learned it's probably Captain Midnight, and he's without doubt a cold-blooded killer. However, that's neither here nor there. What I'm trying to say is, if you give people too much idle time, to think, those thoughts will sometimes turn sour and problems grow way out of proportion. You have to keep people busy and not just with work, with leisure activities too. There'll be enough back-stabbing, even if we do manage to keep most of them content.'

'You paint a very gloomy picture, boss.'

We were immediately back to 'boss' and I left it there, knowing I would be fighting a losing battle.

'Good, 'cause that's what it might be, John, if we don't get on top of it straight away. Now, the first thing I want you to do is arrange a dinner for everyone tonight. I want all the station personnel there, except those on duty. The Afghans to be included.'

John stiffened. 'Some of us won't like that – sharing our table with non-Christians.'

'Too bad. One of those cameleers is a good friend of mine. I won't have them excluded. And you've raised another point there. We obviously don't have a minister here, to do Sunday service. Any lay preachers?'

'Ah, that's where I'm ahead of you, boss. One of the operators, Sam Pickering, he likes to preach. He's a Methodist. A bit fire and brimstone, but he's all we've got. There's quite a mix here, as you can imagine – Presbyterians mostly, but one Catholic. I'm not sure he'll want to join with us, but he may do. We're all Christians, after all.'

'Yeah, sometimes it doesn't work as smoothly as that though. Any Jewish operators?'

'No – an atheist, but no Jews.'

'Well, not much we can do about non-believers. Leave him to his own devices. He may want to walk out and find some peace in the natural world around us, if he's got any soul at all.'

I paused and went into a short reverie as I thought of those times I had stood alone somewhere out in the wilderness of the Australian outback and felt the mystical fingers of the land gently touching my soul. Tim Felix had been vehemently against the idea that the landscape had any kind of spirit, repeatedly saying we had 'left animism behind with the cave men', but for myself, I can never deny the unseen rush of some kind of unfathomable life-force entering my soul when I stand in a wide open wild place amongst the rocks, trees, staring out over a vast varicoloured landscape of an untamed country.

A cough from John Gardner brought me back.

I continued where I left off.

'If we do get any others – like Jews, or Quakers, or whatever, they'll either have to join in or take themselves off and do their own service. We can't work miracles, even if we do want to keep everyone as contented as possible. Now, changing the subject, do we post sentries at night? How friendly are the natives? Are they hostile?'

I was aware that our station was just south of Attack Creek. I was also wondering whether it might not be a good thing to make contact with any tribes in the region, to show we ourselves were friendly and not here to interfere with them in any way. It would not be an easy thing to do, not without someone who spoke their language. Maybe something I would have to leave until an Aborigine tracker or drover came through, someone who could help us with talking to the locals.

'Haven't had any trouble, so far, boss. No, we don't have any guards at night. You think we should?'

'Well, it might be a good idea, at least until those bushrangers have been caught, but don't alarm the women. Tell them it's just a precaution and that there's nothing to worry about.'

'Still, they will worry.'

'Yes, I know. I'll see you at dinner, John. Set some tables outside in the cool. Don't forget my Afghans. You can put them on a separate small table at the end, if you want. They'll prefer it that way, since they eat with their fingers and might feel a bit out of place with us using cutlery. I'm not sure they even like tables, but I'm not putting them on the ground. Place them on the end near me, so I can talk to them on occasion.' I had a sudden thought. 'We have got tables and cutlery?'

John grinned again. 'All the comforts of home, boss.'

'Well, I bet not *all*, but a few, anyway.'

The dinner went well. The two wives did the cooking, one of them the spouse of Pete Goody, the other of a wireman, Dave Davison. It was certainly a change to get tucker that had taste and texture, and didn't require a machete to cut the meat, which was tender. Our cook in the line camp had been barely trained in boiling an egg, let alone making a decent stew or frying an edible steak. Afeeza had fed me on the trail and he *was* a good cook, but he carried bagfuls of herbs and spices with him. He insisted on adding these colourful and piquant ingredients to every meal, saying it was absolutely necessary to season food and was very reluctant to leave them out, no matter how much I protested. Once or twice he yielded to my pleas, but even though he told me he had not put a grain of spice in the meal, I knew he lied, I could still taste them.

After the dinner we had some entertainment. John Gardner played the squeeze-box and we sang along with the tunes. That night I slept in a proper bed for the first time in many, many months. At first it was difficult to drop off, since every time I turned over I could hear the new springs twanging. As a stationmaster I had a bedroom to myself, which also served as an office and a general living room. But the walls were thin and in the adjoining room there was a profoundly loud snorer who started up about one-thirty and did not cork it until six. I almost wished myself back out in the wilderness with Afeeza where the sounds of the night had come from creatures other than humans and were more comforting.

The next week or two went very well. I found I had it in me to supervise people. In the line camps men like me had been regarded by most as trimmings. The really important jobs in the camps consisted of cutting down trees, shaving them, putting them in holes, attaching wire and insulators to them, and then moving on. Yes, they knew the line needed to be tested, but that was of little interest to the gangs whose work it was to erect the structure. Unless I helped with the poling or wiring, I was a frill on the garment.

Here on the station, I was an experienced operator and technician, a man who knew his stuff well, and whose skills were highly respected.

There were new gangs of men coming up the line now, with wagons carrying metal poles made in England. These were to replace those in areas where the termites were ravaging the stripped trunks which we had spent so much sweat and labour erecting. There were poles up north that were rotting with the wet. Those too, had to be replaced, along with the incorporation of new ceramic insulators where necessary. Already the line was undergoing modernisation and Tennant Creek was one of a dozen telegraph stations covering the two-thousand mile stretch between Adelaide and Port Darwin. I was immensely proud to be the Stationmaster of such an up-to-the-minute enterprise.

I had put myself down for shifts alongside the other operators as agreed with John Gardner. On my first watch I delighted in having that brass instrument, the Morse key, between the fingers of my right hand once more. This was no line test, sending messages to myself, this was live communications. I felt like a violinist must feel with a bow between his fingers after a long period without playing. The Morse code came out as music, the dashes quavers, the dots as crochets, filling my head with its rhythmic sounds. It flowed with a beautiful symmetry and made me feel like an artiste whose medium was electricity. It coursed through my arteries, my veins, my very blood carrying vital songs to those up and down the line. O, the singing wire was mine to caress again.

One morning I was busy receiving messages, which I did not ordinarily read with any great interest. Most of them were to and from merchants and farmers who found that their profits had risen substantially due to being able to find markets for their goods a great deal easier and earlier than previously using the telegraph networks. So I was routinely sending and receiving these rather boring epistles, hardly bothering to take notice of the information except to correct words which had been misspelled or to fill in characters which had been missed.

I had woken that morning to find two spear-carrying Aborigines outside, staring along the line of poles, then up at the wire. I watched them for a while until they walked away shaking their heads. I knew what they were thinking: how did these white fellahs believe this stupid fence could keep animals in or out? Their bewilderment with the 'fence' had amused me too and I was in a good mood as I worked. Then around eleven in the morning the name of a ship on one of the messages caught my eye and on reading what followed I received the huge shock that numbed my senses.

> TO COPELAND LINE OFFICES ADELAIDE
>
> MY SAD DUTY TO REPORT *SHEERNESS SANDS* STOP OUT OF HARWICH STOP BELIEVED LOST AT SEA HAVING FAILED TO REACH SINGAPORE STOP JOSEPH SPIERS OVERSEER

Lost at sea? My darling Sally?

I let out a terrible wail that had three concerned people in the operating room within seconds. Tears were streaming down my cheeks. I could hardly blub the words out to get them to understand the reason for my loss of sanity. The women were then called, women being better at handling grief than men. They led me away murmuring words of comfort which hardly even penetrated my reasoning. All I had in my head were images of Sally drowning in a cold green ocean, without me to perish alongside her, as should have happened. I could not but help imagine the terror that must have overwhelmed my sweetheart. Why had I not left her in her safe library, back in England, surrounded by the books she loved and close to the parents who cared for her? What selfish feelings had possessed me to ask her to join me here, halfway around the world, so far from the country of her birth? I alone was responsible for the agony and horror of the manner of her death. I kept repeating these accusations, levelled at me and my actions, to the two ladies who tried to comfort me and who dismissed such words as the natural ravings of a man who was bereft and hopelessly trapped in a cycle of self-blame.

Afeeza came to me, sat with me, prayed for me. It was the custom, he said, in his country, to stay with the bereaved friend until the grief became bearable. He would not leave my side. Refused to sleep until I had lost consciousness myself. When I wept his strong arm was around my shoulders, preventing my body from falling apart, keeping it together so that my soul would not fly out into the ether and be lost to me.

The hours passed and my grief subsided at least to a bearable level. Someone gave me a book to read, to keep me occupied. It was on Australian trees. Why they thought such an edifying work would lift me out of the blackness which had besieged me, I have no idea, but actually just flicking through the pages in a desultory fashion, looking at the drawings of ghost gums, river reds and black box, did seem to calm my agitated state. Without trying I was able to discover there are 700 kinds of eucalyptus trees scattered over this mighty land, along with trees with such exotic names as red bloodwood and lemon scented ironwood. Boppels, cedars, wattles, the pages flowed with beautiful drawings by botanists and did indeed occupy my mind for short periods, but only in the way a passing butterfly might distract a man who is lost in a forest.

In the end, I took a grip of my spirit. I decided the best thing for me was to immerse myself in work. So with the help of my staff I set about improving the station, adding new outhouses and building fences to keep out the wildlife. One morning on a walk around the perimeter I found a blue-tongued lizard and spent an hour watching him at his own work, fascinated by the speed of his tongue. Some rock wallabies came and watched me watching the lizard and got me wondering about who else was watching. God? I wasn't very happy with the Creator, right at that moment, thinking he was more of a Destructor. If he had any responsibility in it all, he had certainly destroyed my life.

I heard the sound of an axe biting into wood and though in truth I lacked any real interest in the activity I found myself wandering into the direction of the cutters. I found two men chopping down a tree which was too close to a new building we had put up. As was the practice, one man was swinging the axe while the other had his hand on the tree. The second man was there for the safety of the cutter. Although an axeman cuts a tree so that it should fall in a certain direction, trees are notoriously fickle and are inclined to change their minds about their destination. You can't always see which way a tree is going to fall, before it actually does begin its descent to earth, but the man touching the trunk can gauge instantly in which direction the lumber is heading. If in a dangerous one, he yells to the cutter, or even reaches out and grabs him by the collar to wrench him out of harm's way.

Watching these two men I could not help but ponder on what might have happened to another axeman, my friend young Tam Donald. Had he been killed and his body left lying in some cleft between rocks? Or had he managed to escape the murderers and got himself lost, and thus thirsted to death? Or, to be more positive, perhaps he was indeed on his way either north or south, to the safety of a town? I hoped Thomas Hamish Donald was safe from harm. He was an innocent abroad, that youth, and did not deserve the kind of death a man could suffer in the outback.

I thought about the conversation I had once had with Tom Smith in his guise as Tim Felix. I now believed it was not about ordering chaos, or chaotic ordering. Order did not come into it. There was chaos everywhere, with no attempt at order to be seen, either from Nature or Man.

That night I had put myself down for dog watch duty. I had just the day before succumbed to the pressure from the rest of the staff to dispense with the onerous sentry duty. It was argued by the others that the local Aborigines had shown no signs of hostility and that there was always the duty operator awake and ready to give the alarm if anything untoward occurred. I did consider, as I sat by my key, which was locked down at the time to enable the current to pass from one end of the line to the other, that there might be a nomadic tribe who could take offence at our presence. Indeed it was possible we were taking water from a source owned by a group we had not met, or had built our station on sacred ground. This was not our spiritual homeland and we were not able to read signs which were obvious to Aborigines, or gauge the changing moods of local men.

A clicking sound in the quietness of the room indicated a message was going through the relay. It required no effort on my part, but I stood up and stretched, my muscles being stiffened by continual sitting. There were sounds outside in the night – animals of one sort or another – but they were more comforting than cause for any apprehension. After over a year I found utter silence more disturbing. I yawned and leafed through some correspondence, knowing I would have to catch up with it sooner or later, having been lax in that direction since the bad news. It was while I was filling in the call log that a faint shadow crossed the page, causing me to look up and towards the doorway. What I saw there caused my gut to constrict with fear: a tall lean figure with Jack Ransome's fancy revolver in his hand.

Walker spoke softly.

'Recognise this?'

I nodded.

'Thought you'd seen the last of me, eh, McKenzie?'

Any answer I might have had in my head remained lodged there. My whole being was transfixed by that weapon, the black muzzle of which was pointed at my chest. He stood tall and languid, stooping a little under the low doorway, a toothless smile on his face. The light from the oil lamp softened his features, shadows filling the hollows of his face, making him less cadaverous than I remembered him, more human. Yet that same sallow lamplight seemed to bring out the evil in eyes that regarded me with contempt and disgust. Why did this man hate me so much? It seemed he did not need a reason, perhaps reasoning did not come into it. Maybe he had taken an innate dislike to me, the moment he laid eyes on me, and was like a wild beast unable to ignore his instincts.

'Cat got your tongue?'

'No,' I managed to rasp, trying to assemble a smile myself. 'How – how are you, Walker?'

His grin widened to reveal the stained teeth.

'You must think I'm fuckin' brainless, McKenzie.'

'No, no.' My voice must have got louder because he gave a quick glance out into the night.

'Keep your voice down, or I'll kill you now.'

I swallowed, hard. 'Are you going to do that anyway?'

He grunted. 'Huh. Did you think I wouldn't come after you? Crowin' were you, that you'd got rid of Sholto Walker?'

'Your name's Thomas.'

He extended the gun hand.

'Don't tell me what my fuckin' name is, I'll tell you, you bastard – understand? I'm the boss now.' He waggled the gun. 'This makes me the boss.'

'I was never your boss.'

'You acted like you was. High and mighty fuckin' shithead. You thought you was Lord Almighty, eh? You want to know what this thing in my hand can do to you? It'll make a hole in you that will have you screamin' for your mother. I'm goin' to kill you now. Look in my eyes, fuckhead. Look in my eyes and see what's comin' you snotty bastard…'

'Oh my God,' I whispered.

'He won't help you, McKenzie.'

I could see the long thin dirty-nailed finger tightening on the trigger and I knew I was going to die in great pain. Then suddenly Walker's eyes widened and he jerked violently, lurching forward. He threw himself at me like a wildcat hurling itself at its prey. His left arm flew in a wide wild gesture, his right arm remained stiffly out front, still pointing the gun at my chest. Then the weapon exploded and I was flung backwards.

I crashed onto the edge of the desk, hurting my spine and this was the only pain I felt at first, until the shock of the fiery agony in my right shoulder seared into my brain. Through the haze of bewilderment over what had happened and dealing with the pain, I realised Tam Donald was standing over me, inspecting my wound, stuffing a wad of cloth into the cavity torn by the bullet. Through his open legs I could see the twitching body of Walker, an axe buried in his back. That axe had no doubt split his spine, its blade hardly visible it was so deep in the bushranger's flesh.

'How are you, Alex? Are you hurt bad?'

'I – I think so, Tam.'

'We'll get you to a doctor, don't you fret.'

By this time I became vaguely aware of other people crowding into the room, some asking what was going on, others staring at the dead body on the floor with the axe handle protruding from its back, each trying to understand what had occurred. One of the less bemused operators was attempting to drag Tam Donald away from me, shouting at him, accusing him of attacking me. It was utter chaos. The world was in chaos and until Afeeza entered the room it would have engulfed me, Tam and everyone else. It was Afeeza who brought the calm, explained who the young Scot was, who the body on the floor was, and that the next most important thing to do was to get the Sikandar to somewhere comfortable so that his wounds could be closely inspected and tended to.

I think I passed out at that point, as they lifted me and carried me into a room with a bed. Even though they must have forced something down my throat to deal with the pain, the agony reached through my unconsciousness and tore at the edges of my brain. Sometime later I woke and screamed as they were digging into my shoulder with something sharp, trying to remove the bullet that was lodged there. Then once again I slipped away on a sea of hurt, wishing I could go somewhere where it was not, even if that place was the world of the dead.

TWENTY-FIVE

I was still on that sea when I came to, on a boat that was being rocked back and forth by the waves. The pain had subsided to a bearable ache, but I knew I was ill in another way. I felt hot, thick-tongued and thick-headed, and realised I had been and still was gripped by a fever. When I opened my eyes the blinding sunlight blazed into my head and it was some time before I could recognise any of the shapes around me. When I did, things began to make a little more sense.

I was not on a ship. I was on a camel. But not perched on top. I was on some sort of stretcher that had been strapped to one side of the beast. I was accompanied by two others, one either side, the left one ridden by Afeeza, the right one by Tam Donald.

'We three kings,' I croaked. 'Where are we going?'

'Ah, you are awake Sikandar my good friend. We are going to Alice Springs, where there is a doctor who waits to make you better.'

Thank God for the telegraph.

'Why couldn't the doctor come to me?'

It was Tam who answered. 'He is, so to speak, Alex. He's on his way up to Alice while we're going down. We'll meet in the middle.'

'Ah. Good.'

I eased my body on the stretcher, which caused the camel to stumble with the shift of my weight.

'Please keep still, Sikandar,' ordered Afeeza. 'My lady has much load on her back.'

'Yes?'

Tam said, 'You're sharing her with Walker.'

My muzzy brain tried to take this in.

'But you killed Walker.'

'Aye, he's dead all right. Your camel needed a counterweight, so we put a stretcher on the other side of her. Can you no smell him? He stinks right enough.'

I thought about it for a few minutes, as I swayed back and forth on the drom's port side, and decided I didn't like it.

'I'm sharing her with a dead body?'

'It's maybe the only useful thing he's done in his life, that Walker,' replied Tam. 'He's no much good for onythin' else.'

I turned my head to the side so that I could see Tam, riding beside me. He was armed to the teeth with a rifle and a handgun at the ready.

'Are we expecting company?' I asked him. 'Why the arsenal?'

'Captain Midnight's out there somewhere,' came the reply, 'and I'm takin' no chances, Alex. He would aye kill us before breakfast and then eat his bacon and eggs with not a regret in his head.'

Tom Smith alias Captain Midnight alias Tim Felix. Still at large. I found it hard to equate a cold-blooded killer with the ex-schoolmaster I had sat and talked with, admired for his learning, even looked up to as the sort of man I hoped to become. They were surely not the same person? It didn't seem possible. Walker, yes, he fitted my idea of a bushranger, but not Tom Smith. The pair surely had nothing at all in common and each must despise the other for his views and opinions. These thoughts swirled around in my fevered brain until I thought my head would burst.

Then I slipped again into that maelstrom of agitated sleep, going down in a dark whirlpool of viscous dreams.

When I next was able to comprehend my surroundings I found myself in bed and though feeling weak and wrung through my head was a lot clearer and my blood felt cooler. My shoulder, bandaged and stiff, contained a dull ache. I was alone in a room whose only other furniture was a rickety chair. At the bed end was a glassless window where a gauze curtain fluttered in a warm breeze. I called out, asking if anyone was there. Tam entered, concern on his face, but when he saw me sitting up he grinned with delight. Close behind him was Afeeza who stood very still for a minute, studied me and then nodded gravely.

As I went to speak my throat suddenly felt like a sandpit.

'Can I have a drink, Tam?' I asked.

'Water. On the table by your bed.'

Sure enough, there it was. 'Are you going to pour it for me?'

'Whut? No. You've got to start doing things for yourself – there's no servants here, y'ken?'

Afeeza nodded again, his mouth curled in a crescent.

I managed to pour the water without soaking my blankets, then I turned to the other two.

'How long have I been here?'

'Six days,' replied Tam. 'You asked the same question the day before yesterday. D'you no mind?'

'Isn't this the first time I've been conscious?'

'You've been in and out the whole six days, Alex. But you seem to have found your head now. The other times you raved a wee bit and chaffed and champed, but you seem better. You've got some colour and your eyes are nay still yellow. Much clearer, eh Afeeza?'

'Like a crystal pool.'

I hoiked myself up a bit higher on the pillow and stared at these two men to whom I owed my life.

'Thank you,' I said, quietly. 'Thank you, both.'

'Och, you'd have done the same for us.'

'Me? No, I would have let you perish.'

Afeeza said, 'He must be well again — he jokes.'

'What did you do with Walker?'

Tam replied, 'We buried him outside Alice. No marker. He didn't deserve one.'

I thought about this. 'He was one of God's creatures.'

'A very low one. Lower than a cockroach. We don't mark the graves of cockroaches.'

'No word of Tom Smith?'

'Not yet, but he'll be caught one day,' replied Tam, his mouth a thin line, 'they all get caught in the end, Alex.'

I wasn't so sure, but I didn't argue.

Tam sat on the edge of my bed, while Afeeza took the chair, which creaked and twisted slightly under his weight.

'Tam, tell me what happened,' I said, 'when you and Jack came upon the two bushrangers.'

Tam's facial muscles slumped and I could see the memory was a painful one for him.

'We were close behind them, thinking they hadn't seen us coming, but when we rounded an outcrop Tim Felix stepped out and shot Jack in the chest, taking him out of the saddle. He was still alive, thrashing in the dust, but Walker rode up and shot him again. Then Walker dismounted quickly and took Jack's gun. "It's mine!" he shouted and waved it in the air, triumphant like.'

'But you?' I said, puzzled. 'They let you go?'

'I was a good twenty yards behind Jack, still amongst a group of gums when he was hit. I'd already turned my mount when Smith fired a shot at me. It hit one of the gums, spraying me with papery bark. After Walker had yelled "It's mine" I kicked the flanks of my horse and was away, weavin' through the trees. One or two more shots came after me, but they didn't hit me. I don't know where they went. After a wee while I realised they were no comin' after me, so I peeled round and went back aways, to find their tracks. I followed them south until they split up, just east of Tennant Creek. One continued south, the other directly west, towards the station. I didna know which was which, but I followed the one going west. That was Walker of course, as you well know.'

'You were following him for a good while, Tam.'

Tam looked a little shame-faced. 'Och, I lost him for a wee bit – more than a wee bit – but I met up with some drovers who'd seen a man who seemed anxious to avoid them, which is strange in the outback where company is welcome. That was two days previous. I went to the place where they saw him and picked up his trail again.'

'You saved my life, Tam.'

He grinned. 'Only just, man.'

'I'm going to teach you the Morse code. When I go back to Tennant Creek, you can come with me. We'll find you a job to do while I'm teaching you and when you know enough, I'll have you on the staff.'

'But what about the Company?'

'They'll know the whole story by now – you'll be a hero. Who wouldn't want a hero on their staff?'

Tam coloured. 'Och, I don't know about *hero*.'

Afeeza put a hand on his knee. 'You are very fine man, Scotty. You kill like a Pushtun. You throw the axe and save Sikandar. You kill better than my brothers, who are very good killers, very proud men.'

Tam looked shocked, squirmed, and his Scottish brogue suddenly grew as broad and deep as it had once been when he had lived in the land of his birth. 'Weeeel, I'll no want that put on mah gravestone, that's certain sure. And I didna throw the axe, I swung at him with it, as if I was burying the blade in the trunk of a tree. Och now, I'll away and get you some tucker, Alex, you must be starved…'

He hurried from the room.

I extended my good arm towards Afeeza.

'Thank you so much, my friend. I owe you my life.'

'A long one, *insha'Allah*.'

'How shall I repay you?'

'My reward is not here, but elsewhere, Sikandar – we shall be friends now for all eternity. I am older than you. I shall die first. When the time comes for you to die, I shall be waiting with my farting camels to take your soul to Heaven.'

'Whose Heaven, Afeeza?'

He laughed, deeply and spread the palms of his hands. 'Heaven. Heaven. What will you care whose Heaven?'

Tam came back with some soup and a hunk of bread, his face restored to its usual ruddy but not crimson colour. He set the tray in front of me, then said, 'Och, I almost forgot. You'll want to read this.' He placed an article cut from a newspaper on the tray beside the bowl of soup. I looked down at the headline and my heart began beating rapidly.

'SHEERNESS SANDS' ARRIVES AT JAVA

The *Sheerness Sands*, believed lost at sea after failing to arrive at Singapore, has arrived safely in a Java port. The ship was caught in a ferocious storm in the Indian Ocean, close to a group of islands called the Maldives, where it took shelter in a lagoon known as Addu Atoll. With the loss of its mizzen mast and rudder it remained there after the storm abated to perform repairs. The ship then set out again for Singapore but problems with the damaged rudder beset the crew and finally the *Sheerness Sands* found itself off the coast of Indonesia. The latest telegraph communication states that the ship is expected to arrive in Port Darwin by the end of the month.

My hands were shaking as I read the report.

'Can this be true?' I breathed. 'Sally safe and well?'

'Must be,' replied my Scottish companion, taking my only piece of bread and absently chewing on the crust, 'says so in the paper, eh?'

In 1878 I happened to read that a 'Thomas Smith alias Captain Midnight' was finally apprehended by two policemen in the bush near Enngonia on the morning of the 5th October. Constable Hatton called on Smith to surrender and when he refused Hatton tried to shoot the brushranger's horse. He failed but his last shot hit Thomas Smith in the side. Constable Gray then used his rifle to finally bring down the horse from under the bushranger. 'Captain Midnight' was arrested and taken to Wapweelah station where he died in the middle of the night. It seemed an apt time to depart this world, considering the nickname he had chosen to ride under. He went out raging with venom on his tongue, cursing the men who had brought him down.

The newspapers printed a picture of the dead man. The gruesome death photograph was of a pale, anxious-looking, clean-shaven fellow, eyes closed, his hair cut extremely short. I could not say whether it was the same man I knew as Tim Felix or not, since Tim had sported long curly locks and a big bushy beard in camp. Indeed, there was mention of only one of Smith's many pseudonyms in the article – Captain Midnight – and that was probably because the editor did not want to distract the reader from the most romantic of his aliases. So the words 'Tim Felix' did not appear and since Sally had just delivered of a baby girl, a delightful prune-faced infant that bawled its lungs out on entering the world, my attention was taken up with things far more important than bushrangers coming to justice, though I did say a prayer for Corporal Jack Ransome of the Adelaide Police Force.

THE IRON WIRE

Garry Kilworth

The following people mentioned in this novel indeed existed, albeit I have used an author's licence to play with their actual words and deeds.

Ashwood, the young man with John Milner when he was killed.

John Bolton, bushranger, colleague of Captain Midnight.

AY Forster, Cadet, Section E.

Constables Hatton and Gray, policemen.

W Harvey, Overseer, Section E.

S Jarvis, Cadet, Section D.

Sophia Jex-Blake, Emily Davies, Elizabeth Garrett – British women working for the rights of their gender in the 1870s.

Ralph and John Milner, stockmen.

Robert Charles Patterson, replacement leader of the Northern Section.

Dr Renner, surgeon for the Overland Telegraph construction teams.

JLM Roberts, Sub-overseer, Section E.

John Ross, bushman, Leader of the Overland Telegraph Exploratory Expedition.

Thomas Smith, alias 'Captain Midnight', bushranger.

John McDouall Stuart, explorer.

Charles Todd, South Australian Government Astronomer and Superintendent of Telegraphs.

Thomas Walker, bushranger, colleague of Captain Midnight.

AT Woods, Overseer, Section D.

MORE FROM INFINITY PLUS

On my way to Samarkand
memoirs of a travelling writer
by Garry Douglas Kilworth
http://www.infinityplus.co.uk/book.php?book=gkiomwts

Garry (Douglas) Kilworth is a varied and prolific writer who has travelled widely since childhood, living in a number of countries, especially in the Far East.

His books include science fiction and fantasy, historical novels, literary novels, short story collections, children's books and film novelisations.

This autobiography contains anecdotes about his farm worker antecedents and his rovings around the globe, as well as his experiences in the middle list of many publishing houses.

The style is chatty, the structure loose - pole vaulting time and space on occasion - and the whole saga is an entertaining ramble through a 1950s childhood, foreign climes and the genre corridors of the literary world.

"Kilworth is a master of his trade." —*Punch*

"Garry Kilworth is arguably the finest writer of short fiction today, in any genre. " —*New Scientist*

"Kilworth is one of the most significant writers in the English language. " —*Fear*

**For full details of infinity plus books
see www.infinityplus.co.uk**

Made in the USA
Charleston, SC
06 October 2014